CRITICAL ACCLAIM FOR THE FRED CARVER SERIES BY EDGAR AWARD-WINNING AUTHOR JOHN LUTZ

TROPICAL HEAT

"Smooth, first-rate...A writer who knows how to seize and hold the reader's imagination from the start."
Cleveland Plain-Dealer

"Lutz has never written leaner prose...
A delight"
USA Today

SCORCHER

"Fast-paced...Superior entertainment"
San Diego Union

"SCORCHER is another reason why John Lutz is one of the best mystery writers of the 1980's, and isn't too far from the best of any other era."
Newport News Press

KISS

"The grip on the reader is relentless until the final, entirely unforeseen shocker...
Lutz's best novel so far."
Publishers Weekly

"One of the best private eye series.
The proof is in KISS."
Orlando Sentinel

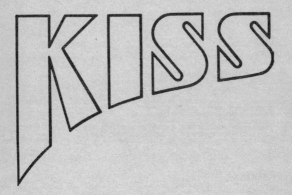

KISS

JOHN LUTZ

AVON BOOKS ◆ NEW YORK

AVON BOOKS
A division of
The Hearst Corporation
105 Madison Avenue
New York, New York 10016

"A Rinehart Suspense Novel"
Copyright © 1988 by John Lutz
Published by arrangement with Henry Holt and Company, Inc.
Library of Congress Catalog Card Number: 88-3074
ISBN: 0-380-70934-1

First Avon Books Printing: March 1990

AVON TRADEMARK REG. U.S. PAT. OFF. AND IN OTHER COUNTRIES, MARCA REGISTRADA, HECHO EN U.S.A.

Printed in the U.S.A.

RA   10 9 8 7 6 5 4 3 2 1

FOR ANDREW

And for every kiss I owe,
I can pay you back, you know.
Kiss me, then,
Every moment—and again.

—J. G. Saxe
"To Lesbia"

1

It was late afternoon but still hot. Carver had poured two glasses of lemonade from the tall pitcher Edwina kept in the refrigerator.

He watched the breeze ruffle the fringe on the umbrella sprouting from the center of the table on the brick veranda. The sun sparked silver off the ocean swells that curled in on themselves to form whitecaps as they neared the shore. Due to the lay of the land, he couldn't see the beach from where he sat, but he could hear the slap of the waves and the rush and roar of surf. Far out at sea something dark, a boat, a bit of flotsam, something, was drifting. Whatever it was, it looked lost and lonely.

Alfonso Desoto sat across from Carver, his back to the sea, his glass of lemonade untouched before him and resting in a circle of dampness on the white-enameled table.

His handsome Latin features had an intense cast to them this afternoon, like those of a bullfighter contemplating grave danger. Desoto was dressed neatly as ever, in a well-tailored cream-colored suit, pale blue shirt, and mauve tie. His gold watch glinted on one wrist, a bulky gold bracelet on the other. He wore a gold diamond ring on each hand, pinkie ring on the right, ring finger on the left. He looked too prosperous and flashy for a cop, but he was a cop. And a good one. A lieutenant in the Orlando department.

He was here in Del Moray because Carver was his friend. Because he was worried. It wasn't like Desoto to worry. Or seem to worry, anyway. It made Carver uneasy. He watched the sea behind Desoto, kept an eye on whatever it was out there drifting.

"Where's Edwina?" Desoto asked casually.

"Out selling condos someplace."

Desoto sighed and sat back. "Not a bad way to earn your bread, *amigo*. Doesn't depend on crime, like our professions."

"You haven't seen some of the condos."

Desoto didn't smile. "What we do for a living, dealing with the kinds of people we see every day, it makes you cynical. Makes you get suspicious when maybe you shouldn't."

"Or when maybe you should," Carver said.

He waited for Desoto to get around to whatever he'd come here to say. The breeze kicked up and snapped the umbrella against its metal frame; the table moved an inch, as if its sail had been filled with wind, scraping over the hard bricks. Carver wondered why the breeze never mussed Desoto's glossy black hair.

Desoto picked up his glass and sipped his lemonade. Put the glass back down and rotated it smoothly in its circle of dampness. He said, "I want to talk to you about my uncle Sam Cusanelli."

The Italian name didn't throw Carver. He knew Desoto wasn't Cuban, as many people assumed. His father had been Mexican, his mother Italian, even though Desoto looked like classic Latin nobility profiled on a Spanish coin. Carver tapped a finger on his own damp, cold glass of lemonade and nodded.

"I never saw much of my father when I was a kid," Desoto

went on. "He was always off somewhere doing whatever mining engineers do—if he really was a mining engineer. It was actually my mother who raised me, *amigo*. My mother and Uncle Sam." He grinned, perfect white teeth a shock in his dark features. "When I was very young I used to think he was the real 'Uncle Sam.' He did nothing to set me straight."

Carver waited. A gull flapped by overhead, screeched wildly, and then soared in a graceful arc toward the ocean to pursue another gull.

"I grew up," Desoto said. "Learned the truth about Uncle Sam. Both of them." He added sadly, "My own Uncle Sam got old, *amigo*."

"We all get old," Carver said. That oughta help cheer up Desoto. Carver sipped his lemonade; it was bitter but he figured he deserved it and took another sip.

Desoto smiled, his dark eyes somber. "From time to time I have doubts that you'll grow old, my friend."

Carver rested his hand on the crook of the hard walnut cane that was leaning against his chair. He remembered the noise and muzzle flash, and the pain of the bullet that had smashed his kneecap and ended his career as an Orlando police officer three years ago. There were times, brief, endless seconds of undeniable mortality, when he wanted nothing so much as the opportunity to become old. "So what happened to your uncle?" he asked.

Desoto shifted his weight and looked uncomfortable. "He stayed with my mother for a while, then after she died he lived alone at an old residential hotel in South Miami Beach. It was a clean place, and Sam was happy there. Then his legs got bad—a circulation problem. Wasn't long before his mind began to slip now and then, but nothing serious. I drove down to see him one day and found out he'd been moved to a retirement home. His sister, in Saint Louis, had arranged for it and was paying the bills."

"That'd be your aunt," Carver said.

Desoto nodded. "My Aunt Marie. Only met her a few times, when I was a kid. She never got along with Sam or my mother."

"Why not?"

"Who knows? One of those reasons you never tell kids, I guess. All I heard were whispers." He curled the left half of his upper lip in a sneer. "Apparently there'd been a reconciliation."

"Happens in families," Carver said. "People grow up, see time dwindling away, and tend to forgive things that happened when everybody's blood ran hotter."

"The home Marie and her husband put Sam in was Sunhaven."

Carver knew the place. A rambling building that looked like a series of pastel cubes or children's blocks clustered at random near the coast highway. Pale cement with lots of tinted reflecting plastic or glass. There was a fancy wooden gate that was sometimes opened, sometimes closed when Carver drove past. Room, board, and medical attention couldn't be cheap at Sunhaven, but it didn't look to Carver like a good place to be while the golden years melted away in the Florida sun. On the other hand, old Sam had to be better off there than in some fleabag art-deco hotel in south Miami. What was Desoto complaining about?

"Aunt Marie must be well off," Carver said.

"Medicare picked up much of the cost," Desoto said, as if eager to minimize Marie's contribution.

"But not all of it," Carver said. Fair was fair.

"No, *amigo*, not all of it."

Carver was suddenly aware that Desoto had used the past tense. "You said 'picked' up."

"Yes," Desoto said. "Two days ago Sam Cusanelli died."

Carver wasn't sure what to say to this. "How old was he?" he asked.

"Seventy-six."

What now? *Well, he led a long, full life?* The pain on Desoto's face concerned Carver. There was a lot more to this than an old man dying on celestial schedule in a nursing home.

"About six months ago Sam began writing me letters," Desoto said. "He knew I was a policeman, but I'm afraid he had exaggerated ideas of my sphere of influence and authority. He wanted me to investigate what was wrong at Sunhaven."

Carver ran his fingertips lightly over the warm, smooth table. "Wrong in what way?"

Desoto shook his head slowly. "I'm not sure. The letters were vague. He was an old man, and it's true his mind wasn't what it had been." Above the pale blue collar and neatly knotted tie, Desoto's Adam's apple bobbed. "I'm afraid I didn't take him as seriously as I should have, and now he's dead."

Carver thought he knew where Desoto was taking the conversation. "Dead how?"

"Oh, natural causes. A cerebral hemorrhage. A stroke, in other words. He'd had them before, and finally a massive one killed him. I talked to the doctor, saw the death certificate."

"But you're not comfortable with the situation."

"I'm not," Desoto said.

"When your uncle was alive, you ever go to Sunhaven to visit him?"

"Sure, lots of times."

"Anything strike you wrong about the place then?"

Desoto's features hardened. "Plenty. But it was like all those places: storehouses for worn-out human beings. Tear your guts out sometimes just to walk through the lobby." He gazed out at the vast Atlantic, older than the oldest Sunhaven resident. "Ah, Jesus!"

Carver shrugged. "Seventy-six. And his mind was slipping, you said. He might get suspicious, maybe a little paranoid, cooped up in a place like that."

"Might," Desoto admitted.

Carver decided to be direct. "You don't think his death was natural?"

"I think it probably was."

"Then what's troubling you?"

" 'Probably' isn't enough, *amigo*. But even if Sam's death came

5

when it was ordained, he was still convinced something wasn't right about the place. I can't get it out of my head there might be something to his suspicions."

"It's normal you should feel that way," Carver said.

"Normal? There's a word shouldn't be tossed around. You and I both know there's no such thing."

"Well, whatever it is, maybe you're just gonna have to live with it."

"Maybe," Desoto said. He flashed his sad white smile. "Or maybe I could hire you to look into things."

Carver didn't like the idea. In his grief, Desoto *was* probably more suspicious than he should be, searching for reason in a random universe. Old people could get the way he'd described Sam Cusanelli. Thinking there was a plot to steal their socks or cheat them out of a prune at breakfast. Damn shame, but it seemed part of growing old. Part of life and death at the places like Sunhaven that dotted the reassuringly bright Florida landscape.

But he felt sorry for Desoto. And what would a few days on this hurt? A few questions asked in order to put Desoto's mind at ease? Carver didn't have anything else to do right now except collect the disability pension for his bad leg and make love to Edwina here in paradise by the sea. And what was Eden without a serpent?

"I'm way over in Orlando," Desoto said, trying to persuade Carver. "I can't snoop around here on the coast. Not my jurisdiction. Listen, *amigo*, I intend to pay."

A sleek yellow speedboat skipped past a couple of hundred yards from shore, buzzing like a hornet furious at being pinned to water. Within seconds the angry snarl became a receding, rising and falling drone, as the boat headed straight out to sea and the prop cleared the surface between waves.

"I won't let you pay," Carver said. "I'm doing it in the service of Uncle Sam."

Out beyond the boat, whatever was drifting had disappeared when he wasn't looking.

2

When Carver awoke the next morning Edwina was leaning over him and kissing him lightly on the lips. He stirred, gripped her shoulders, and drew her closer. Kissed the other side of her neck, her ear. Thought about other places he might kiss.

She said, "Umm," and pulled away from him, smiling.

She was already dressed and had been kissing him good-bye, he realized. There she sat on the edge of the bed, in her tailored blue suit and with her long, dark hair pinned back, her gray-green eyes holding her smile even after her facial muscles had given up on it. She looked crisp and efficient; she was ready to tilt with the world and do real-estate business, all right. She was fierce about her career; it had given her solace and rescued her from the depression of a catastrophic marriage and divorce, and she would give it up only when they pried the condo listings from her cold dead fingers.

"Gotta go," she said. "Beachfront property to show."

"I'll make it more worth your while to stay," he told her, waking up further. The temperature outside was still bearable; the bedroom window was open and he could hear the ocean sighing beyond the swaying sheer curtains and the screen.

7

Edwina stood up and smoothed her skirt over her thighs. Commerce today, not sex. "I'm sure you would," she said.

Carver had an erection. "You wouldn't be sorry."

"But I might be sorry later, when another agent sells the property."

"You could afford to lose a commission."

"It's not the commission."

Carver ran his palm over his bald pate, as if arranging nonexistent hair. "Yeah, I know." There was a distant click and a low whirring sound. The central air-conditioning unit kicking in to begin its day's valiant effort of holding the heat at bay. It was a long war that one summer would end with a burned-out fan motor or broken-down compressor; the heat would prevail. Cool air from the vent wafted over Carver's legs.

"I just remembered, I passed Desoto's car yesterday on the coast highway," Edwina said. "At least I think it was his. Was he coming here?"

"Uh-huh. He wants to hire me."

Edwina cocked her head to the side. This interested her.

"Wants me to look into Sunhaven Retirement Home," Carver said.

"That place about ten miles outside of town? Looks like some building blocks dropped out of the sky?"

"That's the one. Desoto's uncle was in there for a while. He died three days ago."

Edwina ran the tips of neatly manicured fingers along her smooth jaw line. She did that when her mind was turning over. "Does Desoto think there's something wrong with how he died?"

Carver sat up, his stiff left leg extended straight out in front of him. He scooted forward and swiveled until he was sitting on the edge of the mattress. He reached for his cane and leaned on it. "It's not that, exactly," he said. "The uncle, Sam Cusanelli, told Desoto several times there was something not right about Sunhaven. But apparently he couldn't define exactly what was wrong. Desoto didn't take it seriously enough to look into it, even though he and the uncle were close when Desoto was a kid. Cusanelli was seventy-six and his mind played tricks on him sometimes."

"But Desoto takes it seriously now," Edwina said. "Why?"

Carver shook his head. "I dunno. Guilt, maybe, over something he doesn't even remember. Grief, I'm sure. Way people's minds work."

"You going to look into it for him?"

"Starting today," Carver said. "Soon as I get myself up and around."

"You said the uncle died three days ago," Edwina said. "We should send flowers."

That was something that hadn't occurred to Carver. He wasn't good at the amenities. "I'll find out where they should go," he said.

"Never mind," Edwina told him, "I'll check the *Gazette-Dispatch* obituary page. You said, 'Cusanelli'?" She didn't ask it as if she were surprised. She knew Desoto was half Italian. She'd asked Carver about him. Women were always curious about Desoto.

"Cusanelli," Carver confirmed.

She reversed her wrist and shot a cool gray glance at her watch. "Damn! Gotta go."

"Good luck," Carver said.

She was already out the door and in the hall when she called back to him, "You, too."

Carver sat still and listened to the outside door open and shut, then the vibrant hum of the automatic garage-door opener. It sounded like a tenor with a sore throat.

The overhead door hummed closed, and briefly he heard the precision growl of Edwina's Mercedes as she low-geared it down the curving driveway. She'd be heavy on the accelerator when she reached the highway. She was on intimate terms with speed.

After a few minutes Carver got up and limped with his cane into the bathroom, where he splashed cold water on his face to come fully alert. He slept nude, so he had only to sit on the bed again and work into his swimming trunks, and he was ready for his morning therapeutic swim.

After making his way down the rough wooden steps to the beach, he walked with difficulty over the soft sand to where the surf was fanning white, grasping hands of foam on the shore. The sea had always wanted the land.

He moved closer to the ocean and stuck his cane like a spear in the damp sand. Then he lay down on his stomach and, using his arms and good leg to propel himself, inched backward into the cool water. When a particularly large wave roared in, he scooted into it and let its ponderous reverse momentum lift and carry him seaward until he was floating free.

Carver felt exuberant in the water. His upper body had become amazingly strong since he'd been supporting his weight with the cane and had come to rely on his arms and torso. Nature's way of compensating. And here in the ocean, kicking from the hip, he was as mobile as anyone and more powerful than most.

He swam far out from shore. Then he turned his body and treaded water, bobbing on the gentle swells and staring in at Edwina's house with its red tile roof, perched atop the rise where the Army Corps of Engineers had built up the beach with rocks and the developer had graded the land to afford a better view. The sun was like flame on the back of his neck.

After about five minutes he stroked toward shore with his peculiar but graceful Australian crawl.

When he dragged himself back up onto the beach, near where his cane jutted from the sand, he was breathing hard, his chest heaving and each intake of breath a rasping plea for oxygen. That was how he wanted it. Almost every morning since his retirement from the force, he'd been able to swim a bit farther out, each time with a degree of added strength. Occasionally he'd find himself wondering what it would be like to continue swimming straight out to sea, into the tilted, sliding expanses of blue-green ocean and the rushing of water that sounded like the roar of mortality in the blood.

Not today.

Carver grasped the cane and used it to lever himself to his feet. Dripping water, he limped toward firmer ground and the house.

After a shower and quick shave, he dressed in light tan slacks and a black pullover shirt. He put on brown socks and his well-worn moccasins. The crown of his bald head was tanned, but he had thick gray hair curling above his ears and well down the back of his neck. He was forty-four years old, medium-size but trim and cabled with sinew. His features were more harsh than handsome. His nose was straight, he had blue catlike eyes, and a boyhood scar lent the right corner of his mouth a sardonic twist. A strong face, maybe to the point of brutality. Was that why Edwina loved him?

He had black coffee, half a grapefruit, and a piece of dry toast for breakfast. Then he stretched out an arm for the phone and called Desoto in Orlando.

"Still feel the way you did when we talked yesterday?" he asked, when the lieutenant had come to the phone.

"Same way, *amigo*. I know what you're thinking, that my head's not screwed on right at this time. But believe me, I gave the matter a lot of thought before driving there to talk with you."

"It didn't seem spur of the moment," Carver assured him.

Desoto said, "You find out anything?"

"Hell, no. I just got up."

"Hmm." Disapproval.

"Who were some of your uncle's friends at the retirement home?"

"You don't keep friends very long at a place like that," Desoto said sadly. "But I do remember one old guy. Name's Kearny. That's his first name. I think his last name's Williams. He and

11

Sam seemed pretty thick. Took their meals together in the mess hall they call a dining room, played checkers. That kinda stuff. They argued a lot, but they were friends. You could tell by watching them. I was glad Sam had somebody like that out there."

"Kearny still at the home?"

"I guess so," Desoto said. "If he's still alive."

"I'll let you know when and if I do find out anything," Carver said.

"I know you will." Desoto paused. "You be careful, okay?"

"Of what?"

"I'm not sure. I got a feeling about that place. All that sadness, the ends of lives, and in so much sun and brightness. Maybe when you go there you'll know what I mean."

"We'll find out this morning," Carver said.

He stretched his arm again, leaning his weight on the cane, and hung up the phone. Then he limped out to his rusty Oldsmobile convertible, put down the canvas top, and drove through the morning heat toward Sunhaven Retirement Home.

He thought about Edwina kissing him good-morning. And about Uncle Sam, dying among hired help in a place that had made him uneasy.

It felt great to be alive and too young for Medicare.

3

There was a line of palm trees along the perimeter of the parking lot at Sunhaven, but they provided little shade. Carver nevertheless found a space in the dappled light beneath one of them and turned off the Olds's ancient and powerful V-8 engine. In the sudden silence, palm fronds rattled in the warm breeze, speaking an old and indecipherable language.

He got out of the car, set the tip of his cane in the lot's bleached gravel, and limped toward the nearest of the tinted cubes.

A transparent door was barely discernible as the entrance. Its copper tint gave back Carver's reflection as he approached: a slightly crooked, featureless man with a cane, struggling in glaring two dimension. The heat from the gently inclined pale concrete ramp to the door radiated through the thin leather soles of his moccasins. The temperature might hit a thousand today.

But not inside Sunhaven. As Carver stepped in and the door swished closed behind him, the chill almost stopped his heart. All that tinted glass must make the air conditioning more efficient.

The lobby was done in pastels, mostly the pale blues and

13

pinks seen in nurseries, as if to suggest the full circle of nothing to life to nothing. There were several residents seated in wicker chairs. The nearest, an old woman secured with a knotted yellow sheet so she wouldn't topple from her rocking chair, lolled her head toward Carver and smiled as if she recognized him as a long-lost family member. It was quiet in the lobby and the runners on her rocker made soft, rhythmic creaking sounds. Hypnotic sounds. Two old men, one of them with a missing right arm, halted their game of checkers and glanced over at Carver. The nearer of them, hatchet-faced and obviously without his dentures, smiled in the same way as the woman in the rocker. The one-armed man, unnoticed for a moment, darted out his hand and furtively scooted a red checker forward on the board. Carver wondered if it had been his move.

In the center of the blue and pink and mauve lobby was a long, curved reception desk, the lower half of which was covered with what looked like pink industrial velvet. Beyond it were half a dozen tall, pastel dividers, partitioning off what probably were private areas where residents and visitors could talk uninterrupted.

Carver nodded to the checker players and limped toward the tiny, redheaded girl behind the reception desk.

She got younger as he got closer. He figured her for about fifteen, but she had the kind of looks that could confound the guy who guessed ages at carnivals. Her hair was carrot-colored and she had a sprinkling of freckles across the bridge of a miniature, perfect nose. Her eyes were blue and widely spaced, with a dreamy quality and with that pink-rimmed look so often seen on redheads. She had a trim figure beneath her white-and-gray uniform: lean waist and high, small, protruding breasts—a teenage figure. Her hair was medium-length and combed back, arranged in a sort of bun on top of her head and held there with a blue ribbon tied in a large bow. The flared bow resembled an exotic butterfly that had found a suitable flower. There were errant, fiery wisps of hair curling in front of her ears. She looked to Carver as if she ought to be wearing pigtails and orthodontic braces and marching in the junior high school band. The plastic name plaque on the desk read "Birdie Reeves."

She glanced up from the magazine she'd been reading and noticed Carver. She blinked once, slowly, as if there were sand beneath her eyelids and they hurt. Then she smiled. Her teeth were even but protruded; that only added to her Becky Thatcher look. She was so much the opposite of classic beauty that she made you see her own brand of beauty in her blazing youth.

She stood up behind the counter, though it was hardly noticeable, and said, "Can I help you?" There was a lilt to her voice, maybe a midwestern drawl.

"I'm looking for Kearny Williams," Carver said.

Birdie's smile kept splitting her features, causing the flesh at the corners of her eyes to crinkle in a parody of crow's feet. People like her never really appeared old; they simply faded and reminded other people that time was passing. "Uh-hm, we got a Mr. Williams here. You a relative?"

"Friend of a friend. My name's Fred Carver. Tell Mr. Williams I knew Sam Cusanelli."

Birdie's blue eyes widened and her sadness absorbed her smile. "Shame about Mr. Cusanelli," she said. "He was a nice man. I'd say that about most any of the residents, I guess, but it really was true of Mr. Cusanelli. How well did you know him?"

"Very well, when he was younger."

She was smiling again, waiting for Carver to say more. He didn't.

"I see," she said. A man and a woman wearing white uniforms bustled past, discussing something earnestly, oblivious of where they were. The man mumbled, ". . . a drop in the white cell count," and the woman nodded thoughtfully. The old woman in the chair lolled her head and tried to lift a hand to wave but was ignored.

Birdie said, "Well, I s'pose it's okay." She pointed; her thin arm was freckled and dusted with reddish down. "Go on through

15

that door and down the hall, then turn left and you'll come to Mr. Williams's room. I'm sure he's there; he's most always there." She consulted a chart on a clipboard. "Room number's one."

"Easy to remember," Carver said.

"Not for Mr. Williams sometimes."

Carver said thanks and left her to return to her magazine. It had to do with heavy-metal rock stars. There was a glossy cover illustration of an insanely grinning thirtyish man dressed as an English schoolboy and aiming his elaborate guitar like a rifle. Birdie seemed enthralled by the magazine's contents. Her lips moved soundlessly as she read.

A teenager with an MTV mind as a receptionist in an old-folks' home. Well, why not? The place needed a fresh bloom in the midst of all the faded petals.

As Carver made his way cautiously over the slick tiled floor toward the wide door Birdie had pointed out, the door swung toward him and a heavyset woman wearing a uniform like the receptionist's wheeled a very old man in a chrome wheelchair into the lobby. Like the woman in the rocking chair, he was held firmly in place by a knotted sheet around his midsection. His head wobbled and a gleaming thread of saliva dangled from his chin, catching the light. Carver quickly looked away; here was the future for each generation's survivors. It was something nobody of any age liked to think about, but it was there like cold, black reality on every life's horizon.

He pushed open the swinging door with the tip of his cane and went through. Walked down the hall as Birdie had directed and made a left turn. He had to limp only a few feet before he came to a pastel blue door with a gold numeral *1* painted on it. Again using the cane, he knocked.

". . . on in," called a voice from the other side.

Carver rotated the knob and entered a small, sunny room furnished with a bed, a limed oak dresser, and a tiny color TV that was tuned soundlessly to a morning game show. A pretty

16

blond woman on the screen spun an oversized roulette wheel, closed her eyes, and crossed the fingers of both hands. In front of the TV was a brown vinyl chair in which sat a broad, muscular man with wide, squared features. Moving with a difficulty and stiffness that revealed his advanced age, he stood up and turned to face Carver. He had a sacklike stomach paunch, and his throat was scarred and withered from a recent operation. His thick gray hair was precisely and severely parted, as if he'd spent a great deal of time getting it just right, maybe using scientific instruments.

"I'm a friend of Alfonso Desoto," Carver said, leaning on his cane and extending his hand. "Name's Fred Carver."

Kearny had eyes like faded blue marbles. It took a moment for a light to shine in them. "Desoto? Sam's nephew?"

"Right."

A dry, powerful hand gripped Carver's up to the wrist and pumped it almost out of the socket. The old guy was glad to see him. Maybe glad to see anybody. "I'm Kearny Williams."

"I know." Carver retracted his arm; his shoulder was sore. "I came here to see you about Sam Cusanelli."

Kearny motioned for him to take the chair. When Carver declined, he said, "Guess you know Sam's dead. Went three days ago."

"Desoto told me."

Kearny slumped down again in the brown vinyl chair. "Gotta get my weight off these legs after a while. It's pure shit, growin' old. Outlivin' your body. It gets you down, knowin' your good years are behind you. Don't let anybody tell you otherwise, Carver."

The last sounded like a command. "I won't," Carver assured him. "When's Sam Cusanelli's funeral?"

Kearny shook his large head. Light from the window shot silver flecks through his hair. His clothes were neat and clean: loose-fitting jeans with creases ironed into them, a short-sleeved gray sport shirt with an out-of-style wide, wide collar. His shoes were black brogans, work shoes, but they were waxed shiny enough to gleam with reflected images. Carver wondered why he kept so well groomed when he was probably shut away in his room most of every day. "Sam was put in the ground this morning," Kearny said. "Didn't believe in long wakes for himself or anybody else. Told me he'd been grieving in this place long enough anyway."

"He could have left here, couldn't he?"

"He did leave here."

"I mean some other way."

Kearny snorted and looked angry. "Where would he have gone? It was his family in Saint Louis shoved him in here outta sight. That Desoto offered to put him up, but Sam chose not to be a burden. That's us here at Sunhaven, Carver, don't wanna burden the young and living." He added ironically, "As if them and us was all one species."

Carver was surprised Desoto had made such an offer. He lived in a small condo in Orlando. Red carpet, black furniture. A year's salary in stereo equipment throbbing out the damned Latin music he seemed to crave listening to, sometimes in his bedroom with all the mirrors, sometimes with someone. No place for a seventy-six-year-old uncle. A lot of old people would think Desoto's wardrobe alone was a sin.

Of course, Carver hadn't known Uncle Sam and Desoto had. Maybe it would have worked. Casanova and Moses.

Kearny could read minds. "That Desoto, he's a handsome young buck. Got him an eye for the women, right?"

"That's him," Carver said. An eye and anything else he can bring into play.

Kearny grinned and shook his head. "I envy him. He better get it while he can. Everything he can. Life's here and then it's gone. More precious than gold, but nobody knows it till it's too late. Use every damn second of it, you hear me?"

The voice of command again. "Hear you," Carver said. He sat down on the bed.

"How'd you get the bum leg?"

"I was a cop," Carver said. "A holdup man shot me in the knee."

"Desoto's a cop in Orlando. That where you know him from?"

"Yeah. We been friends for years."

"You still a cop?"

"In a way. I'm a private investigator."

A gray eyebrow arched. "No shit? You investigatin' Sam's death?"

"Why? You think there's something suspicious about it?"

"Ah, you're a cop, all right. A question for a question."

Carver knew he had to confide in someone inside Sunhaven. Kearny inspired a certain degree of trust. Kearny seemed mentally sharper than Birdie had intimated. Kearny had been Sam's buddy. Kearny was the guy.

"How close were you to Sam Cusanelli?" Carver asked.

Kearny's gruff façade slipped for a moment. The blue eyes misted and he turned away to stare out the window into the blasting sunlight. "Close enough I cried when he died." The voice had risen an octave, with shrill panic in it. "I'd tell you I ain't cried in a long time, but that ain't so." Kearny's broad, square shoulders rose, then fell heavily as he blew out a breath. "Damned stupid, gettin' to be friends with somebody in a place like this."

"I don't think so."

"You will someday. Time'll do it to you. When you're young it buries your mistakes and works the rough edges off you. Then one day you find out it's worn you down to within a shade of nothin', and you can't stand any more loss. You'll learn what I mean."

"I'll ask again if there was anything suspicious about the way Sam Cusanelli died," Carver said gently.

"And I'll ask again if you're investigatin' his death."

Carver jumped into deep water. "You might say I'm working for Sam. Desoto told me his uncle had hinted there was something wrong here at Sunhaven. He hired me to find out if Sam was right."

Kearny turned away from the glaring sunlight and clumsily rubbed his eyes with his thick fingers. "A cop hiring a cop. Don't make much sense."

"The only way," Carver said. "Desoto has no jurisdiction here on the coast, and his superiors might not like him making inquiries about his uncle's death, since it isn't even listed as suspicious. The Del Moray police wouldn't like it, either, and Desoto doesn't want them tromping through here and putting whoever might have something to hide on their guard. Main thing, though, he's in Orlando and I'm here."

Kearny wrestled the chair around so he was facing Carver, aiming a glance at the door to make sure it was closed. "Yeah, Sam told me what he thought."

"Which was . . . ?"

Kearny looked momentarily bewildered. "That something's very wrong here."

Carver was getting tired of this. "*What* did he tell you was wrong?"

Fear slithered like live shadow across Kearny's aged, stubborn features. "Twenty years ago I was a truck driver and a teamsters organizer. Break the arm of a man raised his fist against me. Back then I wasn't scared of a thing, Carver. I am now."

"Sam wasn't afraid to tell Desoto."

"And Sam's dead."

"You think that's why? Because he was talking about Sunhaven?"

"I don't know. People die here all the time. That's what we wait for here. I don't know that talkin' too much *isn't* why Sam died." He massaged his gnarled knuckles; he'd been a rough man, long ago. "A natural death, in his bed. Ain't that what we all want?"

"Sooner or later, I guess."

"Sam wanted it later. He wanted to live a lotta years more."

"He'd want you to talk," Carver said.

"Ever meet Sam?"

"Never had the privilege," Carver admitted.

"Well, you don't know what you're talkin' about. Sam wouldn't give a shit if I talked or not. 'I'm dead, Kearny old sport,' Sam'd say, 'so nothin' matters to me. Ashes to ashes. Ever seen a cigar butt gave a damn about anything? Do what you fuckin' want.' " Kearny smiled. "He'd mean it, too. Sam'd say what he meant, then he'd shut up. One of the reasons him and me got along."

Carver sensed he'd come to the end of the conversation. He planted the tip of his cane and stood up. The bedsprings sang as his weight released them.

"Hey, I'd tell you what I know," Kearny said, "only I don't really know anything. Just got my suspicions. Like Sam."

"Suspicions of what?"

Kearny shook his head in frustration. "Hell, I ain't even sure! You believe that? Well, it's true. I don't know any more than Sam did."

"Okay," Carver said. "Do me a favor and don't tell anyone why I was here."

"You got it," Kearny said. "Last thing I want is for Nurse Rule to learn I was jawin' with a cop."

"Who's Nurse Rule?"

"Head nurse here. Damn near runs the whole place. Sam didn't like her."

"You don't either, I guess."

Kearny's features hardened into a seamed mask; his eyes looked inward and back along the years that had brought him to where he was, the people he'd known. "Not many here'd say they like Nurse Rule."

"Mind if I come back to talk to you again?" Carver said. "Nobody'd be suspicious. I told them at the desk I was an old friend of Sam's."

"Hey, don't you be seen talking too much to Birdie!" Kearny said in a hasty, hoarse whisper. "That little thing don't deserve no trouble. She's got no idea what goes on around here."

"Nobody seems to," Carver said. This wasn't going according

to his script. The deceased's best friend was supposed to help try to avenge his death, if something really was wrong at Sunhaven.

He tightened his grip on the hard walnut crook of his cane and angled toward the door.

"You can't blame an old man for being afraid, Carver." Kearny's voice was rising again. "You can't."

"I don't," Carver said, and went out.

As he was passing through the lobby, the old woman tied in her rocker with the yellow sheet stared up at him with vague, moist eyes and said, "In 'thirty-two I was elected homecoming queen at Tulane University and my sister Dolly got so jealous she slit both her wrists. Arm flopped outta the bathtub and bled under the door, or Daddy'd never have found her in time to save her. Lord, that was some day! You believe that?"

"Sure," Carver said.

"Well, none of it's true." The old woman turned withered hands palms up and feebly extended her own scarred wrists.

Carver limped faster and pushed through the tinted glass door into the glare and crushing heat outside.

Sunhaven was a lot like the rest of the world, he decided. Uninhabitable.

A walk through there did wonders for the mood.

4

Edwina was still out trying to match buyer with condo. Carver got a can of Budweiser out of the refrigerator, popped the tab, and sat at the oak table in the kitchen. He stared out the window at the gulls doing aerobatics over the glittering sea and wondered if they somehow sensed how free they were. Free of a foreseeable future.

After a while he took a long, cold swallow of beer that made the back of his throat ache. Edwina had phones all over the house; she didn't want to miss a potential deal because it took her an extra few seconds to answer a call. Carver dragged the one on the kitchen table over to him. It was a functional-looking gray model with oversized buttons. It remembered the last number called; it kept forty numbers in its permanent memory and would reach any of them automatically at the touch of a button; it chirped or rang or buzzed or whistled, however you set the controls. Its taped voice warned you if you punched out too many or too few digits in the number you were trying to code in. It would call someone you didn't like and give them a shock over the line and then laugh at them. High tech was wonderful.

Carver used the phone for the simple task of calling Desoto. It made short work of that.

"Been to Sunhaven?" Desoto asked immediately.

"Just got back," Carver said. "I talked to Kearny Williams."

"He's a sharper old guy than they give him credit for around there," Desoto said. "What's he think?"

"He thinks what your uncle thought."

"And you, *amigo*? What do you think?"

"That it's too early even to make guesses."

"Ah, you called to tell me you have nothing to tell me."

"Not exactly. I called to ask. I need a rundown on some of the people out at Sunhaven. A Nurse Rule—don't know her first name. She's the head nurse there. And the receptionist, young girl name of Birdie Reeves."

"Don't forget Dr. Lee Macklin."

"Who's that?" Carver asked.

"Sunhaven's chief administrator."

"The doctor who signed Sam Cusanelli's death certificate?"

"No," Desoto said. "A young staff doctor named Pauly signed it."

Carver looked out at the clouds scudding eastward, away from him, over the wide ocean. "I get the impression you might already have used the resources of the law to check on some of these people."

"Only Macklin and Pauly," Desoto said.

"And you came up with?"

"Nothing surprising. Macklin has the sort of background you'd expect. Administrator of a nursing home in Chattanooga before coming here with glowing recommendations. Married. No kids. Pauly, first name Dan, is a thirty-nine-year-old bachelor and earned his medical degree at Washington University in Saint Louis. Did a general medicine internship in Miami, practiced there for a while at a medical clinic, and two years ago opened his own practice in Del Moray. He has a contract with Sunhaven and calls on patients there daily."

"It all sounds okay," Carver said. "Nobody with an arrest record or a mail-order medical degree."

"Sounds okay far as it goes. But I don't have all the answers yet. I'll feed the names you just gave me into the wonderful world of the computer and see what happens. Shouldn't take long. You be around wherever you are for an hour or so, I'll call you back. You home?"

"Yeah," Carver said. It still felt odd to realize he, and others, now thought of Edwina's house as his "home." Carver's official home, a ramshackle cottage on the beach twenty miles north, was where he'd lived until he became involved with Edwina. He still slept there occasionally, when he had business in that direction and it was convenient, but less often every month. "I'll be here till you call."

"Get back to you," Desoto said, and hung up.

Carver replaced the receiver, shoved the kitchen phone back to its customary place near the wall, and downed the rest of his beer. It was already going flat and warm.

He'd limped over to the refrigerator and was about to draw out another can when he heard the diminishing snarl of Edwina's Mercedes as she downshifted to make the turn into the driveway. Then the faint swishing of tires on the hot concrete, soft against hard.

A car door slammed solidly out near the side of the house. She hadn't parked in the garage; she was going out again soon.

Carver decided to forget the second beer. He gingerly shoved the refrigerator door shut with his cane, careful not to dent or scratch its gleaming white surface.

"Too early to drink," Edwina said. She'd seen his car parked in the shade alongside the garage and knew he was in the house. And when she'd entered the kitchen she immediately saw the opened beer can on the table.

"Imagine me a thousand miles east," Carver said. "It's later there."

"Wetter, too," Edwina said. "Unless you want me to imagine you on an island."

Subject-changing time. "Show the condo?"

She put down her purse next to the Budweiser can and walked over to the sink. "Looks like I've got a contract. I'm supposed to meet the buyer at Quill this afternoon and write it up officially." Quill Realty was her employer and the beneficiary of her uncommon determination. "It's a close enough offer I think it'll be accepted without a counter."

"Congratulations," Carver said.

"Not yet. Maybe this afternoon. How'd things go at Sunhaven?"

"It's a depressing place."

"It might not be that way from the inside."

"Oh, it is," Carver assured her, "despite the cheery decor."

"I didn't mean inside the building," Edwina said. "I meant inside the heads of the residents. Your outlook and your expectations change when you get old. The things that make you content are different from when you were young."

"I've noticed that already," Carver told her. When he knew she was watching he ran his gaze down her body, to the elegant swell of calf and curve of ankle beneath the severely tailored blue suit skirt. "Then, too, there are things that stay pretty much the same."

"I only came home for a moment to get my listing book," she told him.

"So you say."

She gave him a grin he recognized, a sudden flash of wickedness across her strong, serious features. Her gray eyes were direct and challenging. "It's someplace in the bedroom. Want to come help me find it?"

That had been the idea. But suddenly Carver realized he didn't really feel like going into the bedroom with Edwina. He was still thinking about the old woman in the rocking chair. About all the misdirection in his world. *Well, none of it's true.*

Not much about Sunhaven was true, he suspected. The smiles, the soothing designer "up" colors, the lulling sense of bureaucratic routine. Something about the place . . .

"Fred?"

"Sorry," he said.

His abrupt change of mood puzzled her.

"I think I'll take time out for a drink myself," she said, stalking to the refrigerator in her high heels. She was of average height but appeared taller. She had a marvelous walk. "You want another beer?"

"No thanks."

She gazed into the refrigerator for a while, then poured lemonade into an on-the-rocks glass. She never drank alcohol when she was working, so she didn't add gin, as was sometimes her practice. She didn't even bother adding ice.

After closing the refrigerator door, she stood where she was and downed half the lemonade, as if she'd been parched and hadn't known it until she'd touched the glass to her lips.

"You don't realize what it means to grow old until you visit someplace like Sunhaven," Carver said.

Down went the rest of the lemonade. The tendons in her throat worked beneath the smooth flesh as she swallowed. "Tell me about it. Cheer me up."

Carver smiled. "Sorry, didn't mean to be glum. But you go to an old-folks' home, the experience stays with you for a while."

"Retirement home," Edwina corrected. She put the glass down on the sink counter.

"Well, that's the most favorable if not the most accurate thing this one could be called," Carver said. "You know how voodoo works?"

"I think so. Someone you believe in tells you you're cursed and going to die. So you accept it and slowly kill yourself from the inside."

"That's how it seems to be at Sunhaven. The residents are already chalked up, crossed out of life, and it's only a matter

27

of time before breathing stops and it's official. Death with a capital D, looking for a place to lie down."

"Not everyone's relatives think of them as already dead when they get past seventy," Edwina assured him.

"But too many do," Carver said. "Too many give them up to time because they know time always wins."

" 'Scuse me," Edwina said. She left the kitchen and returned a minute later carrying the listing book she'd gotten from the bedroom. "I don't think I want to hang around here while you're in this melancholy mood."

Carver smiled at her. He knew he was too cynical; he was trying to change that in himself. A lot had happened to him in the past three years. His divorce, the maimed knee and his new occupation, the death of his eight-year-old son. And on the plus side, Edwina. "I don't blame you for leaving," he told her. "I'm sorry. Maybe I'm not the right man for this case."

"You're not," she said, "but you're the only man. Desoto's your friend and he trusts you." She walked over to Carver and kissed him on the mouth. She tasted like lemonade.

"See you tonight," she said, and turned and swayed out of the kitchen.

He heard the side door open and close, and he waited for the sound of her car starting.

Instead, the side door opened and closed again, and someone walked across the carpet toward the kitchen.

Something cold moved through Carver, like the ghost of ancient premonition. Something beyond thought.

Edwina was in the doorway. She was frowning.

Carver set the tip of his cane and limped toward her.

"A car coasted down the driveway as I left the house," she said.

He stopped and stood near her. Why had what she'd seen upset her?

"Someone turning around," he suggested.

"No, it was far up in the driveway, near the house."

"What kind of car?"

"I'm not sure."

"Big? Small? What color?"

"It was a fairly large car. White. There was only the driver in it. A man. I only saw him for a moment, from the back, so I couldn't say what he looked like."

"Could be someone drove up here to see you, then changed his mind," Carver said.

"It's possible. Only there was something . . . furtive about the way he drove away. The car was just rolling down the driveway, already turned around and pointing that way. As if he'd backed up to where he'd been parked. I'm sure the engine was off."

Carver said, "I wouldn't worry about it. Just one of those things that happen without apparent reason. But if we knew more we'd understand why. Might be a number of explanations. Someone was coming to see you—or me—lost his nerve, and didn't want us to know he'd been here."

Edwina clutched her purse close to her body, as if she'd heard pickpockets were all around her. "Doesn't that strike you as a bit peculiar?"

"Sure. It's a peculiar world. Maybe your condo customer wanted to see how the saleslady lived. Maybe somebody at the office has a crush on you. You know how beautiful women attract this sorta thing."

Edwina didn't seem soothed by that line of reasoning.

He kissed *her* this time. Gently. On the forehead. "It's okay," he told her.

"Has to be, I guess."

She pushed a dubious smile his way and left the house again. He listened closely. This time she got in the Mercedes and drove away. He followed the wavering sound of the car's engine until she'd turned out of the driveway and accelerated.

Edwina's house wasn't visible from the coast highway. Someone who'd followed him here from Sunhaven might have wanted to get a look at what was at the other end of the long, winding drive Carver had turned onto. Seeing Edwina steer her car into the driveway shortly afterward might have piqued his curiosity and provoked action. Contemplating a quick getaway, the watcher might indeed have turned his car around and backed up the drive toward the house, then parked near enough for observation but far enough away so the sound of the engine wouldn't reach whoever was inside.

A pro would do it that way. That concerned Carver.

The phone jangled, startling him.

Probably Desoto.

5

But the caller wasn't Desoto; it was Alice Hargrove, a real-estate agent from Quill, trying to get in touch with Edwina. Carver had met Alice a few times, the first a long time ago when he'd pretended to be a customer so he could talk to her about Edwina's former lover Willis Davis. Willis was dead now, which was a condition he deserved.

Carver told Alice she'd just missed Edwina, made some polite and inane small talk, and hung up. He hated small talk.

A few hours later, he was dozing on the sofa with his shoes off when the phone brought him quickly awake. In his stocking feet, without his cane, he balanced himself with a palm on the sofa arm and lunged the few feet to where the ringing phone sat on an end table. Half asleep, he'd momentarily forgotten he was crippled.

This time the caller was Desoto. Carver could hear Latin music pulsing softly from the portable radio the lieutenant kept on the windowsill behind his desk. A sad guitar backing a woman's melodic lament. Love was full of drama on Desoto's station.

"Nurse Rule is Nora Rule," Desoto said. He told Carver her address in Del Moray. "She's been working at Sunhaven three

31

years. Before that she worked at a medical clinic in Miami."

"Wait a minute," Carver said. "Not—"

"Not the same clinic where Dr. Pauly practiced," Desoto interrupted. He began to read directly, apparently from his computer printout. Cop voice, cop talk. "Single female Caucasian, brown and blue, thirty-seven, five-feet-six, a hundred fifty pounds, born Camden, New Jersey. Father and mother deceased since she was twelve. They died in an auto accident."

"How can you know so much about her?" Carver asked.

"Told you, *amigo*, computers."

"Computers shit," Carver said.

"Okay, so she was in the military. They got records on her. The army. She was a sergeant. That's where she learned nursing. Got out in 'seventy-six and furthered her education, got a job, wound up with a better job at Sunhaven. The American way, to be upwardly mobile."

"What about the others?" Carver asked.

"Ah, there we weren't so lucky, my friend. Kearny Williams seems to be what he says he is: a retired over-the-road trucker from New Orleans. Ask me, everything about Kearny sets right. Nothing more pertinent on the doctors Pauly or Macklin. And nothing at all on Birdie Reeves."

Carver wasn't surprised about Birdie. The check did reveal she'd never been arrested. Someone that young, if they hadn't been in the military or been fingerprinted by the law or worked for the government, had nothing on them in the data banks that fed law-agency computers.

"Got any idea what her real first name is?" Desoto asked. "Surely can't be Birdie."

"Wouldn't think so," Carver said. "I'll find out."

Desoto read in his police lieutenant's monotone the addresses of the principal staff at Sunhaven. Then he said, "What now?"

"I'm going back to Sunhaven, but first I need a little background information. Your uncle express any fear for his life when he was at Sunhaven?"

"If he had," Desoto said, "I'd have gotten him outta there.

He did say a couple of times he thought somebody had tossed his room, gone through his things and then tried to put them back the way they'd been so he wouldn't know."

"Funny thing," Carver said. "Edwina was leaving here a few hours ago and saw a car glide down the driveway, she thinks with its engine off. A big car. White."

"Hmm. You maybe stirred the pot, *amigo*. Brought something to the surface." Desoto seemed glad, but at the same time somewhat regretful that he'd brought this kind of possible trouble to Carver. Or to Edwina.

"Why you hired me," Carver reminded him.

"Yes. You'll keep me informed?"

"Sure. Also why you hired me."

Desoto was quiet for a moment. Carver could hear the sounds that empty houses make: the breezy, rushing hum of the air-conditioning unit, the higher-pitched drone of the refrigerator. Now and then a low groan, creak, or snap. The noises made by materials heating and expanding beneath the malicious Florida sun.

Then Desoto said, "There's something you don't know, my friend. Something I should have told you."

Carver waited, not liking the icy sensation on the back of his neck. Friends were more dangerous than enemies. They came with obligations and they knew the chinks in your armor.

"There's another reason I wanted you to handle this," Desoto said. "If you didn't, it'd all be up to Lieutenant William McGregor."

Carver felt his stomach roll over. McGregor was a Fort Lauderdale police officer who'd been in on the investigation of the murder of Carver's son last year. He had this idea he'd saved Carver's life and solved the case, and parlayed that into a lot of publicity that resulted in his being hailed for heroism and then promoted. Those had been his goals all along. Justice wasn't of much interest to McGregor.

"I thought McGregor was a captain," Carver said. "In Fort Lauderdale."

"So he was," Desoto said. "But things do change. A few months ago there was some question about the fidelity of a Fort Lauderdale politico's wife. An older woman, but not without beauty."

"She was seeing McGregor?" Carver asked. He couldn't imagine the towering, homely McGregor as a lothario, stealing someone's wife. Not unless the woman liked her men vulgar and unscrupulous. But then, some women did.

"She was paying McGregor to keep quiet about her affair with her brother-in-law," Desoto explained. "Then one day she broke down and confessed everything to her husband, who was in a position to force McGregor's resignation from the Fort Lauderdale department. The only thing McGregor could do was accept a position in a smaller department at reduced rank. The Del Moray department."

"Why the hell would anyone hire him?" Carver asked.

"He's an acquaintance of your fair city's mayor," Desoto said. "And my guess would be the mayor doesn't have any choice. You know McGregor; kinda guy collects secrets and turns them into currency of one kind or another. Listen, I was afraid if I told anyone but you what I thought, what Uncle Sam had told me, there mighta been an investigation by the Del Moray law, with McGregor having a hand in it. I wouldn't want that. I don't like McGregor."

"Only folks who like poisonous snakes like McGregor," Carver said.

"Ah, then you understand."

"Yeah, but I'm not crazy about it. Sooner or later I'll have to deal with McGregor. Once he finds out you and I are in this—two cops, and not his best buddies at that—he'll get curious."

"You can deal with him; you have before."

"I'll keep him out of it as long as possible," Carver said. "Do my nosing around quietly."

"I'll let you get to your work, then, *amigo*, and I'd better get busy with mine. Crime's picking up here."

Carver said good-bye and hung up, leaving Desoto to his Latin rhythm and his busy day. Orlando was a rapidly expanding city with growing pains, and the police department was hard-pressed to keep up. It had been that way even when Carver was on the force. Always more crime than time.

He put on his shoes, then limped into the bathroom and rinsed away the sleep-sour taste in his mouth with some kind of blue, minty liquid Edwina had bought. He squinted at himself in the mirror. A dusty swirl of sunlight streaming in through the window highlighted his graying stubble and made it evident he hadn't shaved closely enough that morning. So what? Scruffy guys were in style. They were everywhere, like dressed-up bums, and women couldn't get enough of them. He raked his fringe of hair back with his fingers and told himself he was ready to do business. Told himself twice, so he believed it.

But as he stepped outside, the heat sapped him of much of his resolve. For a moment he thought it would be nice to go back in the house and stretch out again on the couch and breathe cool air. Then he gripped his cane with a sweat-slippery hand and reminded himself that the weather forecast called for rain sometime this afternoon. That would cool things off for a while, before it became steam. There was a price that went with beaches and palm trees, and it could be calculated in Fahrenheit.

He made his way across the wide driveway to where the Olds squatted half in sun and half in shadow.

The big engine fired right up and clattered loudly for a moment before the heat-thinned oil built pressure. Carver wristed perspiration from his forehead and jammed the shift lever into Drive.

He knew how to tail suspects, but his police training hadn't included spotting someone following him. When he jockeyed the Olds in a sharp, rocking left turn out of the driveway, he gave no more than a glance at his rearview mirror.

It was Satchel Paige who'd suggested people not look back because something might be gaining on them.

That kind of advice could cause trouble.

35

6

What Carver needed was a clearer picture of the people involved in this. What sorts were they? Where and how did they live? What were their interests? Their virtues and vices? Who were their friends? Every problem, almost everything in life, sooner or later came down to people. And what they did to each other and why.

Birdie Reeves lived in an apartment on the west side of Del Moray, away from the beach and the expensive neighborhoods of the young and successful and the wealthy retirees. Her building was on the corner of West Palm Drive and Newport Avenue. It was a low, rectangular structure of beige stucco with a brown tile roof. The stucco had been chipped away here and there by time and weather and needed paint. A large sugar oak grew in the front yard and cast dappled, shifting light over the grounds. Off to one corner a couple of grapefruit trees that long ago had been planted too close together rustled in leafy embrace. The building sat well back from the street, and the entrance was a cedar gate in an ornate wrought-iron arch that served as a trellis for vines on which bloomed brilliant red and yellow roses. The gate, and the curlicued iron arch, also needed paint. Some oil on the hinges, too. There was a piercing squeal as Carver shoved the gate open and pushed into a courtyard overgrown with weeds and more roses. Somebody here liked roses, all right. There were red and yellow ones to match the blossoms over the gate, but these bloomed on bushes instead of vines. Here and there a white rose or a purple hollyhock peeked out from between high weeds that bent over the brick walk.

Careful how he set the tip of his cane on the uneven bricks, Carver limped to a wooden door with a metal *D* nailed crookedly on it. To the left of the door clung more rose vines; they'd scaled the cracked and patched stucco wall by climbing from one rusty nail to another. The long nails were hammered in a staggered pattern to provide maximum coverage. Someday the wall would be nothing but roses, like a parade float.

In the middle of the *D* on the door was a round glass peephole. Carver knocked loudly and stood so he was visible to anyone inside. Birdie was working at Sunhaven; he figured the apartment was empty, but there was always the possibility of a roommate or long-term guest. If anyone answered his knock, he was ready with an insurance-salesman cover story to explain his presence. Carver could be full of bullshit when it was necessary.

The only sound came from the unit next door: a radio tuned to an Atlanta Braves day game. A huge mosquito lit on Carver's arm and drew about a pint of blood before he realized what was going on and slapped at it. He missed. The insect flitted at his nostrils as if angry with him and then droned away.

Carver tried the knob and wasn't surprised to find the door locked. This was the kind of neighborhood where people pinched their pennies for everything else, but spent lavishly for locks and window grilles. Even if he'd considered breaking and entering, he'd have had a difficult time picking the bulky, shiny Yale dead bolt that had recently been installed. He glanced at the door to the unit where the radio was playing. It had the same kind of apparently new dead-bolt lock.

The sportscaster's excited voice inside the apartment said,

"Deep, *deep* to left! Back, back, *back*! . . ." A much calmer voice behind Carver said, "She ain't home."

He turned and was face-to-face with a stocky, sixtyish woman in a limp tan housedress. Her broad face would have been plumply pretty except for half a dozen warts on her cheeks and the sides of her nose, and the glint of suspicion in her narrowed blue eyes. Carver knew he ought to do something to alleviate that suspicion. Muster up some charm.

He smiled. A beautiful smile that came as a surprise on such a fierce-looking man. "Know where she is?"

"At work. I'm Mrs. Horton, the building manager. Didn't catch your name."

"Didn't throw it," Carver said, still with the smile, "but it's Elmont. Roger Elmont." The name of the broker who handled his car insurance. "I'm in the insurance business." He nodded toward the new heavy-duty lock. "Theft insurance'd be a lot cheaper if more people put that kind of hardware on their door."

Mrs. Horton's eyes stayed narrowed; Carver saw they might simply appear that way due to the fleshiness of her florid face. She didn't offer her first name; she thought of herself as "Mrs. Horton," and expected Carver to address her as such. Hers was a righteous and proper world.

She said, "We had some burglaries in this area about six months ago."

"This building?"

"Nope. But right down the block. Fella walked in on two punks ransacking his apartment. They gave him a bash on the head took twenty stitches to close. So I got in touch with the building owner—he lives in Miami—and told him I wasn't gonna keep living here and managing the place 'less he furnished me and the other tenants with pickproof locks. He didn't want to at first, but he gave in."

"A wise move on your part," Carver told her. "And the owner's. Statistics show the burglary rate's up all across the country, but especially here in Florida."

"All them drugs, I reckon. People hooked on them's gotta steal to support their habits."

"That's a big part of it," Carver agreed. "It costs my company plenty, I can tell you."

"That what you wanna see Birdie about? Insurance?"

"Is that what her friends call her? Birdie?"

Mrs. Horton nodded. Her shrewd eyes flicked up and down Carver, lingering for a moment on the cane; he wondered if she thought he should be wearing a dark suit and carrying an attaché case full of boring material.

"Actually, all I wanted was to talk to Mrs. Logan about her statement on the crime she witnessed in February.

Mrs. Horton frowned, sniffed, and backed up a step. "Birdie's last name ain't Logan. And she ain't no missus. Hell, she don't look any older'n twelve. Little bitty thing, she is."

Carver gave her his alarmed, then puzzled expression. "Hmm. The main office told me to look up Mrs. Betty Logan, 126 Newport."

"This building only sides on Newport," Mrs. Horton said with a hint of triumph, as if they were in a game and she'd made a point by knowing something Carver had gotten wrong. "Address here's West Palm."

Carver leaned hard on his cane and wrestled his wallet from his hip pocket. He drew out one of his own business cards and stared at it. He said in an apologetic voice, "What they have written here is West Newport."

"Ain't no *West* Newport. Street runs north and south." She was smiling faintly; she was even one up on the bigger brains at the main office. Not a bad day for her.

Carver shook his head and gnawed his lower lip, as if suddenly irritated. He stuck the business card back in his wallet, the wallet back in his pocket. "I've wasted a lot of time."

Mrs. Horton shrugged and backed away a few more steps, allowing Carver room to move around her toward the gate. There was no mistaking the gesture. Obviously he'd wasted some of her time, too, and she was calling a halt to it.

He probed for firm ground with the cane and moved around her. She was wearing cheap, cloying perfume that mingled with the stale smell of perspiration. "At least I've seen some beautiful roses," he told her.

"Manager before me planted 'em," Mrs. Horton said. "Damn things come back year after year."

"Perennials," Carver said.

"I ain't sure what kind they are. Don't know one rose from another."

He apologized again for invading her iron-fenced domain to see a tenant who wasn't home and had a different name and lived on a different street and was someone else's tenant. He stopped short of telling her there was no Betty Logan on Newport Avenue. It would have been small satisfaction.

The landlady seemed to feel the same protectiveness toward Birdie Reeves that Kearny had displayed at Sunhaven. Maybe it was because of Birdie's youth and country-girl naïveté. Or maybe she was simply the kind of vulnerable kid who brought out the parental instinct in people over fifty. He wished he could get Mrs. Horton drunk and pump her for information about Birdie, but he doubted that she drank anything stronger than grapefruit juice squeezed from the fruit of the two trees at the south corner of the building. And that without sugar.

As he played the cane over the brick walkway and awkwardly sidestepped around the inward-swinging gate to the street, he was sure Mrs. Horton was watching him from the other end of the wild garden. They weren't her roses. He shouldn't be her thorn. She was glad to be rid of him.

Nurse Nora Rule lived in a different sort of apartment, on Osprey Avenue in the opposite end of town. It was a tan, three-story brick building constructed in a U around an oval swimming pool. The place was well tended and clean and the rent had to be high. There was a long, low carport along the west side of the building, shaded by a line of palm trees planted five feet apart. The trunk of each tree was painted white, the paint ending evenly about four feet above the ground. No one had ever given Carver an adequate explanation as to why people would want to paint the bottoms of tree trunks white. He'd stopped asking.

Each tenant had an assigned parking space. The carport was stocked with late-model cars, a few of them expensive Porsches and the omnipresent Cadillacs and Lincolns. Carver watched a blue Lincoln with darkly tinted windows back from its parking slot and drive away. Windshields and chromed bumpers that weren't shaded by the carport's roof glinted in the brilliant sun and hurt the eye.

As he limped toward Nurse Rule's apartment, he saw that the people poolside were mostly middle-aged and prosperous-looking. Sleek, tanned women lounged about with feline haughtiness in designer swimsuits and sunglasses. Some of the men wore gaudy matching beach outfits of trunks and pullover shirts or light jackets.

A few of the pool people interrupted their chatting and splashing to glance at Carver, but no one said anything about, or to, the gimpy guy dressed like a Paris hoodlum.

A blond woman with short, spiked hair, wearing a skimpy red suit over a deep brown tan, paused on the end of the diving board and grinned with toothy wickedness at Carver, then did a neat swan dive into the pool. Nifty. Hardly made a splash. She surfaced still grinning, but made it a point to ignore him as she swam toward the shallow end of the pool, where a couple of preteenagers were swatting around a white-and-yellow-striped beachball. She had a nice stroke. Nice everything.

There was an empty brass mailbox next to Nurse Rule's door with "Nora Rule, #3" neatly lettered on a white card under clear plastic set in a slot. All the units had similar fancy mailboxes. A large bee droned about the mailbox momentarily, saw that no one had sent any pollen, and buzzed away in concentric circles toward a flower bed in front of the unit next door. Wondering if anyone at the pool was watching him, Carver rang the doorbell.

41

No one came to the door. What a surprise.

A few minutes passed, and he casually stepped off the walk and stood shielding his eyes from the sun while he peered in through the front window.

The furniture looked new and expensive; it was modern, lots of glass and chrome on the tables, sharply angled arms and legs on the low, cream-colored sofa and matching chairs. One of those metal-shaded floor lamps that resembled bulging eyes on long, curved stalks arced above one end of the sofa, as if eager to read over someone's shoulder. Carver could see into part of the kitchen: a wooden table with gleaming steel legs, an uncluttered sink counter, fancy oak cabinets with brass hardware. There was a gigantic wall clock above the sink, pale blue and shaped like a frying pan, whiling away empty time with its red, oversized second hand. The apartment had about it a decorator's touch and an almost military neatness.

Carver pushed down on his cane and leaned away from the window. He glanced at his watch, as if he'd had an appointment with Nora Rule and was curious as to why she hadn't answered his ring. Then he shrugged and made his way back toward where he'd parked the Olds.

No one around the pool paid any attention to him. The kids at the shallow end were arguing over the striped beachball; the woman with the blond spiked hair was standing hipshot, busy sipping a tall, green drink with an orange peel splayed on the glass rim. She was listening raptly to a gray-haired, paunchy guy who apparently swam wearing half a dozen gold chains draped around his neck. Across the street, beyond the palm trees gently swaying in the breeze, lay the white-flecked, undulating blue of the ocean. A few sailboats and expensive cruisers were visible frolicking beyond the breakers.

Sun, sand, sails, drugs, God, and the army of the retired. Social Security checks worth hundreds of dollars, and execution-style murders over millions.

Ah, Florida!

7

Dr. Dan Pauly lived not in an apartment but in a house on Verde Avenue, in a moderately wealthy part of town. It was a very small, brick-and-stucco home with wooden flower boxes beneath the front windows and a curved stone walk that led from the driveway to the front porch. Perfect red geraniums, and some kind of leafy vine, thrived in the flower boxes, which were in glaring sunlight. The grass in the front yard was thick; it was so weed-free and uniform in length that it appeared shorter than Carver found it to be when he probed the ground with his cane. How high could it get and still look like a putting green?

He went through his friend-come-to-call act again. Appeared curious as to why no one had come to the door. Went to a window and peered inside, as if concerned that something might be wrong or that Dr. Pauly maybe had the TV on too loud and hadn't heard him. Then a walk around back, to see if maybe Pauly was in the yard. Another bold peek in a window. All for the benefit of any neighbor who might be watching.

The Pauly home was expensively furnished, but it wasn't

nearly as neat as Nurse Rule's apartment. There were newspapers stacked on the sofa, a glass and a coffee cup resting on an end table. A pair of shoes, or maybe house slippers, was on the floor near a chair, one of them flipped upside down as if it had been removed hastily and forgotten. A bachelor lived here, Carver reminded himself. A busy and not very tidy one.

Feeling as if he had a better idea of the who and what of Dr. Dan Pauly, as well as of the other Sunhaven staff members whose homes he'd seen today, Carver negotiated the curved walk back to the street. Dr. Macklin's home wasn't on his agenda; the Sunhaven administrator had family quarters at the retirement home itself. The better to rule the kingdom of the old.

It would have been convenient if Carver had seen something through a window that gave him some idea of what was going on at Sunhaven and who was making it go on, but real-life detective work didn't fall into place that way. Real detective work was more routine, and usually uneventful. Something like real police work, until when you least expected it a hyped-up punk with a cheap handgun zapped a bullet through your knee.

Carver had parked the car around the corner from Dr. Pauly's house, near a Chinese carry-out restaurant. Across the street from the restaurant was a small park with a playground, but it was too hot today for even kids to play outside. The grass was burned brown. Plastic swing seats swayed gently in the warm breeze. An American flag rippled just enough to send ropes and pulleys clanking rhythmically against its metal pole.

When Carver was a few feet from the Olds, his cane suddenly flew out of his grip and he was on the hot concrete before he realized what had happened. The heel of his right hand stung, where he'd caught himself and for a second taken the weight of his fall.

A medium-height but incredibly broad Latin man was standing about six feet away and smiling down at him. He had on faded Levi's and a sleeveless black muscle shirt. Had muscles, too. His arms were leg-size and layered with brawn in a way

44

that only years of weight training could provide. His shoulders were stacked with the same hard muscle. The man's thighs threatened to pop the stitches on his strained jeans. His waist was slimmer than Twiggy's.

He was holding Carver's cane delicately with both hands, as if he might decide to tap-dance and use it as a prop. Maybe tell a few jokes. His thick black hair was waved high in an attempt to make him appear taller. It made him look as if his head came to a point. No matter; he was a mile short of handsome anyway.

Carver worked his way up to a sitting position, his stiff leg extended awkwardly in front of him. He felt foolish and knew he couldn't get up all the way without his cane.

The Latin with the muscles looked around. Carver looked around. They were alone beneath the cruel sun. Across the street, the rope and pulleys clink-clanked lazily against the metal flagpole.

"You should find some other way to spend your time, *compadre*," the man said. He had a Spanish accent and a smooth voice that was oily with meanness and a dark kind of humor. He was getting a tickle out of this.

Carver wished he'd get near enough so his legs were within reach. If he could grasp a handful of Levi's and drag the man down with him, so they were both off their feet . . . well, the guy would probably dismember him like a Colonel Sanders chicken. Sometimes it was wise to admit you were outclassed. Sometimes it meant survival.

The wide man was irritated by Carver's neglecting to answer. He gripped the cane like a baseball bat, swung it as if trying to hit the ball out of the park, but whipped his hands back halfway through the powerful swing. The cane snapped in half, and the end with the crook flew into the street and clattered against the opposite curb. The laws of physics had defeated hard walnut. Carver had even seen the cane bend before it had reversed direction and split apart.

"You should pay closer attention to what I say, eh, fuckface?"

"Right," Carver said. "Better way to spend my time."

"Some other way's what I said. I don't much give a shit if it's better. It's your time. But it just goes to show how you don't pay close enough attention when you're told something."

"Other way," Carver repeated dutifully.

The man's smile broadened. He had deep-set and twinkling cruel eyes. He was a menace, all right. A *bandito* who'd stumbled upon Nautilus training. "Be some bad luck if your one good leg got broke up, you think?"

"Bad luck," Carver agreed. He felt a hollow coldness in the pit of his stomach.

"Human bone, it don't take much to snap it. Not like this cane." He tossed the broken end of the cane on the sidewalk in front of Carver, within reach. "Sharp. A weapon. You want to use it?"

"I'll pass." *Come closer, you bastard!*

"You got no guts, my man?"

Carver didn't answer. See if the musclehead would lose his temper. Carver was prepared to grab the broken piece of cane and use its sharp tip to penetrate flesh. His body was tensed, his fingertips almost tingling with anticipation. For the moment, fear was pushed to a far part of his mind.

The broad, smiling man edged nearer, but not quite near enough. He'd had experience. He was playing a familiar game. "Fuckin' cripple, you got no right to live anyway. Law of the jungle, you be dead meat in no time, you know?"

Carver stayed quiet, looking the man calmly in the eye. The Latin stared back at him in the way little boys observe insects being devoured alive by ants. No mercy. In fact, if any help was offered it would be to the ants.

"Goddamn straggler some bigger animal get an' eat. Chew up the good parts of you, spit out the bad." He spat a large glob of phlegm on the street to lend emphasis to his words.

"There a point to this?" Carver asked.

"Point is, fuckhead, you're playin' in a jungle. You understand?"

With a speed and grace Carver would have thought impossible, the man danced in, kicked him in the good leg, and danced out before Carver could react. Pain sliced like a hot blade deep into Carver's thigh. Then the leg started to go numb. Fear shriveled him. He didn't want to lose all mobility. *Not my one good leg! Oh Christ, no!*

"I guess you got the message, my man," the muscular Latin said. He spat again, artfully, through his broad white smile. Some of the warm spittle struck Carver in the face; a fleck of it got on his lower lip. "You take care of yourself, hear? Way to do that is to change your work habits. Maybe change your job, you think? You gonna do that?"

Carver began rubbing his leg, trying to coax feeling back into it. "Whatever you say."

"Thought so."

The broad man swaggered away toward the corner, proud of his bulk and what it had just enabled him to do. Should be wearing a truck license and he knew it. He didn't bother glancing back at Carver; he was moving on to more important matters and fresh game.

Carver dragged himself to the Olds, managed to get the door open, and struggled inside.

God, it was hot in there! Sweat was rolling down his face and the back of his neck. Within seconds his shirt was plastered to him. His arms were doing all the work; his hands were raw from clutching the sidewalk. He slapped at his thigh where the man had kicked him, glad to feel pain. Anything but numbness, helplessness.

Finally he managed to sit up behind the steering wheel. His eyes stung from perspiration, causing him to squint. But he saw a white Cadillac flash past the intersection, his assailant in the driver's seat.

He smiled grimly and started the Olds.

8

The white Cadillac stayed dead on the speed limit, cut east toward the ocean, then drove north along Beachside Avenue for a while, parallel with the shore. The wide and gleaming Atlantic made the car look small.

After about five minutes it leaned into a left turn and headed inland. Carver stayed well back and didn't think the Caddie's ominous driver had seen him, but there was no way to be sure. The broad and powerful Latino seemed to be an expert in his dubious profession of intimidator.

In the older, industrial section of Del Moray, the Cadillac suddenly picked up speed and rounded a corner with a scream of rubber on pavement. That was okay; the Olds could keep up. Carver goosed the vintage convertible up to sixty, played the brake and accelerator, and two-wheeled it around the corner in pursuit of the Cadillac.

Another screech of heat-softened tires on concrete. He leaned forward to peer intently through the windshield.

But the Caddie wasn't in sight on the narrow street. It must have taken the corner at the end of the short block, at the north side of a long, abandoned building that looked as if it might have been some kind of factory but was now obsolete and gradually surrendering to weeds and weather.

Carver sped to the intersection, braked to a skidding halt, and glanced east and west. No white Cadillac. The driver must have realized at some point that he was being followed and driven to this area of narrow avenues where he could lose Carver. The knowledge gave Carver the creeps; maybe the Latino had cunning in proportion to his muscle. Which would make him very dangerous indeed.

Carver cursed, made a left turn, and decided it was time to drive back to Edwina's and think things through. Past time, actually. This hadn't been one of his better days. He was feeling distinctly mortal.

Whack!

The right side of the Olds's windshield shattered and fogged. Tentacles of the webbed crack zagged over to the driver's side and tiny, glistening shards of glass fell and sparkled like bright sequins on the dashboard.

Carver sucked in his breath and dropped low in the seat, scrunched sideways and half on the floor. He did this almost instantly, but not before he saw the white Cadillac filling the rearview mirror. Fear shot through him with the suddenness of the bullet through the windshield.

With his head just high enough so he could peer over the dashboard, he kept one hand on the steering wheel and used the other to press down on the accelerator. All he could really see was the long expanse of the Olds's gleaming hood. He tried to picture the straight, narrow street, tried to remember if there were any parked cars. Any oncoming traffic. Tried to forget his fear.

Hell with it. No choice but to stay close to the center line and go.

Go!

The Olds jumped forward, engine roaring and tires screaming. Carver's heart kept pace with the racing engine. His hip battered against the transmission hump. After a few seconds, he chanced bouncing up high enough to get a fix on what was ahead, ducking back down immediately so he wouldn't provide a target.

It looked clear all the way to the intersection. He risked giving the car more gas, picking up speed. Flying low! He was going to make it!

There was a loud grinding sound and the steering wheel bent his thumb back painfully and jerked out of his damp and slippery hand. The Olds lurched sideways, rocked, shuddered, stopped. The engine died.

Carver didn't want to die next, but that seemed to be the idea.

Wishing like crazy he'd brought his old Colt automatic that was taped to the back of a dresser drawer in Edwina's bedroom, he lunged sideways and worked the passenger door handle. He shoved the door open, gripped the side of the seat and pulled, gaining enough leverage to help him clamber out the right side of the car.

As soon as he struck the pavement he was up on one elbow, looking in every direction, tensed for a bullet, trying to figure out which way to roll. He swiveled his head this way and that so violently he hurt his neck.

The white Cadillac was gone.

He was alone in the middle of the street.

It wasn't the kind of neighborhood where citizens rushed outside at the sound of an accident, even when the temperature *wasn't* in the nineties. There weren't many people living in the degenerating industrial neighborhood at all. He thought he heard a door slam. An old man carrying a bottle in a crinkled paper sack glanced over at him and shuffled on out of sight. A dog began barking incessantly in the next block, as if to warn everyone that something unusual was going down and for God's sake don't get involved.

The Olds was angled at forty-five degrees in the street. Carver used the side of the car for support to lever himself to his feet. The elbow he'd landed on was throbbing, but he didn't think it was broken. But what the hell, he wasn't a doctor. Better wait to see if it swelled.

On the left of the Olds and slightly behind it was an old black pickup truck. Carver had sideswiped it, adding to its lifetime collection of dents. The driver's-side door was creased, and flakes of rust jarred loose from the impact lay like dried blood on the street.

No choice but to stay inside the law. Carver kept his palms on the Olds's sun-heated metal and limped around to the damaged truck. He fished in his pocket and got out one of his business cards, then reached through the truck's open window and got a yellow stub of a pencil that was lying on the dash. He wrote "Sorry—call me" on the back of the card and stuck it beneath one of the truck's wipers, then tossed the pencil back inside. He didn't really expect to hear from the truck's owner, who might not even notice the new dent.

The man in the Cadillac had only been trying to frighten him further, he was sure. The bullet that had starred the Olds's windshield had penetrated the plastic rear window in the convertible top and snapped over the passenger seat next to Carver. The white Cadillac had been only a few feet behind the Olds; the shot had been a deliberate miss.

Carver could still see out the driver's side of the smashed windshield, and damage to the Olds from the accident was minimal. Anyway, the car was almost as dented and rusty as the truck it had hit. Here was an accident to make an insurance adjuster shake his head.

Carver eased his sore body back behind the steering wheel, started the Olds's engine, and slipped the shift lever into Drive. He was tentative at first, but within a few blocks he was sure the massive and outdated car was running as well as ever. It was a rolling symbol of Detroit's long-ago best; it wasn't easy to harm a monument.

After winding around side streets in the depressing neighborhood, he found his way back to Beachside Avenue and drove home.

He knew Edwina would still be out trying to sell real estate, but there was someone seated at the table on the veranda. It was dusk and Carver couldn't make out who it was.

There was an old umbrella on the backseat of the car. Carver twisted around and managed to reach it.

Using it as a cane, he climbed out of the car. The unopened umbrella supported him okay, but he had to stoop slightly to walk, and he had to be careful to plant the pointed metal tip on hard surfaces.

He swung the gate open and limped toward the seated figure, trying to think who it might be. A man, very tall—basketball-player tall. Loose-jointed and slouched in a casual—almost insolent—attitude. As if this were *his* home and Carver was dropping by to see *him*. Though almost entirely in outline, the man was familiar to Carver. Familiar in a way that stirred something unpleasant in the murky depths of memory.

When he got closer and the figure raised a can or glass in a mock toast, Carver still didn't know for sure who it was. Didn't know until the man spoke:

"Heard my old asshole buddy had some trouble, so I hustled right over here. Lock on your cunt's house is cheap shit, easy to pick, so I wandered on in and helped myself to a beer while I waited." A loud belch. "Knew you wouldn't mind."

McGregor.

9

Carver limped toward the table where McGregor sat sipping beer. McGregor watched him silently, and when Carver was about ten feet away extended a huge foot and shoved out the chair opposite him in an invitation to sit down. Playing the genial host as if he lived here. The grating noise of the metal chair legs on the bricks irritated Carver. He said nothing as he scooted the chair nearer to the table and sat down. He hooked the handle of the unopened umbrella over the back of the chair next to him.

McGregor hadn't changed much since Carver had last seen him. He was a lanky tower of a man, awkward yet with a suggestion of coiled strength. Homely, elongated face to match his long body, with a prognathous jaw, pale blue eyes, and straight blond hair and bleached-looking eyebrows. Nobody had ever told him about good grooming. His clothes were always wrinkled, he substituted cheap lemony cologne for bathing, and he looked as if he gave himself haircuts with a dull knife. There was a wide gap between his front teeth, contributing to the most lascivious grin Carver had ever seen. He gave no indication that he'd noticed anything about Carver, but Carver knew he'd noticed everything.

Without glancing at the umbrella McGregor said, "Think it was gonna rain?"

"Couldn't be sure it wasn't," Carver said.

"Where's the cane?"

"Broke it."

McGregor chewed on something infinitesimal for a moment, clicking his eyeteeth together and gazing out over Carver's head. "Walnut cane, wasn't it? That's hard wood. Not easy to break."

Carver wondered if McGregor would believe how the cane had really been snapped. He wasn't sure if he believed it himself; it had been astonishing, like witnessing a magic trick. That kind of strength and hand speed was only barely possible. "Ran over it with the car," he said.

"Careless."

"Yeah, not the sort of thing I'd do on purpose."

"Where's your lady friend?"

"She's working late. Putting together a real-estate deal."

McGregor showed Carver his lewd grin and let it linger. "You sure?"

"Sure as I need to be."

"I guess in that business the customers gotta work and can't get away during regular hours, so they meet all them sexy real-estate ladies in empty houses most anytime day or night. Some of those display houses, Carver, they even got water beds, mirrors on the ceilings. You'd be surprised what's done to close a deal."

Bastard, Carver thought. It was time to make McGregor uncomfortable. "How come you're not still a captain in the Fort Lauderdale police department?"

McGregor didn't look uncomfortable or embarrassed. Few had ever remarked on his sensitivity. He pursed his lips and spat out whatever it was he'd been chewing on. "Politics. Something you never understood. Now, I tell you, this ain't a social call. I'm on the Del Moray force these days."

"A lieutenant, aren't you?"

"Politics again. And again something you wouldn't grasp, old pal. Point is, like your live-in Edwina, I'm working tonight. Report came in a while ago of a fight over on Ashland Avenue. Real lively one. This guy had a stick or a cane, swung it and broke it on something, maybe the other guy's cranium. Couple of cars sped outta there before the police came. One of the cars was seen close enough that somebody gave us the license number. We run a make on the car, and it turns out it's a prehistoric Oldsmobile registered to you. Christ! I think. My old buddy in some kinda jam? So I drive over here and figure I'll ask you. I'm now asking."

"I'm not in any sort of jam," Carver said. He watched the darkening ocean behind McGregor. Far out at sea the lights of a ship glistened in the void of an indistinct horizon.

"Could be the witness read the license plate wrong," McGregor said. "They do get excited and make mistakes. And you got no injuries. None I can see, anyway. Other hand, you got no cane, either. Tough gimp like you, it don't seem logical you'd limp around all the time with an umbrella. Kinda sissified, you know what I mean. And I gotta say, it don't look a bit like rain." He tilted back his long head. "Hey, check out that moon!"

"I told you I ran over my cane," Carver said.

"Yeah. Thought it was a snake, I guess." He lowered his head, then tipped it back again to drain his beer can. He set the empty can down hard on the metal table and fixed his creepy pale eyes on Carver. "You on a case?"

"Sure. How I earn my bread."

"Got anything to do with this scuffle over on Ashland you weren't in?"

"No."

"Do me any good to ask you to fill me in on the facts?"

"Nothing to fill in. No concern of the law. I know my professional boundaries. It's not an open case with the police, and no crime I know of has been committed and needs reporting."

"I guess a domestic thing's what it is," McGregor said.

"That's right. Family matter."

McGregor grinned. "Family, hey? Well, there's all kinds of families. You ain't fucking with the Mafia, are you, Carver?"

"If I was, I'd sure tell them about you and let you in on the deal."

"And you'd let me in, too, I'm presuming, if there turned out to be a crime committed. Or if you stumbled across anything the law'd like to know. Being a relatively new man on the force, it'd be to my advantage to bring in a prize soon as possible."

"Way I hear it," Carver said, "you don't need to crack a case and make an impression here; you know the mayor. Know him even better than he'd like."

"Nothing wrong with using a little suck to attain a position, Carver. But it still wouldn't hurt if I made it evident I'm better at my work than anybody else in this piss-ant department. Hell, that shouldn't be hard. I don't plan on being a lieutenant all my career. I caught your name when the plates were run, knew you weren't the type to foul your own nest, so if you were working on something right here in Del Moray it must be important."

"It's nothing for you," Carver said. "If it turns into something, you'll hear about it."

"I better," McGregor said. "And hear about it personally and confidentially, you to me, for my ears only." His close-set little eyes got intense and mean. He was no hypocrite. He was a man who knew what he was and reveled in his own evil. "Even a mere police lieutenant can make things tough for private heat in the old hometown, hey?"

True enough, Carver had to concede.

McGregor stood up in sections, in the manner of six-and-a-half-feet-tall misplaced basketball centers. He extended his long arms and stretched languorously. Then he looked around and nodded approval, as if he were some kind of city inspector and everything checked out fine. "Hell of a nice place," he commented. "You hooked yourself one with money. Hey, maybe you oughta marry her before she gets wise to you."

"I'd show you out," Carver said, "only I can watch from here and be sure you're really gone."

"S'okay. I wouldn't want you following me around like a disabled Mary Poppins anyway." He reached awkwardly behind his back, inside his ill-fitting suitcoat, and withdrew something and tossed it on the ground. Carver recognized the clatter of hard wood on bricks. He looked down and saw both halves of his broken cane. "Case you might wanna walk on your knees sometime," McGregor said.

He ambled toward the gate, calling back over his shoulder, "You stay in touch."

"Count on me," Carver said.

He sat on the veranda and listened to McGregor's car start. The bastard had parked it around behind the garage so it wouldn't be visible and he could take Carver by surprise when he arrived. Maybe get him to say something while he was off guard. Gaining the advantage was McGregor's way of life.

The smooth, pale roof of the unmarked Ford dipped out of sight as the car descended the winding driveway.

Carver sat where he was and stared out at the ocean while it got completely dark and the moon took over. It made luminous the whitecaps of the breakers rolling in. One day like today was enough in anyone's life, he thought. The rush of surf on the rocks below was like the hectic whispering of gossips.

Where *was* Edwina this late?

Damn McGregor!

He got up and hobbled into the house, then to the front hall, where he got his spare cane from the back of the guest closet.

Carver felt whole again with the cane, more confident. It bothered him that he'd grown so dependent on it. He was a man who loathed dependency more than loneliness. That had caused problems in his life.

He heard the garage-door opener's wavering hum, and he limped into the living room and waited for Edwina to come in.

When she saw him she did a double take, smiled, and said wearily, "The buyer brought his attorney to the closing with him. Lawyers! They don't do anything but make things more confusing so they take four hours instead of one."

She tossed her purse and attaché case on a chair and walked over to Carver and kissed him. He pulled her down, held her tightly, and kissed her back. They were the sort of kisses that might lead to something.

They did.

Carver was lying nude beside Edwina in the soft glow of the bedside lamp, perspiring and listening to the ocean's now kindly whispers, when the phone rang.

Edwina stirred sleepily and beautifully. She kissed him on the arm, and then rolled to her side of the bed to stretch so she could lift the receiver. McGregor was right: the real-estate business knew no regular hours.

She mumbled a hello, then let her head drop back on the pillow and held the receiver out toward Carver. Her breasts and stomach were still reddened from the friction of his body. "For you. Dunno who."

Carver pressed the receiver to his ear; the plastic was cool and gave off a dry, acrid scent.

Before he could say hello a voice asked, "Fred Carver?"

Carver said he was.

"Name's Amos Burrel. I live out at Sunhaven." The voice was aged but still vibrant, with an edge of irritability and defiance, as if its owner wished he could simply disregard the years but knew that was impossible. "You the Fred Carver visited Kearny Williams here this morning?"

"The same."

"I got the room next to Kearny's. Walls are paper thin. Heard everything the two of you said."

Carver smiled, but at the same time made a mental note to speak more softly at Sunhaven. "You shoulda come over and joined the conversation," he said.

"Nope. I think you and me better have our own conversation."

"When?"

"Tomorrow morning suit you?"

"If it's convenient for you," Carver said.

"Hell, anytime's convenient for me. I never leave here. Catch me when I ain't on the pot, we can talk."

"I'll be there around ten," Carver said.

"Anybody asks, tell 'em you came to visit Kearny," Amos Burrel said. "But you come see me instead. Got that?"

"Got it," Carver said, and hung up.

"Who was it?" Edwina asked, half asleep and staring blankly at the ceiling.

"You know that old caution about the walls having ears?"

"Sure."

"That was Ears."

10

Birdie Reeves recognized Carver immediately and brightened the already brilliant reception area with her country-girl smile. Even her freckles seemed to glimmer. "Here to see Mr. Williams?"

Carver nodded and mumbled and gave back the smile. Birdie had been leafing through a sheaf of papers on the curved reception desk and diligently returned to the task as he limped past. Like yesterday, there were several Sunhaven residents in the lobby area. But the cast had changed except for the two men playing checkers, who again stopped their game to observe Carver's passage. No one had to be restrained in their rocking chair or wheelchair with a knotted sheet. No one was drooling or rambling incomprehensibly. The great dignity of age lay over the place today, and not the physical infirmities that assaulted that dignity.

In the hall, a white-uniformed attendant gave Carver a head-peck hello and bustled on. Carver passed Kearny Williams's closed door and knocked on the next one. The knock sounded surprisingly loud.

The door opened immediately and a once tall, now stooped man with gravity-drawn features stared out at Carver. His face was long and jowly, as if it were melting, and there were wattles of flesh beneath his chin. He was wearing old-fashioned horn-rimmed glasses that made him look like an owl after an all-night binge, yet there was a hint of defiance in his unblinking brown eyes and even in the way he held his emaciated bent body. Not defiance of Carver, but of diminishing time. Of where his world had finally cornered him. It was a defiance that rang hollow because it was born of his personal realization of mortality and his abject fear of it. Courage had become bluff.

"Amos Burrel?" Carver asked.

"Me," the man said.

"I'm Fred Carver."

"Hell, I know that. C'mon with me." He stepped into the hall and shut the door to his room. "Wish I could lock that damned thing, only they won't let us do that here. People steal any loose item they can get their hands on in a place like this. Steal a wart right off your ass just for the joy of it if they thought it could be removed. Get their jollies that way, some people. Figure you might not be around long enough to accuse them if you ever do work out who's the thief. Damned senior-citizen punks!"

"I thought we might talk privately in your room," Carver said.

"Why in hell would we do that when I told you it was you and Kearny talking in *his* room prompted me to phone you? Think the wall's any thicker from the other direction? Huh?"

"Guess not," Carver said, extending the cane as far in front of him as he dared with each step and struggling to keep up. Amos was at least in his mid-seventies, but he had a long-legged, awkward stride, a kind of rhythmic lurching that covered ground amazingly fast. If the Senior Olympics had a hall-walking event, Amos would be the guy to beat.

They left the building and crossed to another by way of a

walkway walled with pink plastic panels. Beyond the tinted panels were pink-hued palm trees, a pink resident gliding past, pushed in her wheelchair by a pink attendant. Beyond pink palms rolled the endless pink ocean. In the hot sunlight streaming through the panels, Carver glanced down at his hand gripping the crook of his cane. Pink.

A sign read VISITOR CENTER. An extra-wide pneumatic door hissed open, and fast Amos led Carver inside. It was much cooler in the visitor center, a relief. Carver was breathing hard. Amos wasn't.

The color of the panels had changed; everything here had a slight copper tint. It added color to some of the residents being visited by family and friends, made them seem almost robust despite the wheelchairs, canes, and metal walkers. Despite the infirmities dragging them down. Carver wondered if there were green plastic panels anywhere at Sunhaven.

The copper-hued rectangular room was one large area where vinyl sofas and chairs were clustered about in conversation groupings. So visitors wouldn't feel as if they and the aged residents were being eavesdropped upon, or too closely overseen by the uniformed staff that roamed casually about. Care was taken so the attendants didn't bring to mind the word *guards*. The building had long, thick brown drapes along the west wall, almost like theatrical curtains. The floor was carpeted in beige. The ceiling was white acoustical tile. Sound didn't carry well here, as Amos knew.

"Siddown, Carver," he said, dropping into a low brown vinyl sofa so hard Carver was afraid the old guy might snap a bone. The sofa sighed in protest, realized Amos didn't weigh more than a hundred and forty pounds, and immediately shut up.

Carver sat opposite Amos in a matching brown armchair. He glanced around. There were about a dozen other residents in the room, chatting with visitors whose dark hair and supple bodies made them seem as out of place here as extraterrestrial beings. The nearest of these was a young woman talking to an older woman in a wheelchair. They both had wide cheekbones and identical turned-up noses. Carver was sure they were mother and daughter. The young one looked infinitely sad, then momentarily panic-stricken, as she studied the woman in the chair, whose faded eyes had for a second been averted. The future was as real as the past. Waiting.

"We can talk okay here," Amos said. "Far as the attendants know, you're my son from Syracuse come to visit me."

"You got a son in Syracuse?" Carver asked.

"Could have. I was a policeman there forty years ago, before I became a paint salesman."

"What's being a policeman got to do with fathering a son?"

"Not s'posed to have anything to do with it, but it did. That's why I left the force and sold paint. First it was all oil-based and didn't move for shit, then when we started carrying a latex-based line I made a damned good living out of it. Stores can't sell people paint they gotta spend the whole day washing off themselves and everything else after they change the color of a wall. Latex is water-soluble and don't cause that problem. Know that?"

"Know it," Carver said. "You're not still selling paint, are you, Amos? You didn't lure me here so you could talk me into two-coating my house?"

Amos adjusted the horn-rimmed glasses where they rested on his ears and looked angry. "I tend to ramble now and again," he admitted. "It aggravates the piss outta me, Carver, even while it's boring you. But don't worry, I don't lose my place. I know why I asked you here."

"You overheard the conversation I had with Kearny Williams," Carver said.

"No need to remind me. Nor to remind me what was said. So Sam Cusanelli suspected there was something wrong with this place, did he? Well, lah-de-dah."

"That's what he told me yesterday. But you know that; you were listening."

"Well, Sam was right. When I heard you were private heat and a friend of that Lieutenant Desoto, I figured you'd be the one to tell."

"Tell what?"

Gray bushy eyebrows shot up in irritation. "Why, that there really *is* something wrong here in this colored ice-cube tray of a hell." Amos wasn't going to be used in any testimonial ads by Sunhaven.

"Why don't you leave here?" Carver asked.

Amos's jowly chin quivered and then became firm. "I as much as been told by my no-good daughter and son-in-law that if I do, they'll start legal proceedings to have me declared *non compos mentis*, unable to handle my own affairs."

"Really? Could they do that?"

Amos grinned, the loose flesh of his face arranging itself into a thousand creases. A light danced in his brown eyes. "It ain't a hundred percent certain. So they'd rather keep footing the bill for me here, while they wait patiently for me to die so they can inherit my money."

"How much wealth does a latex paint salesman accumulate?" Carver asked.

Amos's grin turned foxy. "Question is, how much do some people *think* he can accumulate?"

Carver was getting tired of this; he decided to drive to the point. "Can you tell me what's going on here that had Sam Cusanelli suspicious?"

"Same thing had me suspicious, maybe. 'Bout a month ago old Jim Harrison died. Nicest fella. From Eugene, Oregon."

Carver waited, watching Amos, whose eyes remained alert yet somehow disengaged, as if looking at some portion of the past that had abruptly materialized around them and that Carver couldn't see.

"People die here, Amos," Carver said gently.

"Yeah, it's that kinda place. And Jim had been sick. Like half the folks inside these walls. He had the room right opposite mine, and the night before he died I heard noises, somebody coming and going there. Wouldn't have struck me as odd, only it was three in the morning."

"Maybe Harrison felt sick and called for a doctor."

"No, I heard voices, but they weren't talking that way at all. Not like doctor and patient."

"Talking how, then?"

"Not arguing, just talking normal, but I couldn't make out the words. I happened to be awake, took the wrong goddamn pill for my arthritis and it got me hyper as a cat."

And maybe imagining things, Carver thought.

"It seemed to me I sniffed a burning smell, too. Like somebody'd just struck a match and lit a cigarette. Hell, I ain't smoked in years."

"Maybe that's why it's been *years*."

"Anyways," Amos went on, "next morning they found Jim dead in his bed. Stroke, they said took him. It can happen anytime, I guess, but Jim seemed healthy as Hercules the day before he died. Then I got to thinking about that late-night visit, and what I'd seen the night before that."

"You do a lot of observing at night," Carver remarked.

"My window looks right out on the parking lot. Besides, I got insomnia."

Not the wrong pill.

"But I don't tell nobody," Amos said. "Had it since I got the same uneasy feeling Sam Cusanelli had that something doesn't set right around here. They don't know here I was a cop long time ago. A detective-sergeant, matter of fact. I remember how to investigate. Night before Jim died I heard a car out on the lot and seen Nurse Rule talking to a fella had driven up by the main building. She got in the car with him and they sat and talked for a long time. Then out she climbed and went back in the building. A little later I heard her drive away in her own car."

"How long did they talk?"

"I'd guess about fifteen minutes."

"Maybe she met her boyfriend," Carver said. "Talked with him a while, then came back inside to do some late-night work. See any romance inside that car?"

"Romance? Nurse Rule? You shitting me?"

"I don't know the woman," Carver explained.

"Well, I wouldn't call her homely, but she's the type might cut off your balls after you put it to her. Know what I mean?"

Carver wasn't sure if he did. "Was it unusual for her to be here that time of night?"

" 'Course it was. Why I brought it up."

"She was never on the night shift?"

"Not Nurse Rule," Amos said, with the same undercurrent of respect Carver had heard in Kearny Williams's voice. "She's the boss."

"What about Dr. Macklin?"

"Hah! We don't see much of Dr. Macklin around here. It's Doc Pauly makes the regular rounds."

"What kind of guy is he?"

"Good man, Doc Pauly."

"Good doctor?"

"That, too."

"Birdie Reeves?"

"Just a real sweet youngster. Reminds me when I was a teenager couple of million years ago. Kinda girl when you're fifteen you're sure you're gonna marry someday." A change crept into Amos's worn voice. "Sometimes it even works out that way, but not often. Sure as hell didn't for me."

Carver tapped his cane on the carpet, rotated the tip a few times, and stared at the indentation it had made. "That's it?" he asked. "All you have to tell me?"

"That, and my cop's instincts are screaming there's something going down in this place."

Amos bit off his last word and clamped his lips together. Then he beamed and said, "This is Miss Jane Worthington."

66

There was something about the way he pronounced her name, like a sailor saying the name of his ship.

An old woman with cottony white hair and parchment skin was standing over them. She looked almost as tall as Amos and had a face from a Renaissance painting, oval and pure and somehow noble. She had the kind of beauty that never faded but instead settled in deeper with the years and made a mockery of superficial attractiveness. It had nothing to do with button noses or long eyelashes; it had to do with what she had been and was now, and how she would play in memory.

Jane Worthington waited a few seconds and saw that Carver wasn't going to be introduced and wasn't about to volunteer his name. Without commenting on this breach of etiquette she said, "Amos, you telling your lies to this fine young man?"

Amos didn't answer. Carver smiled. "What lies are those?"

Her wise gray eyes flicked to his cane but registered nothing. She'd seen handicaps before and knew what they did and didn't mean.

"I confided in Jane," Amos said in a near whisper. "Had to tell somebody what I thought. Damn it, I ain't Catholic—I couldn't tell a priest."

Jane shook her head. "Tell you the truth, Amos, I think you got two bolts and a nut loose. But it isn't hard to understand why. It's just that we don't like to think our friends should die and leave us, even in a place like this. It doesn't seem natural, though it's the most natural thing in the world."

"You don't think there's anything wrong here?" Carver asked.

"No, I don't. But I play along with Amos and don't tell anybody about his harebrained suspicions."

"I told you Sam Cusanelli had the same suspicions. Somebody else around here does, too. I ain't alone in this, Jane."

"I know you're not. It's the kind of thing that spreads. An undercurrent of gossip."

"Some gossip's true."

"Most isn't. That's why it's called gossip."

"See enough smoke," Amos said gloatingly, "and you look and you'll find a fire."

"And sometimes an arsonist."

Amos put on a huffy expression and leaned back in the sofa. He clearly didn't like being one-upped. This was a difficult woman for sure.

"I've heard enough and played enough games for today," Jane Worthington said. "Morning, Mr. Carver."

She left them, moving regally, her tall, lean body still graceful and not acknowledging her years.

Amos looked embarrassed. "Well, I did tell her who you were and that I'd invited you here to talk. She's the kinda woman you talk to and secrets sorta slip out."

"Amos, I think you've got a crush on Miss Jane Worthington."

The old man's long face turned tomato red. "Piss on you, Carver! I was married to Mrs. Burrel forty-three years before she died of a liver infection in 'eighty-two. Besides, Jane's too young for me. There's damn near five years' difference in our ages. I thought you'd take what I had to say serious instead of funning around."

"I do take it seriously," Carver said. "But what if I take what Jane Worthington says just as seriously? According to her, you tend to exaggerate now and then. Lies, she called them. But I don't figure you for a liar."

Amos's face creased into a grin. "Then you believe me?"

"I do more or less. You're the second person I've talked to who thinks Sunhaven's something other than it should be. And we've got to include Sam Cusanelli's opinion."

"Sam seen the fella once, too," Amos said.

"What fella?"

"Why, the fella Nurse Rule was talking to in the big white Cadillac night before Jim died. One you said mighta been her boyfriend."

Amos suddenly drew in his breath in a gasp and his eyes fixed on something behind Carver and then wavered and dropped. He was staring at his lap as if he'd just spilled food there.

"Who's your friend, Amos?" a crisp female voice inquired.

Without looking up, Amos said, "This is Mr. Fred Carver, Nurse Rule."

Though she was stockily built, she didn't give the impression of being a large woman; yet she filled her space in the world. She was wearing a white uniform with a squared blue collar and carrying an empty clipboard with a pen clamped to it. Brown hair, narrow blue eyes, very thin lips that were probably always curved in a smile that meant nothing. A face like a lumpy potato, yet, as Amos had said, for some reason not exactly homely. Her hands were surprisingly small but strong-looking. Square-fingered and without nail polish. Functional tools of her trade.

She trained her dead but bright eyes on Carver and he felt a current of cold, primal knowledge; she was the stuff of black widow spiders and feral animals. She repelled and frightened and fascinated people more as they got to know her and depend on her.

"Are you a relative?" she asked Carver.

"He's a friend," Amos mumbled. The son-from-Syracuse story was forgotten. It wouldn't wash with Nurse Rule.

She stared at Amos, her flat, bland features registering mild curiosity. "Amos?"

His head trembled on the stalk of his neck, but he looked up at her with effort.

Her curved lips arced in a wider smile that gained no warmth. "Have a nice visit, Amos." Her gaze swung to Carver again. It meant something when she looked at people, every time, or she wouldn't have bothered. "You, too, Mr. Carver."

She walked away. A no-nonsense stride, no excessive arm-swinging and very little hip motion. Her white shoes trod soundlessly on the earth-colored carpet.

"Why are you so afraid of her?" Carver asked.

"My bath . . ." Amos said, still obviously shaken by the possibility of having been overheard by Nurse Rule.

"What about your bath?"

"Last time my back went out and I couldn't move, I wrote a letter of complaint to the state about the way I was ignored all night when I kept ringing for help. Nurse Rule gave me my bath the morning after that and threatened to scald me bad if I wrote any more letters. She'd say it was an accident, something wrong with the hot-water thermostat. She'd get away with it, too; you can be damned positive of that."

Carver wasn't sure he was hearing right. "She *what*?"

"You heard," Amos said softly. "I ain't never told anybody till now. Not even Jane." He stared into Carver with eyes that had completely lost their glint of defiance. "My back goes out from time to time. Never can tell when. Jesus, it makes me feel helpless! I'm counting on you, Carver."

Carver stood up and leaned on his cane. He rested a hand on Amos's thin shoulder but withdrew it hastily when the shoulder began to quake. Amos quickly shoved something into the hand. A damp scrap of white paper, tightly folded.

"What's this?" Carver asked.

Amos wasn't going to answer. Wasn't going to look up from staring at his lap again. He was crying soundlessly when Carver limped away.

Was Jane Worthington right about Amos's overactive imagination and his suspicions? Was the story about Nurse Rule and the bath true? Maybe Carver had wasted his time listening to the paranoid delusions of an old man haunted by the past.

An old man who'd seen Nurse Nora Rule sitting with someone in a white Cadillac.

Or thought he had.

The sun was still beating down outside, but Carver was chilled.

In the parking lot, he stood near the Olds and laboriously unfolded the scrap of paper Amos had given him. Scrawled in light pencil was a series of numbers. Carver knew immediately where Amos had copied it from.

A license plate.

11

When Carver left Sunhaven he drove south on Route 1, then west on the Bee Line Expressway toward Orlando. He left the convertible's top up to block the sun, but all the windows were cranked down and the wind whirled and roared like a hurricane in the speeding car, whistling through the cracked windshield, slapping taut canvas against the steel struts above Carver's head. *Mach one! Mach two!*

At much slower speed, he maneuvered the Olds through downtown traffic in Orlando to the tan brick and pale stone Municipal Justice Building on Hughey. He parked in the side lot, near a row of dusty tan patrol cars.

When he went inside to talk to Desoto, he was told by a desk sergeant named Markus that the lieutenant was at lunch. Carver knew Markus slightly from his time on the force, and Markus wanted to pass the time of day with cop talk, but Carver had things to do and got out of there as soon as he could.

He limped from the building and made his way toward Orange Avenue, where he was sure he'd find Desoto in Rhonda's Restaurant. Heat rose in waves from the city's baked concrete,

71

which never cooled completely this time of year, except in the early morning hours or after late rains.

It wasn't much of a walk, even for a man with a cane, but by the time Carver pushed open the door to Rhonda's and basked in the rush of cool inside air he was soaked with sweat and felt slightly light-headed. He wondered how people had managed to live in Florida before air conditioning. And why. Heat, alligators, and mosquitoes weren't much by way of attractions. Standing just inside the door, he back-wristed perspiration from his forehead, then looked around in the dimness.

Rhonda's specialized in spicy Italian food, a weakness Carver and Desoto shared. The restaurant had a small bar off to the left and about twenty white-clothed, round tables arranged along the walls. There were half a dozen more tables on a raised area accessible by three wide, carpeted steps. The lunch crowd was still evident; there were only three or four empty tables.

As the headwaiter was angling over to seat him, Carver heard Desoto say, "Your aging eyes going bad as your leg, *amigo*?"

Desoto was sitting alone at a table not five feet from Carver. He'd finished eating; dishes were spread out in front of him, pushed back on the table, and he was enjoying a stein of beer. It was dark beer with no head on it.

Carver waved the waiter away and sat down opposite Desoto. He decided not to acknowledge that crack about his eyes. Sure, it wasn't really so dim in Rhonda's, but he'd trudged all the way up here from Hughey in bright sunlight. Because it took a while for his eyes to adjust didn't mean they were going bad, that he was getting old. But it occurred to him that everyone was getting old. Nobody got off the treadmill. And the treadmill never stopped.

"Had lunch?" Desoto asked.

"Don't want any. Too hot to have an appetite."

"It is hot out there. You've worked yourself into a lather pursuing my case, eh?"

"Exactly."

A waitress popped out of nowhere, a middle-aged woman

72

with a dour expression and gray-brown hair bunched with over-sized bobby pins in a bun like a bird's nest on the back of her head.

Carver asked for a draft beer. Not much of a tip in that, the woman's face seemed to convey, as she nodded and ambled away on sturdy legs to place the bar order.

After she'd returned with his drink, Carver brought Desoto up to date on everything that had occurred since they last spoke. He described in detail his morning visit with Amos Burrel.

Desoto listened without once interrupting, his head slightly bowed and his dark eyes serious. It was as if something on the tablecloth had gripped his attention. Now and then he sipped at his beer. When Carver was finished, Desoto signaled the dour waitress for another drink.

"Did Sam ever mention Amos Burrel?" Carver asked.

Desoto shook his head no. He held what he was going to say until the waitress had delivered the fresh beer and then left, juggling an armload of dishes as she waddled toward the back of the restaurant. "This Amos. From what you say he sounds like some of the others I met out at Sunhaven."

"What others?"

"Residents. Friends of Uncle Sam. Some of them, I tell you I don't know about. Sad. People get old, they begin suspecting everyone's out to get them. They think people are talking about them, stealing from them. I know Sam wasn't like that, but the others I'm not so sure. Old age can be like a curse, *amigo*. Primitive societies used to think old people got irrational because in their enfeebled state they became possessed by demons. Some religious folks here in Florida still believe that. You believe in God and his angels, it follows there's a devil and his demons, eh? It divides the world nicely and makes things simple."

"I can't judge whether Amos is senile," Carver admitted. "He's suspicious and unpredictable, but maybe he's been that way all his life. Maybe he's telling the truth right on the mark and has good reason to be afraid."

Then he told Desoto about the folded scrap of paper Amos

had thrust into his hand as he was leaving. He gave the paper to Desoto, who studied it, shrugged, and excused himself.

Carver watched him, a tapered, elegant figure that turned female heads, walk to the end of the bar and ask to use the phone. He was going to run a make on the license number. It wouldn't take long.

Five minutes later, Desoto—pale suitcoat buttoned, tie neatly and securely knotted, looking like the coolest thing in the room—returned to the table and said, "White 'eighty-seven Cadillac sedan registered to Raphael Ortiz. Address in Del Moray."

Desoto sat back down, tried a sip of beer, and then set the stein in the center of the table as if the taste disagreed with him. "This Raffy—as he's called—is a major-league bad-ass, *amigo*."

Carver was surprised by the distress in Desoto's voice. "How bad can he be?" he asked.

"Ah, you might say he's almost a legend. Anyway, I and many others know him by reputation. He's a Marielito who came over in the boat lift from Cuba. Computer says in Cuba he was convicted of murdering his brother. Then, while in prison, he gouged out a guard's eyes with a broken bottle, and his sentence was changed so he could never be released. He built himself up with weights in prison—not weights like Nautilus equipment; he used stones. Then he became an expert in martial arts. Made himself into the baddest of hombres. No one would cross him. He ran the place—the warden, the guards, everything. Castro must have been overjoyed to be rid of him. That's Raffy Ortiz."

Carver waited, his wrist resting on the curve of his cane.

Desoto leaned forward and his handsome face took on a somber look. "Now, there's something I know that isn't common knowledge or part of Raffy's sheet. Four years ago in Miami a crooked pharmacy was robbed of some designer drugs. Ecstasy, Eve, that kinda crap. A hostage was taken, young girl who was working behind the counter and was the wife of one of a rival faction in the drug trade. She was found in the swamp a week later. Usual things had been done to her, the M.E. said, but also some *un*usual things. While she was alive. Miami said she had to have been looking forward to finally dying. Said they had it on good authority it was Raffy's work. But there wasn't enough evidence to charge him."

"Means he's sick, not tough," Carver said.

Desoto tilted back his head and arched a dark eyebrow; he wasn't finished talking. "The dead woman's husband went berserk and vowed revenge, went looking for Raffy. The story is Raffy came to him. With Raffy's buddies looking on, Raffy and the husband had their left wrists tied together and commenced to carve themselves up with knives. You know the ceremony: test of machismo. We of Latin temperament do that kinda stuff. Some of us."

Carver was familiar with the bound-wrist method of knife fighting to the death. It made Roman gladiators seem like pansies.

"Raffy enjoyed it, they say. And was very skilled. After slitting the husband's throat he castrated him and stuffed what was cut off into his mouth. That's the supreme insult in Raffy's world."

"Hard to insult somebody who's dead," Carver observed.

Desoto stared hard at Carver. "You hear what I said, *amigo*? Please don't take it light. This Raffy, he *enjoyed* all of what I described. I heard he gets a hard-on when he fights." Desoto touched his beer stein but didn't lift it. He sat back. "Thing is, I regret getting you into this, my friend. It's time we give it to the Del Moray police, eh?"

"There's nothing to give them," Carver said. "The word of an old man that he saw somebody in a car he thinks had that license-plate number, talking to the head nurse at Sunhaven. No crime there. And remember, Amos's family's about an inch away from having him declared legally insane so he'll be committed. Some potential witness."

Desoto sat silently for a moment and considered what Carver

had said. He didn't seem impressed. "The fight you had, Carver. If you can call it a fight. The assailant you described fits Raffy Ortiz. Got to be him. This is more than I wanted from you. Let's give it to McGregor, let him deal with Raffy." Desoto smiled. "It could be interesting: J. R. Ewing versus Godzilla."

"Not yet," Carver said. "You hired me, so I'll do it my way."

"*Your* way? Don't hand me that Frank Sinatra shit."

"Lyrics are Old Blue Eyes's, sentiment's mine."

"He won't bleed, you will."

"I'll try to approach this so it doesn't work out that way."

"I can fire you, *amigo*."

"Someone who hasn't paid somebody can't fire them," Carver said. "Though I admit it's a fine legal point."

A tragic expression slid into Desoto's liquid brown eyes. He knew Carver. "So that's where we are. You can't turn loose of this one, can you?"

"Won't turn loose."

"Same thing. You don't know the difference; that's your problem."

"I'm in it till it's settled," Carver said.

Desoto sighed.

"That's how it is," Carver said. He spoke calmly but there was no compromise in his voice.

"Then I'll give you more information about the people you're dealing with at Sunhaven," Desoto said. "I checked further on Birdie Reeves. She's a fifteen-year-old runaway from Indianapolis. Playing big girl, driving around Florida without a license. Real name's Beatrice Reeves."

And her landlady knows about it, Carver thought. That explained the suspicious, protective attitude when he'd gone to her apartment building. And someone in administration at Sunhaven might know Birdie's true age and her past.

"We could turn her in and see she's sent back," Desoto said, "but she fled a hellhole. Mother beat her since she was an infant, and her father was a sicko who found her impossible to resist when she got to be eleven. The court sent her to a foster home two years ago and she was molested there. She ran. Who could blame her?"

"She seems to be doing okay here," Carver said. "Got a job, her own apartment. Not much, but something. Best thing to do is leave the kid alone, let her pretend she's grown up. She really will be soon enough."

"My recommendation also," Desoto said. "Though not officially. We never talked about this, okay?"

"Talked about what?" Carver asked.

Desoto stood up and tossed two folded bills, a ten and a five, on the table. "Beer's on me."

"I'm grateful."

"I'm grateful, too," Desoto said sincerely. "Also fearful." He smoothed nonexistent wrinkles in his coat and pants. "I'm glad you decided not to order anything to eat. I'd have felt like I was dining with someone during their last meal."

"I'll report to you again soon," Carver said, "if for no other reason than to get my confidence restored."

Desoto flashed a smile that was very white in the dim restaurant and clapped Carver on the back. "My way of saying be careful, *amigo*. Please don't underestimate Raffy Ortiz. This is a guy can make your childhood nightmares seem pleasant."

He left the restaurant hurriedly, looking straight ahead, back and neck rigid, like a kid who'd just as soon not glance at shadows. Handsome in his tailored suit. Dashing as a movie star.

The glum waitress coasted in, scooped up the bills from the table, and asked Carver if he wanted anything else. He told her no. She seemed glad as she set off toward another table.

He sat quietly and finished his beer. He couldn't specifically recall any of his childhood nightmares, but he knew he'd had them. Was sure he had. He was no exception. They were part of his experience, vague and undefined and still with him. Submerged in a dark tidepool of his mind.

And closer to the surface than they'd been in years.

12

Carver had barely crossed the city line into Del Moray when a siren gave an abbreviated yowl behind the Olds, like a yodeler who'd suddenly had a hand clamped over his mouth. He looked into the rearview mirror and saw the whirling red and blue roof-bar lights of a patrol car flashing feebly in the sunlight. Immediately his gaze flicked to the speedometer. He was driving a few miles per hour below the limit. While he was in Orlando, he'd gone to an auto salvage yard where he often got used parts for the Olds and had his cracked windshield replaced in almost a matter of minutes. Hadn't violated any traffic laws, he was sure. Not in the ten seconds he'd been in Del Moray before the patrol car had slid in behind him.

He slowed the Olds, let it roll onto the road's sloping shoulder, and coasted to a stop. Gravel crunched beneath the tires and pinged off the insides of the fenders until the big car ceased motion.

Carver watched in the side mirror as the patrol car's door opened and a tan uniform climbed out and swaggered toward him, arms swinging wide to clear the nightstick, cuffs, and holstered gun bobbing on his hips. As he got nearer, Carver heard gravel scrunching beneath his soles with each measured step. The inexorable stride of the law.

"You Fred Carver?"

The voice startled Carver. It came from right over his shoulder. The cop had been much closer than he'd appeared in the mirror; mirrors did that, distorted distance.

Carver acknowledged who he was and waited for the uniform to ask for his driver's license.

Instead, the dry, official voice said, "Lieutenant McGregor wants to talk with you."

Was *that* what this was about?

"He knows my address," Carver said. "My phone number, too."

"All I know," the uniform said, "is my job's to see you come to headquarters and be interviewed. Immediately."

"What's with McGregor? He doing this to demonstrate his authority?"

The cop's beefy, perspiring face almost broke into a smile. They were getting to know McGregor in the Del Moray department. Getting to fear him, too. "He's got the authority to demonstrate, Mr. Carver," the uniform said. "So do I, you want to make things difficult. No sense creating a problem, though. Will you follow my car, sir?"

"All right," Carver said. Why fight this? He'd see McGregor and get it over with as soon as possible. "I'll be in your mirror, officer."

Now the ruddy-faced cop did smile. It was an almost apologetic flickering in the blue eyes and at the corners of the mouth. He didn't like this. He had more important things to do than errand-boy bullshit for the higher-ups and he was relieved Carver was cooperating. McGregor must have suggested there might be an argument; take the hard-ass line with that rebel Carver, if you have to. No need. Carver had kept it as cool as possible in ninety-degree heat.

The uniform said, "Thanks, Mr. Carver."

Carver started the Olds engine and waited until the patrol car had pulled out onto the road and moved in front of him.

Though he knew where police headquarters was, he kept the Olds's long hood aimed at the cruiser's back bumper all the way. Make the uniform feel useful.

Del Moray police headquarters occupied a converted brick house with tall white colonial pillars supporting a miniature porch roof. The roof wouldn't be of much use in providing shade or shelter from rain. The booking area was in what had been the living room. A curved stairway led to offices and holdover cells upstairs. Lockers, the squad room, and briefing and interrogation rooms were in the basement. There were more offices beyond the booking desk, small ones, made by partitioning the area that had been the dining room, kitchen, and a downstairs bedroom. Despite the presence of uniformed police, the institutional green paint on the walls, and the crackling background chatter of a dispatcher, to Carver the place still felt more like someone's home than a police station. Beaver Cleaver might burst in to get his bat and glove any minute.

There was an Amoco service station across the street that kept the patrol cars running. On the left of headquarters, a parking lot and then the intersection. On the right was a grassy, vacant lot, and then a row of houses similar to headquarters, only these were real houses, where families lived.

The uniform who'd summoned Carver had gone on about his business, and it was a short, young, blond policewoman who ushered Carver into McGregor's office. She was overweight but well proportioned and walked lightly, on the balls of her feet and with her toes pointed out, like a dancer. Very official in her tan uniform and beige-tinted nylons. Carver noticed she didn't carry a side arm.

"Thanks, Myra," McGregor said from behind his desk. "That's all for now, babe." Myra looked slightly ill and withdrew without speaking.

McGregor said, "Small-town bitch thinks she's Cagney or Lacey and wants to be out on the street her first year on the force. I'm keeping her here till she gets more experience. Let her type reports, do filing. Office stuff. Best thing for her at this point."

"For her own good," Carver said, leaning on his cane.

"Mine, too. 'Cause I'd rather look at her ass all day than at some spread-hipped copper who's spent half his life squatting in a cruiser. See you got a new walnut cane, Carver. Siddown, why don't you, before you break that one, too."

The office was tiny, not what McGregor had gotten used to as a captain in Fort Lauderdale. It was painted light green, like the rest of headquarters, and had brown linoleum and a gray steel desk. The linoleum was supposed to look like hardwood floor but didn't. There was a copy machine and file cabinets along one wall. A plain oak chair off to the side of the desk. The single window was dirty and afforded a view of the parking lot. There was wire mesh over the glass, in case a prisoner or Myra tried to escape. Headquarters had central air conditioning, but it was warm in the office and smelled like McGregor's cheap lemon-scent cologne.

Carver lowered himself into the oak chair, extended his stiff leg out in front of him, and rested his cane against his thigh lightly, holding it so it wouldn't slide to the floor.

"Got a phone call about you," McGregor said, making a tent with his long-fingered hands, pressing the fingertips together hard enough so they whitened. Carver wondered if McGregor could palm a basketball. If he'd been a star in high school, getting cheerleaders drunk and taking advantage of them.

He was running with the ball now. Carver waited for him to continue.

"Call came from, of all places, a retirement home. Nurse in charge out there was wondering about you."

"Complaining about me?"

"Oh, not complaining," McGregor said. "Wondering, is all.

81

Said you been hanging around the past few days, talking to some of the old fuckers out there. Thought you might be some kinda con man. Maybe working the pigeon drop on the old marks. Hey, I explained to her you were an operative of the law. She said she wouldn't trust a private detective to give her change for a dollar. Know what? Neither would I."

"You must have had a bad experience," Carver said.

McGregor crossed his long arms and sat back. Worked at looking thoughtful. "Now, why would a guy like you be floating around a retirement home? Maybe developed a yen for older women. Maybe wanna pick up some pointers on hobbling around with a cane. I dunno. Gee, I just flat dunno. Maybe you'd be so kind as to tell me."

"I'd be so kind. It's simple. I know one of the residents and went to visit him."

"No," McGregor said, "that ain't it. I checked. You don't really know anybody out there. I did learn a few things, though. Old fella that died there last week was related to our mutual friend Alfonso Desoto. Uncle or some damned thing. That have anything to do with your uncommon interest in the place?"

"No," Carver lied. He knew he'd eventually have to tell McGregor he was working for Desoto, but this wasn't the time.

"Keep in mind you're licensed to do your sleazy kind of work. That license can be revoked."

"I'm within the rules," Carver said. "No crime I know about's been committed. No evidence is being withheld."

McGregor began rocking back and forth gently in his chair. "You say so, I believe you. Not because you're a Boy Scout but because you're just smart enough to know I'm not bluffing, so you won't step over the line."

"Your threats don't mean shit to me," Carver said. "Reason I stay legal is a yard beyond your grasp: professional ethics. You probably hear rumors of them from time to time."

McGregor laughed, opening his mouth wide to reveal his gapped teeth. His breath was so sour it cut through the sweetened lemon scent of the cologne and nauseated Carver. "We both know there's no such thing as ethics, asshole. Only people who can claim them are the ones ain't been tempted strong enough to give in."

Carver said nothing, thinking McGregor might be right. It was a depressing prospect.

McGregor ran his tongue around the inside of his cheek, distorting his features. He concentrated on trying to suck something out from beneath his molars for a while, then apparently succeeded and said, "You know Hitler had only one nut? Monorchids, they call people like that."

"Didn't know," Carver said.

"Caused a lot of trouble for a guy with one nut, hey?"

"History time?" Carver asked. "Or biology class?"

"Freshman law enforcement. Pay attention. Raphael Ortiz has got three nuts."

McGregor looked so serious Carver had to try not to smile.

"They examined him when he did a short stretch in Raiford Prison. Three nuts. No kidding. Three—count 'em."

"You count 'em."

"Know what that means?"

"Special underwear, I guess. For whoever this Ortiz guy might be."

"By the by, I checked the license-plate number a witness to that fight on Ashland gave us. Tussle that took place near where you accidentally drove over your cane. White Caddie, belongs to Ortiz. Then there was a rumor of a shooting in the west end of town. Fella did the banging sped away in a big white car. You say you don't know Ortiz?"

"Heard of him," Carver admitted.

"I'm not surprised. Most every cop in Florida has."

"Supposed to be a tough guy, isn't he?"

"Goes way beyond tough," McGregor said solemnly. "If he'd wanted to kill you, you'd be dead. He's a scary guy. Three nuts. He ain't like you and me."

"Nice of you to warn me," Carver said. "But now that you have, I think I'll leave." He set the rubber tip of his cane on the linoleum and raised himself to a standing position. He was looking down at McGregor now. McGregor didn't like that. He stood up and looked down from his six-and-a-half-foot height at Carver.

"Didn't have you brought in so I could warn you," he said. "I don't much give a shit what happens to you, Carver. Thing is, I'm curious. You're snooping around a nursing home, and Raffy Ortiz is snooping around you. Only ones not doing any snooping are the police. That don't seem right."

"Now you're snooping. The world's been set straight."

"I'm putting you on notice, Carver. Don't forget I'm interested in this matter. You find out something the police oughta know, better see I hear about it. I mean ten seconds after you find out." He grinned, for a moment inserting the pink tip of his tongue in the gap between his front teeth. Made him look devilish and somehow obscene. " 'Course, you won't be able to do that if Raffy Ortiz has ground you up and fried you for breakfast."

He sat down and lifted a file folder from his desk, as if he'd abruptly dismissed Carver from his mind and was moving on to important matters. Busy man with an important job. "Nice talking to you," he said, opening the folder and burying his nose in it. "Now, get the fuck out."

"Always a pleasure," Carver said, and limped toward the door. He knew McGregor wasn't concentrating on the folder's contents. Might as well have been Shakespeare.

Outside in the relentless sun, he made his way toward where the Olds was parked and thought about his conversation with McGregor. If Sunhaven had brought Carver to the law's attention to discourage him from investigating, someone out there must feel he was on track. And feel that whatever was being covered up was serious enough even to risk using the police as a temporary ally. They might also be trying to spike Carver's guns before he turned over any evidence to the law. Portray him as a nosy nuisance bound to try causing a fuss sooner or later. Not to be taken seriously. That way the denial of any accusations would seem more plausible. No one knew Desoto had hired him. Here he was, working for nobody, a character hanging around and stirring up the old folks. Drawing wrong conclusions and planting dangerous ideas in age-eroded, suspicious minds.

But McGregor knew better, and it worried him.

And McGregor worried Carver.

13

Carver decided he'd stay away from Sunhaven for a while, starting with that evening. Instead, he'd wait for Nurse Rule to leave work and then follow her. Whatever was going on, she seemed deeply involved. Judging by the fear and respect she engendered around Sunhaven, the dominant force of her personality, she might very well be one of those in command. All Carver had to figure out now was what and whom she was commanding.

His armpits were sweating and his pullover shirt was stuck to him. The sun had made it across Florida and hung poised to drop into the Gulf, and the temperature had plunged all the way to eighty-five; it was miserable sitting in the parked Olds and becoming molded with perspiration to the leather seats.

Where Carver was parked, well off the side of the road, he could see the top of Nurse Rule's black Peugeot sedan gleaming in the sun like polished onyx. She was still at Sunhaven, even though it was almost eight o'clock. Working late. Maybe taking blood just for the hell of it, or flogging one of the attendants who'd spilled a bedpan.

On Carver's right, beyond a stretch of weedy land that fell away and became barren as it got sandier, the blue-green ocean rolled, darkening gradually as the sun sank. He wasn't in position to see the beach, and from this distance the surf sounded like a series of contented sighs. He knew there were a few expensive private homes down along the shore. And not far north a large condominium project was in the initial stages of construction. It would no doubt be another of those drab, stacked architectural clones repetitious with balconies that do wonders for the skyline. There was probably a condominium built every minute in Florida. The damned things multiplied like bionic bunnies.

A gull swooped in low, screamed, and soared out toward the ocean, jeering at Carver. He was hobbled and confined to land, and it could goddamn *fly!* A breeze kicked up and rustled the palm fronds, but it only sent warm air through the parked car. Carver licked the salt of perspiration from his lips and glanced as he had a hundred times toward the Sunhaven staff parking area.

The black curve of the Peugeot's roof was gone.

Damn! He slammed a fist against the steering wheel, causing a dull pain in the heel of his hand. It was pain he knew he deserved. He'd been sitting here in the heat sweating and feeling sorry for himself and Nurse Rule had managed to drive off without him seeing her. She must have made a right turn, away from Del Moray. *Wrong business! I'm in the wrong business!*

But even as he was admonishing himself, the black Peugeot emerged from the Sunhaven driveway, slowed, then nosed onto the highway in his direction and accelerated. It had been out of sight beyond the gentle rise of ground near the lot. Nora Rule was staring straight ahead; she seemed preoccupied and didn't notice Carver's car.

Feeling a rush of relief, he started the engine, U-turned, and stayed well back of the Peugeot as he followed.

Nurse Rule drove fast and with a sure touch. She braked

firmly at stop signs, and when it was her turn to cross intersections she did so with smooth acceleration. If there was any polite hesitation it wasn't on her part; driving was a chore to be dispensed with as soon as possible. The whole idea was to get from A to B.

When she reached the Del Moray city limits, it took Carver only a few minutes to realize she was driving toward her apartment. He'd figured on that, but there was no way to be sure, so he'd had to pick up the tail at Sunhaven.

Now he decided to take a chance. He ran the Olds up to forty-five and made a left and then a right turn, so he was traveling parallel with Nurse Rule's car. This way he reduced the chance of being seen by her, and he'd be parked near her apartment waiting when she arrived. He hoped Raffy Ortiz wouldn't also be waiting.

Nurse Rule pulled into her private parking slot, climbed out of the Peugeot with a flash of chunky white thigh, and still with her preoccupied, self-important air strode into the building. She was wearing her white uniform with the blue collar and sleeves and carrrying a small black vinyl portfolio. She was the type who'd take work home.

When it was almost dark, the blond, spike-haired woman Carver had seen diving at the pool yesterday emerged from the building. She kept herself in shape, all right. Her dark skirt was tight and showed off slender, rounded hips. Her stiltlike high heels lent her nyloned, athlete's calves and slim ankles a muscular but attractive turn. Yummy. Leg art of the highest order.

She lowered herself into a red Porsche convertible parked two spaces down from Nurse Rule's slot in the carport, and half a minute later sped past where Carver was parked in the Olds. He scooted low in the shadows so she wouldn't see him and maybe recognize him. Didn't straighten up until he heard the Porsche hit third gear down the block.

When it was almost ten o'clock, Carver figured Nurse Rule had decided to spend a quiet evening doing her homework and then going to bed. That's what he should be thinking about, getting into some air conditioning and then into bed. Edwina should be home by now.

Tonight hadn't panned out. He wasn't really disappointed. That was what his job mostly consisted of, waiting in quiet places for people who never showed and things that never happened. Much more boring than in detective novels and TV shows. Except maybe "Barnaby Jones" reruns.

The Peugeot was past him almost before he knew it.

Caught daydreaming again. Nightdreaming.

He started the Olds, pulled into the street, and rode the accelerator hard until he caught sight of the Peugeot's distinctive horizontal taillights.

Nurse Rule drove to the coast highway, then north along the shore. Yellow moonlight played off the black ocean, and shadowed clouds towered like dark-stained cotton mountains above the sea. Carver held a constant distance behind the red slashes of the Peugeot's taillights. The Olds's powerful engine throbbed as if it loved speed, sending a steady vibration through his buttocks and up his spine.

They drove for almost an hour. Then the Peugeot slowed and made a right turn beneath a gold neon sign made to look like an antique Spanish coin or medal engraved with a helmeted conquistador. Carver knew it wasn't an authentic reproduction, though, because it had red letters across it that spelled ME-DALLION MOTEL.

He turned the Olds into the seaside motel's parking lot, killed his headlights, and skirted the perimeter of the lot until he could park where he wouldn't be noticed observing Nurse Rule.

The motel was new, but it was built to look old and featured small individual cabins that appeared to have been constructed out of driftwood. The office, however, was modern, as was the swimming pool with its two diving boards and curved plastic slide. There were only two people, a man and a woman, splashing around in the softly illuminated pool, and only a few cars parked in front of the cabins. Carver suspected the Medallion Motel hadn't been here long and business was still slow.

Nurse Rule didn't stop near the office. Instead, she drove the Peugeot to the end cabin and parked next to a black or midnight-blue late-model Lincoln. Carver was relieved it wasn't a white Cadillac.

Even before she'd climbed out of the Peugeot, the door to the cabin opened.

In the light streaming from inside stood a slim, dark-haired woman in a severely cut blazer and skirt, probably a business suit. Carver couldn't discern her features but suspected she was a knockout. She held herself with the unconscious poise and self-confidence of women who'd been venerated for their beauty since childhood.

Nurse Rule approached the woman and stood close to her. They tentatively touched hands. Nurse Rule, who was four inches the shorter of the two, raised her right hand and gently clasped the back of the slim woman's neck, then drew her head down not so gently and kissed her on the mouth. There was something so blatantly possessive about the maneuver that it embarrassed Carver, made him feel like a voyeur. Which he guessed he was. Nurse Rule's sex life—and the other woman's—should be nobody else's business.

The kiss lasted a long time. One of the women kicked out a leg and closed the door. It made no sound when it shut. A few seconds later one of them lowered the blinds.

Carver got out of the Olds and limped silently through the darkness to the blue Lincoln. He could smell the ocean and hear it crashing over and over behind the cabins. The temperature was still high, but the breeze off the sea was cool now.

Cars occasionally swished past out on the highway, and there were lights in two of the other cabins, but there was a sense of isolation about the motel. There was something lonely, something sad, about using it as the site of a furtive romantic rendezvous.

He committed the Lincoln's license-plate number to memory, then on impulse he tried the gleaming passenger-side door. It opened and the interior of the car lit up brightly, startling him.

Carver looked over at the pool. The two swimmers were paying attention only to each other. He stooped low, his stiff leg almost beneath the car, and wedged his cane between the ground and the steel doorframe so it held in the button that allowed the interior lights to blink on when the door was open. The car was dark again.

The Lincoln had the new-car scent people always talked about; probably didn't have more than a couple of thousand miles on it. In the moonlight, he opened the glove compartment and groped inside. Felt a pair of glasses—probably sunglasses—and some papers and a small box of tissues. A pen or pencil. A cheap plastic disposable lighter. He pulled out a few folded papers and studied them in the faint light.

They were service records made out to the Lincoln's owner, Dr. Lee Macklin.

When Carver returned home he found Edwina sleeping deeply in their king-sized bed, with the ceiling fan slowly revolving and the window open. He was exhausted but he wasn't quite ready to join her. After standing for a moment watching her sleep, he backed out of the bedroom and soundlessly closed the door.

Using the living-room phone, he called Desoto, who'd gone to bed and seemed irritated about being awakened at midnight.

"Need to ask a question," Carver explained.

"One that couldn't wait till morning, *amigo*?"

"Could have, but I'm curious."

Desoto yawned. " 'Bout what?"

"Ever see Dr. Macklin's wife?"

Desoto didn't answer for a moment. "Huh?"

"Dr. Macklin's wife. Dr. Lee Macklin, the chief administrator out at Sunhaven. You told me he was married."

"Married, yeah," Desoto said. "But Dr. Macklin doesn't have a *wife*. Thought you knew—Lee Macklin's a woman."

Carver was quiet for a while. "With a husband," he said thoughtfully.

"Nothing odd about that. Other than the husband. He's a former flower child, rumored to be into drugs. As a user, not a seller."

Drugs. Florida. Carver wondered, if suddenly all illicit narcotics were made legal, would the state's economy collapse?

He apologized for waking Desoto and hung up.

14

West Palm Drive was dark, but there was a light glowing in Birdie's window. After his brief conversation with Desoto, Carver had immediately gone back to his car and driven here. It was 12:30 A.M., but he knew the young kept late hours. And this time of night—morning—it was unlikely he and Birdie would be disturbed. The respectable Mrs. Horton was probably fast asleep.

Carver parked the Olds a hundred feet beyond the rambling apartment building and made his way over the shadowed pavement to Birdie's door.

West Palm could have used a few more streetlights. The main source of illumination on the deserted block was the yellowish floodlight peeking through a thick growth of bougainvillea clinging to the corner of the old apartment building. Moths circled about the dim light, occasionally flitting too close and bouncing off it with enough force for the *tap*! of impact to carry to Carver. The dim bulb wasn't exactly the flame that lured and devoured, but it would have to do. And it gave the moths a second chance to flirt with destruction. More than most people got.

Fearing the arrival of the protective and suspicious Mrs. Horton, Carver pressed the button alongside Birdie's door and heard a sputtering buzzing from the depths of the apartment.

The door opened on a chain and Birdie peered out. She squinted up at Carver and recognition flared in her blue eyes. "Why, you're Mr. Carver, from out at Sunhaven." She said this as if it were quite amazing. Made him feel like Marley's ghost in *A Christmas Carol*.

"I know it's late, but I'd like to talk to you, Birdie."

She frowned; it made her look at least twelve, the little dickens. "Nurse Rule pointed right at you and said to let her know if you came to Sunhaven again. I dunno if we oughta talk, Mr. Carver."

"We're not at Sunhaven."

"Well, that's a fact."

"You do everything Nurse Rule tells you?"

"Heck, yeah. It's my job."

"Let me in, Birdie. Nurse Rule won't find out. Nobody'll find out. And my intentions are honorable."

"I'm kinda uneasy letting strangers into my place this time of night, Mr. Carver. I mean, it's not like you're *really* a stranger, but still it don't seem a fitting thing to do. I mean, I don't know a blessed thing about you."

"I know things about you, Birdie. But I won't use them to harm you, I promise. I know about Indianapolis. Listen, all I want's a conversation. Nothing more."

She stared at him with eyes gone wide and then gone narrow and cold. The door eased all the way shut and he heard the muted rattle of the chain against wood. She opened the door all the way and stepped back to let Carver enter.

She was wearing a blue terrycloth robe with a sash yanked tight around a waist that couldn't measure more than twenty inches. He was sure he hadn't awakened her. She was barefoot and her red hair was mussed and still damp. Her freckled face was pale but it glowed. She looked and smelled fresh, as if she'd just stepped from the shower, or maybe been born only a few hours ago.

What he knew about her past couldn't be true; a fifteen-year-old with her kind of wear should show scars. The things that had been done to her—Christ! Carver knew how Mrs. Horton felt; he also wanted to protect little Birdie, pat her on the head and tell her comforting lies about the world that had dumped so much shit on her. Carver reminded himself there was a fighter inside the frail figure before him. There had to be. Here she was, supporting herself and living out an independent existence when most girls her age were thinking about getting braces removed or whether some boy whose voice hadn't changed had a crush on them.

She backpedaled to a worn-out, sprung gray sofa, as if doing a dance step, then bent gracefully sideways from the waist to toss an old *National Enquirer* on the floor. Carver caught a glimpse of headline: DI SECRETLY GIVES BIRTH TO CHILD WITH GOAT'S HEAD. Those things happened in the best of families.

Birdie hadn't taken her young eyes from him. "Wanna sit down, Mr. Carver?" There was something intense and slightly irregular about the rhythm of her speech, as if she were pumped up from gulping half a dozen cups of coffee.

Carver sat where the *Enquirer* had been and propped his cane against a sofa cushion. Sitting, he'd be less intimidating to Birdie. In front of him was a produce crate, painted bright green and serving as a coffee table. There was an ashtray on the crate, and a plate crusted with dried egg yolk. Birdie wasn't the neatest of housekeepers, but then she was young and had problems more pressing than floor-wax buildup.

She sat down in a wood-and-canvas director's chair facing the sofa. Clasped her hands tightly, welded her knees together beneath the robe. Her bare toes were white and scrunched down into the carpet. There was a hairpin on the floor near her left big toe. In a voice that held the slightest quaver, she said, "You mentioned Indianapolis."

"Where you ran away from," Carver said. "From what I know about the situation, I don't blame you for leaving, and I wouldn't act to send you back there. You seem to be making your way okay here in Florida."

Her lower lip trembled, then she gnawed on it and stared hard at him, sizing him up. He could feel himself being categorized and cubbyholed. Though he'd used Indianapolis mainly as leverage to get in the door, he realized he wanted to know more about what had happened to Birdie there.

"You want something in return for not telling on me, don't you?" she asked, as if she knew the answer. She drew up her legs until she was hugging her knees, as if she wished she could curl herself into a tighter and tighter ball and then disappear.

"I didn't come here to harm you or make a deal," Carver said. "I only want to find out some things."

"Such as?" She was suspicious; men the age of her father and foster father didn't act this way. Wasn't normal.

"Tell me about what happened in Indianapolis."

She seemed puzzled. "Because you wanna know, or because you're kinky?" The question was matter-of-fact and serious.

"I want to know," Carver said. He smiled. "I'm usually not kinky with women under thirty."

"You sure?"

"Stretch marks turn me on. Indianapolis?"

Her face went blank and she gazed toward the dark window, as if her past and her hometown were right outside. "Me and my dad never got along. Argued a lot. You know how it is. Then, when I was almost twelve, he came into my bedroom one night after we had a big fight and apologized. He'd whammed me in the back with his fist, and while he was sitting on the edge of the bed he started to massage where he'd hit. To make it feel better, he told me, but it didn't help at all. Then he started rubbing . . . other places. One place led to another. I wanted to make him stop but I didn't know how. I was scared. He warned me not to tell my mom when she got home."

"Did you?"

"Not at first. He seen to it I stayed scared. Threatened me all the time about what'd happen if I talked, how everybody'd know I was bad and hate me, and all the trouble I'd cause. Other times he'd be nice to me and tell me how pretty I was. It got so he'd come into my room two or three nights a week. Wake me up sometimes with his mouth on me. Kissing me on the ear, sticking his tongue way in. After a while I didn't wanna tell on him. Know why?"

Carver said nothing. He was beginning to wish he hadn't asked Birdie about this. But it was as if she were wired to an irresistible energy and couldn't stop talking. Something had control of her.

"I got to thinking, Mr. Carver, that despite all the hurt and sin, those nights in my bed were the only times my father or anybody else showed me any love." A tear zigzagged down her cheek and dropped onto one of her drawn-up knees, leaving a dark wet spot on her robe. She didn't seem to notice she was crying. Somebody else was here in the room with Carver; not Birdie. Somebody from the nightmare.

"Oh, I knew it was wrong. Specially when I got to be about thirteen and seen how the other girls were with their fathers. My dad wasn't like theirs; not at all. I asked, like it was for somebody I knew, if anyone else's father did to them some of the things mine did to me. One of the girls said yes, but the others thought the questions were crazy. I wonder how many of them was scared to talk. Scared the way my dad had scared me. He was getting rougher and rougher with me in bed, too. Started to tie me up. Then he started hurting me bad. That's when I decided to stop what was happening, to tell my mom."

"What did she say when you told her?"

"Got mad at me. Said she didn't believe me. That I was like sick in the brain and hated my dad and wanted to break up their marriage and ruin her life. I found out since that's how a mother acts sometimes, Mr. Carver; she didn't wanna believe. Couldn't stand the thought of it, and of him leaving her."

97

Carver said, "She would have believed you eventually. Did she confront him?"

"Oh, sure. But he denied it all. Everything. Then he found an excuse and beat me bad and did things to me so I could hardly walk. Said I fell down the basement steps."

"And what did you say?"

"Nothing. I ran away from there to a shelter I'd heard about from some other kids. The people there believed what I told them and called the police. Both my dad and mom denied everything, though. Nothing could be proved. The shelter was gonna send me back to live at home, because they had no choice legally. So I ran away. Went to another shelter. A social worker, Linda Redmond was her name, raised hell and got me placed in a foster home. That lasted a month, and I woke up one night and found the fat bastard who lived there in my bed. My guardian, so called."

Carver found himself clenching the worn material of the sofa in anger.

"When I ran away from there," Birdie went on, "they found me and things got all snarled up in the courts and I wound up at home again. I soon got outta there, though, finally and forever. Outta the city. I never wanna go back."

"You're older now, Birdie. Smarter. Why don't you get a lawyer and formally charge your father with child molestation? Get yourself out from under what happened."

She shrugged and seemed to come back to her living room. Wiped a tear from her cheek and dragged her wet forefinger over her terrycloth robe. "Well, he's dead—it don't matter now."

"Maybe it matters to you. It's something you should get resolved."

"It's all in the past, Mr. Carver. I read a magazine article once that said time was like a river with an S-shaped curve in it. We're all drifting on that river. Can't see ahead into the future or behind into the past. I figure we can't go back upriver around the bend, even if we want to. So what difference does it make what's there?"

"Contamination washes downstream."

"It don't if you don't let it. Built a dam, is what I did, and I'm busy getting on with my life. If only people'd let me."

"Who won't let you?" Other than limping private investigators.

"People in general, is all. I gotta be careful and not even use my real name. Bea's what I used to be called. I've used a couple of names. Nobody knows me as Birdie except here in Florida. It was Dr. Pauly started calling me that after I answered a classified ad and got the receptionist job out at Sunhaven. Said I reminded him of an injured bird. The name kinda caught on, and I been Birdie ever since. My Florida name. Think of myself as such."

"Do they know out at Sunhaven you're a runaway?"

"Some do. They have for some time. I told 'em I was just turned eighteen when I applied for the job, but them kinda places check on their employees. Somebody found out about where I was from. Dr. Macklin called me into her office one day and told me she knew. I broke down and cried and like caused a big scene. Told her everything. My side of what happened. She said she'd look into my story, and if it was true she wouldn't turn me in. That was almost a year ago, and she hasn't said anything about it since. I don't think she will. She likes me, I can tell. And I'm a real good receptionist."

Carver wondered just how much Dr. Macklin liked Birdie, and in what fashion. "Dr. Macklin ever flatly told you how she actually feels about you? I mean, the way she thinks of you?"

Birdie seemed slightly puzzled. "No, I wouldn't say that. But she seems to have a kinda big-sister attitude toward me. Tell the truth, Sunhaven might be the closest thing I ever had to a home and family."

"What about Nurse Rule?"

"Well, what about her?" Wary now.

"Is she, ah, friendly toward you?"

"You talking about her being a bull-dagger?"

Carver blinked. "Right, Birdie. She ever made a play for you?"

"Oh, sure. She was all over me till I told Dr. Macklin. The two of them had a private talk in Dr. Macklin's office, and that stopped that. We been on a business-only relationship ever since. That's what Nurse Rule said she wanted, after Dr. Macklin talked with her. And that's fine with me. I do what I'm told. Nurse Rule's not the sorta supervisor you cross, if you know what I mean."

"I know," Carver said. "Does she hold a grudge about you going to Dr. Macklin?"

"Not any more than she seems to hold a grudge against most everyone. She's a hard woman. But I gotta say she's fair as she is firm."

"You ever seen her with a man named Raffy Ortiz?"

Birdie shrank back into her chair; the canvas and wood creaked. "Never," she said, too quickly. Fear darkened her midwestern features like a rain cloud over a wheat field.

"You know Raffy Ortiz?"

"Know him enough I can say he gives me the creeps. He's a friend or something of Dr. Pauly. Comes out to Sunhaven and sees him every great once in a while."

"How often's that?"

"Maybe once, twice a month. They don't like him to come around there."

"Who doesn't?"

"Just everybody. I get the idea even Dr. Pauly ain't all that crazy about Mr. Ortiz."

"What have you heard about Raffy Ortiz?"

She stared at the ceiling for a moment, letting him know she was thinking hard. "That he'd killed somebody once. One of the residents said he thought he recognized Mr. Ortiz and he heard he'd once killed a man in a knife fight down around Miami."

"Which resident?"

Birdie almost squirmed with nervousness. She was running on a compulsion to blab, but not about this. "I can't recall. It was just some loose talk."

"Is that why you're afraid of him?"

"Of the resident?"

"Of Mr. Ortiz."

"That, and the way he looks at me. I caught him a few times staring at me the way I used to be stared at sometimes by my father. Like he wanted to do those same things to me."

Which might be exactly what a sicko like Ortiz had in mind, Carver thought. Birdie's instinct for survival had been working well when she'd formed her opinion of Raffy Ortiz. A man who hurt people, and who found in their pain a dark and visceral amusement.

Carver looked at Birdie and wished it had been different for her, wished she'd had a father who felt about her as Carver did about his own daughter, living with his ex-wife, Laura, in Saint Louis. What kind of man would systematically rape his own child? Something that had developed in the human race over millions of years, something in the evolutionary process, must be missing in men like Birdie's father—the thing that had helped ensure the survival of the species by shorting out sexual desire for one's own offspring. It was difficult to understand or forgive such people.

Birdie had spent enough time reliving her agony, Carver decided. She'd been made a victim as a child, and would probably remain a victim all her life. He could never fully understand her pain, but he didn't want to compound it.

"Thanks for talking with me, Birdie." He angled his cane to support his weight and stood up. "I mean what I said. I won't mention you to the authorities."

She stood also, drawing the robe's sash tighter around her waist. She smiled as if he'd just offered to buy her an ice cream cone at the carnival. She'd always have that kind of smile; it came with desperate hope. "I believe you," she said. "Don't know why, but I do. Guess you want me to keep quiet out at Sunhaven about our talk here tonight."

"It's up to you. Neither of us broke any laws by having a conversation."

She crossed her bare feet, wriggling her toes. The nails were painted pink. "I'd just as soon we made it our secret, if you don't mind. Nurse Rule wouldn't like it, knowing I let you in and told you things."

"Our secret, then," Carver said.

He resisted the urge to pat her shoulder and made his way across the room. When he opened the door the warm night air enveloped him, carrying with it the sweet, wild scent of flowers. He could hear the growl of distant traffic, and a radio or TV tuned too loud somewhere in the building. The darkness seemed ripe with struggle, a void where humans grappled blindly with each other and with themselves.

"Mr. Carver?" Birdie said when he was ready to step outside.

He twisted his torso so he was looking back at her, his cane set firmly on the wide threshold.

"You can come back again and talk if you want. Guess what I'm trying to say is, I could use a friend."

"You've got one to use," Carver said.

He limped out into the night.

Less than an hour later he stretched out on the cool bed next to Edwina. He lay on his back, his fingers laced behind his head, and listened to the repetitive thunder of the ocean. Moonlight softly outlined familiar forms in the room—a chair, Edwina's dresser, the tall chest of drawers—and lent them a pliant, dreamlike quality. Carver felt that if he closed his eyes he might wake up.

Edwina's bare, pale leg stirred, rustling the white sheet. Keeping the rest of her body still, she turned the dark shape of her head on her pillow so she was facing him. Her hair splayed over white linen. He couldn't see her eyes, but he sensed she was awake.

"Where've you been?" she asked.

"To see a child."

Edwina had a knack for knowing when not to ask questions.

She lay quietly. He could see, stark against the moonstruck wall, the silhouetted length of her body. Her stomach and breasts were rising and falling almost unnoticeably as she breathed, in subtle but profound rhythm with the breaking sea.

He knew she'd been physically abused by her former husband. Edwina didn't talk much about that time in her life, and it was something Carver didn't pry into. It had all ended more than a year before he and Edwina had become lovers, and he had never met her ex-husband. Knew his name was Larry, but didn't know much else about him. He used to spend a lot of time thinking about Larry, hating him. He'd seen what Larry had done, and how long it took for it to be made right again.

"Can you ever really forgive someone who's violently sexually abused you?" he asked.

"You mean as a child?"

"Not necessarily. A man and a woman, maybe. Or a man and a young girl. His daughter."

"The two situations aren't alike."

"Aren't they?"

"I don't think so."

He didn't speak for a while. She was thinking about Larry. And who knew what else? She'd always be a mystery. Maybe that was why he loved her.

In the dim, cool silence she said, "A woman might forgive being abused by her husband. She can eventually understand it. And after that maybe she can forgive. I doubt it happens often. There's usually no reason to forgive."

"So an abusive husband is seldom forgiven. What about an abusive father? One who sexually molests a very young girl over a stretch of several years. Is he ever understood by the victim and forgiven?"

Edwina's answer came instantly across the shadowed bed. "A father? Never. The only thing is for the victim to get as far away from the situation as possible, and never go back."

Carver thought about what she'd said, then he slept soundly.

15

Not the phone, the doorbell.

At first Carver hadn't been sure what had awakened him. There was a breeze sighing through the bedroom window, but it was a warm one. The doorbell was quiet now; he could hear the sea gushing on the beach.

He lay in bed and watched Edwina struggle into her gray silk robe and stumble from the room. She was still half asleep, walking stiffly and bent forward slightly at the waist, like an actress in a low-budget zombie movie. Some zombie, even in the morning.

A minute later her voice drifted faintly to him from the foyer, mingled with that of a man. The male voice sounded vaguely familiar to Carver, but he couldn't place it. He rotated his body, sat up on the edge of the mattress, and reached for his cane. He used the crook of the cane to snag a belt loop on his pants, which were folded on the chair near the bed. He drew them to him and put them on. Pulling on his pants involved half sitting, half lying on the bed while working his stiff leg through to the cuff. It was a knack. He'd gotten used to it, then good at it.

Hardly thought about it now. Routine. Shoes were no problem; he almost always wore the kind without laces. Usually moccasins. But socks required effort, so he decided to remain barefoot until he found out what was going on.

He glanced at the clock: 9:15. At his reflection in Edwina's dresser mirror. Tanned, oily complexion. Wavy hair around his ears mussed. Where were his eyes? There! Blue things way in there. He smoothed back the wings of gray hair with his hands, then stood up with the cane. Shirtless, he limped down the carpeted hall to the living room. The soft carpet felt great beneath his bare feet.

The uniform who'd driven Carver to see McGregor yesterday was standing just inside the door with Edwina. He looked fresh and cool this morning, as if he'd just been manufactured. There were sharp creases in his short-sleeved shirt and brown uniform pants. He spotted Carver over Edwina's shoulder, flicked a smile, and nodded a good morning. An amiable public servant.

"You're here to give me the bad news," Carver said. "McGregor's been shot."

The smile again, but brief. Guy had control. "Don't know what the news is, but it's not that. McGregor's the one gonna tell you the news."

"The news for him is this," Carver said. "Even a police lieutenant can't send one of his men around on a whim to drag citizens off to the station so they can chat at his convenience. Where does he think he is—Mayberry?"

"No need for anybody to get dragged anyplace," the uniform said patiently. Here he was again trying to pacify Carver. This wasn't why he'd become a cop. "The lieutenant's waiting for you right outside in the cruiser. Wants for you two to talk in private. Guess he figured you'd object to another ride to headquarters. He wanted me to tell you that this time you'd be glad you and him got together."

Carver took two lurching steps to a side window. There was a Del Moray patrol car, parked in the shade of the three closely grouped palm trees near the gate. There was the elongated, looming form of McGregor, bent over in the backseat. The car's whip antenna was vibrating in time with its idling engine and the windows were up. McGregor had the air conditioner on.

"Had your morning coffee?" Edwina asked the uniform.

"Some. Wouldn't turn down another cup, ma'am."

"In the kitchen," Edwina said. "It'll have to be instant."

"I was told there was no other kind." He followed her from the living room, studiously looking away from her swaying hips.

Carver stood still for a moment, then he went outside to talk with McGregor. The gravel driveway was hot and sharp on his bare soles. He walked gingerly, flicking some of the larger pieces of gravel aside with his cane. The temperature had to be well into the eighties already. Today would be warmer than yesterday. Maybe the weather would continue to heat up until there was spontaneous combustion.

"Don't it hurt your feet to walk around without shoes or socks?" McGregor asked when Carver had slid in next to him in the back of the cruiser.

"Only tickles. Trick I learned in India."

McGregor gave him a long, appraising look, wondering if he was kidding. Decided it didn't matter. He stared straight ahead out the cruiser's windshield at the vast ocean. Even though the air conditioner was whining away, it was warm in the car. "You been keeping busy on this Sunhaven thing?"

"Sure," Carver said. Throw McGregor for a loop with the truth.

McGregor didn't act thrown. He picked almost daintily at the gum line of his front teeth with a little finger, keeping his head bowed so he wouldn't bump it on the car's sloping roof. "Then I guess you know about the death out there last night."

Something cold moved in Carver. He was tired of dealing with McGregor's selfish, twisted attitude. His callow disregard for people he couldn't use. Sharks had more compassion.

"Who died?" Carver asked simply.

"Old fucker name of Williams. Kearny Williams. Girl out

there, little cunt behind the reception desk, said you was a friend of his. Came to see him."

"How'd he die?"

"Oh, some sort of stroke or attack."

"What sort?" Carver asked levelly.

"Aortal aneurysm, the doctor said it was. Fibrulation caused a ruptured wall of the main artery leaving the heart. Heart wore out, is what it all means. Fucking cardiac arrest."

"Did Williams have a history of heart problems?"

"Hey, he's your friend; you tell me. You say you knew him well enough to go out there and see him. Old Kearny ever mention a bum ticker?"

"No," Carver said. "There gonna be an autopsy?"

" 'Course not. Law don't provide. Natural death. Nonviolent. Not at all unexpected, according to the doctor. How come you figure there should be an autopsy? Think the medical examiner's got time instead of internal organs on his hands?"

"What if the family requested an autopsy?" Carver asked.

"That'd be different. Thing is, they was asked if they wanted to have the dear departed laid open and looked into. Talked to them myself just this morning by phone. They said no. Said Kearny Williams's been living on borrowed time the last five years 'cause of his bad heart. Said let the poor old bastard rest in peace. Not them words exactly."

"I bet they felt better after you talked to them."

"Cheering up mourners ain't my job. Protecting the dumb-ass public is. Speaking of which, have you noticed Raffy Ortiz hasn't tried to crush your windpipe or peel back your fingernails lately?"

"I owe you for that benign neglect?"

"Not exactly. But since you and him are, in my estimation, linked in some way possibly illegal, I had him followed the past couple days. He took a short trip. Flew up to New Orleans early yesterday and got back last night. Guess he had more important things to do than bounce you around."

"Where'd he go in New Orleans?"

"That I don't know. I contacted the New Orleans police and they sent someone to fall in behind him, but they weren't even out of the airport before Raffy'd slipped away." McGregor paused for a moment and ducked his head for a better angle to peer out the windshield at a pelican winging past over the ocean. The morning sun was striking sparks off the water, making it hard to stare in that direction. Still squinting at the pelican, McGregor said, "You got any idea why your rough playmate would up and fly to New Orleans?"

"It's a big city," Carver said. "Lots of reasons to go there."

"Sure. You can listen to hot jazz, or poke a southern belle, or dine in fine fashion. But hell, you can do all them things right here in Florida and have some fresh-squeezed orange juice before and after."

"Maybe Raffy likes Cajun cooking," Carver suggested.

"Maybe this is no time for you to be a smart-ass."

Carver said, "I don't know why Raffy went to New Orleans."

"Well, you *do* know he's back. I just told you. It oughta give you something to think about. He's a regular wrecking machine. Into martial arts. Knows karate, kung-fu, all that slant stuff that makes people dangerous even if they ain't natural killers from the get-go. Which, in fact, he is." McGregor scooted around to face Carver directly. The sickening odor of cologne and stale perspiration was almost overpowering in the stifling car. "Another thing I want you to think about is our last conversation. Anything you find out, I get to learn next and in a hurry. Understand?"

"Yeah. But will you be able to retain it?"

McGregor faced forward and folded his long arms across his chest. "Out, assface. Conversation's over. Go in the house and send my man back out here. I was you, I'd get limping. He's got a way with the ladies. And you know how some of 'em drop their drawers soon as they see a uniform."

"There's a special place in hell for you," Carver said. "It's just like here on earth only it never ends."

"Hey, you think I'm unhappy?"

"You gotta be miserable being you. Anybody would be."

McGregor turned and gave Carver his leering, gap-toothed grin. "You got it wrong. I'm a contented man. I *know* what I am, and I know the truth about things. Got no illusions. You're just like me, Carver, only you got illusions. You put yourself on. Sorta guy makes me wanna puke. People are only out for themselves, and that includes the two of us. It's a shit world. I see it and you don't. I roll in it and even kinda enjoy it, and you can't. Your hard luck."

Carver suddenly had to get away from McGregor, from the sight and sound and corrupt smell of him. He flung open the cruiser's door, swiveled on the seat, and planted his cane on the gravel driveway.

"People are all alike," McGregor said. "Life teaches you that. Grinds it into you. Ask your feeble friends out at Sunhaven; they been around awhile and they'll tell you. A shit world, all right. That's the reason most of 'em are actually looking forward to dying even though they're scared to piss in their pants."

"Jesus!" Carver said. He straightened up out of the car.

"Him? He was invented for fuckheads like you."

Carver slammed the door and limped toward the house. McGregor was some way to start the day.

16

"What's McGregor doing in Del Moray?" Edwina asked when the cruiser had driven away. She was standing at the sink, rinsing the uniform's coffee cup. Her own cup was still on the table half full, steam rising from it like an unformed thought.

Carver told her. Then he told her where he was on the Sunhaven case, and the reason for McGregor's visit.

"I loathe that man," Edwina said, not for the first time.

"Most everyone does. He prefers it that way. As long as everybody's his enemy, he can feel justified doing anything to anyone. A foolproof system."

Edwina nodded. She understood. Larry, maybe. Or perhaps she was thinking about herself during the first year after her divorce, when she was fighting to establish her own identity and her territory in life. That was when she'd made big mistakes, and then made things right again and became for the first time the real Edwina. It hadn't been an easy passage.

After breakfast out on the veranda, Carver phoned Sunhaven and asked Birdie if Dr. Pauly was there. It was Dr. Pauly's day off, Birdie informed him. No, the doctor didn't have any practice other than at Sunhaven and he'd probably be at home.

"Not on the golf course?" Carver asked.

"Dr. Pauly's not the golf type," Birdie said.

"What's he usually do on his days off?"

"I dunno, Mr. Carver. Never heard him talk about it. But I'm not really around him that much; he's busy when he makes his rounds. Says 'hi' and 'bye' to me, is all. But he's a nice man. Always smiles as he hurries on past the reception desk. Now and then gives me a look when a resident does something really crazy, like only me and him understand what's going on. Stuff like that."

"Birdie—"

"Gotta hang up. Sorry." The last in a whisper.

Click . . . buzz.

Someone must have been approaching her desk. Birdie didn't want anyone at Sunhaven to know who was on the other end of the connection. Instincts of a survivor.

Carver had a second cup of coffee, kissed Edwina, and then made his way to the garage, where the Olds was parked next to her Mercedes; a hulking heavyweight has-been next to a trim young middleweight.

As he drove from the shadowed garage into the glaring morning, he glanced over at Edwina sitting gracefully at the outdoor table, holding her coffee cup poised while her hair caught the sun and her silk gown flowed with the currents of the breeze. Beauty crystallized in memory.

For one instant, he felt sorry for McGregor.

The wooden flower boxes beneath the windows of Dr. Pauly's Hansel-and-Gretel house were dripping darkly and the geraniums stood at glistening attention. Someone had recently watered the plants. Overwatered them.

When Dr. Pauly answered Carver's knock, he was wearing a pair of those leather sandals with recycled tire-tread soles, faded blue jeans cut off just above his knees, and a white T-shirt with "WHY ME?" printed across the chest in black letters. Not the kind of guy you'd want to see stroll into the operating

111

room as you drifted off under an anesthetic, but on the other hand, it was his day off.

Carver identified himself.

Dr. Pauly smiled. "I know who you are. You've been out at Sunhaven a few times. Caused something of a stir." He was a fortyish man with dark hair that had receded. There was no way to know how far, because it was combed straight down onto his forehead in sparse bangs, Roman emperor style. His features were sharp but pleasant, with gray eyes deep-set and friendly beneath symmetrical bushy black brows. His chin was as sharply pointed as his nose; when he got very old, like his patients at Sunhaven, chin and nose would strive to meet.

"Stir?" Carver said.

"Maybe that's an exaggeration," Dr. Pauly said. "C'mon in where it's cool." He stepped back to let Carver move inside.

The tiny house's living room was neat now, but through an open door Carver could see into a bedroom strewn with clothes and newspapers. A corner of a bed with tangled sheets was visible. There was a large wicker laundry basket heaped with wrinkled clothes next to it, with a wadded pair of gray sweat-socks on top as if for dour decoration. In the doorway to the kitchen stood an upright vacuum cleaner and a maze of spiraled hose and attachments. A faint pine disinfectant scent hung in the air, probably from some sort of cleaner or floor wax. Apparently Dr. Pauly cleaned house on his day off, working front to back.

Carver sat down on a small brown sofa and propped his cane against his leg. Dr. Pauly stood smiling with his hands clasped behind his back, at military parade rest, and said, "Rumor has it you think something's wrong out at Sunhaven."

"*Is* there something wrong?" Carver asked.

"Sure."

Carver waited, aware he'd edged forward on the sofa. A picture of expectation.

Should have known better.

Still smiling, Dr. Pauly said, "But not any more wrong than at any other nursing home, Mr. Carver. Old age can be a trial sometimes, but we try to make it as pleasant as possible. That means 'merely endurable' for those in a badly deteriorated condition. Oh, I know how younger people feel walking through a place like Sunhaven. The depression, the sympathy. There's something personal working there because we all know we're going to get old ourselves. But believe me, in general the residents are contented. At least as contented as we can make them."

"I understand Kearny Williams died last night."

Pauly's bushy dark eyebrows almost knitted together for a moment in a look of surprise and concern. "How'd you know that?"

"I was told by the authorities. You signed the death certificate."

Dr. Pauly nodded, then raised his very expressive eyebrows and said, "You're not suggesting there was anything suspicious in the way old Kearny Williams died, are you? Good Lord, is that the sort of thing you mean by 'something wrong at Sunhaven'?"

"Not suggesting," Carver said. "He died of heart failure?"

"Pure and simple, Mr. Carver." The eyebrows formed a severe V again, this time in obvious frustration. "You've got to understand, these people are aged; the human body wears out, develops afflictions." Did Pauly glance at Carver's bad leg? "Kearny Williams's death was anything but unexpected. His medical records will attest to that, even from before he came to Sunhaven."

"What do you know about a man named Raphael Ortiz?" Carver asked.

Dr. Pauly brought his hands around in front of his body, tucked his thumbs in the side pockets of his cutoff jeans, and stood hipshot. It was a defensive posture. He looked more like a street-corner lounger than a doctor. "Mr. Ortiz came to me as a patient in Miami a few years ago."

"What was wrong with him?" Carver asked. "Bearing in mind the Hippocratic Oath."

"He'd suffered a series of deep cuts."

"From a knife fight?"

"I didn't ask."

"You must have asked how he'd gotten hurt."

"I did. All he'd say was that it was accidental."

"Could the wounds have been sustained in a knife fight?"

"I don't think I'll answer that one, Mr. Carver. Mr. Ortiz has seen me since, and he's still my patient. He was more or less forced to see me the first time; you have to understand, a man like that, he's suspicious of doctors. Once he went to one, though, he became grateful for the treatment. He developed an excessive idea of my capabilities. I'm the only doctor he'll see. It's something of a fixation, actually, and not uncommon in people like Mr. Ortiz."

"So if he happens to skin a knuckle on somebody's teeth, he runs to you for treatment."

"I wouldn't put it that way," Dr. Pauly said. "But I guess maybe it *is* that way."

"Then you're aware of his history of trouble with the law in Cuba and then here? What he does to get his money? The kind of man he is?"

"What Mr. Ortiz does is none of my business. A man comes to me in need of treatment, I'm not going to interrogate him before administering to him. I don't moralize or sit in judgment before I set broken bones or stop bleeding. That's not what being a doctor's all about."

" 'Course not," Carver said. "But what if he came to you with, say . . . a gunshot wound?"

"Mr. Ortiz has never asked me to treat a gunshot wound. If he did, I'd be suspicious and notify the police according to law." He frowned, made a thin, straight line of his mouth, and searched for words. "Mr. Carver, there's nothing unethical about my treatment of Raphael Ortiz. Nothing unethical happening at Sunhaven, either."

114

"That you know of."

"Well, sure. But I think if there were, I *would* know it. I'm the doctor the patients see most frequently; they trust and confide in me. And I know the rest of the staff quite well. They have their individual characteristics and personal problems, but they're professionals and damned good at their work."

"Including Nurse Rule?"

"Especially Nurse Rule. So she's not every man's idea of the ideal dinner date. She runs Sunhaven's nurses and attendants with the uncompromising efficiency of a Prussian officer. Is that bad?"

"Not if the Prussians are on your side."

"You've met the enemy and it's not Sunhaven, Mr. Carver. It's old age. It's hardened blood vessels and stiff rheumatic joints. And suspicion that's had enough incubation time in the brain to hatch paranoia. It's senility. It's loneliness and constant discomfort."

"You talk as if you don't want to grow old," Carver said.

"But I do. What I just described is the dark side; not all residents are that way. For most of them these really *are* their golden years. We do everything possible to see to it. Their responsibilities are behind them, their families visit them frequently, and Sunhaven relieves them of their anxieties. If they're in reasonably sound health for their age, they're happy, Mr. Carver. Happier than they'd be anywhere else, for the most part. I'm not saying some of the residents aren't leading miserable lives; it happens, and, eventually, to most of them—until death puts an end to it. That's the sad reality of the world. But if you think Sunhaven's hell, drive through the bad side of town, any town, and catch glimpses of the aged who are homeless and in obvious need of attention they aren't going to receive."

Carver thought the doctor had a point.

Pauly withdrew his thumbs from his pockets. He scratched his chest through the T-shirt. Seemed nervous.

"They pay you well at Sunhaven?" Carver asked.

"None of your business, of course. But I feel I'm fairly compensated. Though as you can see, I'm a long way from wealthy."

"What do you know about Dr. Macklin?"

"She's competent and kind. I enjoy working under her supervision."

"Would you say she needs somebody like Nurse Rule to actually run Sunhaven? I mean, an assistant tough enough for the dirty details?"

Dr. Pauly didn't know what to do with his hands, so now he slid his fingertips into the jeans pockets and stood erectly with his elbows pointed out. He looked like a space shot ready to be launched. "Oh, I wouldn't describe it as that kind of arrangement. Dr. Macklin can be quite firm when it's necessary. Nurse Rule never usurps Dr. Macklin's authority. I'd say they have a good working relationship."

"Are you aware that Nurse Rule went to the police so they'd question me about my talking to Sunhaven residents?"

"I am," Dr. Pauly said. "And to be frank, I think she acted needlessly. She's a bit of a zealot about her job, Mr. Carver. Many managing nurses are. It's what makes them good at their work, and what sometimes causes problems. At times they tend to overreact. You'll find at least one Nurse Rule in almost every major medical facility."

Dr. Pauly sighed loudly and ran a hand over his face. It was suddenly too warm in the small living room. He walked over and adjusted the thermostat for more air conditioning. There was a soft click, and a low hum from the back of the house. "If you don't mind, Mr. Carver . . . I've been up most of the night and I'm pretty much exhausted."

But not too tired to do housework, Carver thought.

He said, "I understand. Sorry to bother you, doctor." He used his cane to raise himself to a standing position.

"I'm glad to help, naturally," Dr. Pauly said, "but the thing is, you're trying to find a crack in something that isn't broken. Sunhaven might not be run to perfection—not many institutions are—but we do try, honestly."

Carver moved the short distance to the door. Dr. Pauly stepped over to usher him out, but he didn't open the door for him, didn't make his passage easier because of the stiff knee and cane. Point for Pauly.

"One thing before I go," Carver said. "When and where is Kearny Williams's funeral?"

"I couldn't say for sure," Dr. Pauly told him. "Mr. Williams's family's had the body shipped to them in New Orleans."

Carver thanked the doctor for his help. Apologized for taking up his time.

"Wish I could help you more," Dr. Pauly said. He seemed to mean it. "I don't know who's given you the notion something unsavory is going on at Sunhaven. I can understand why they might, though. Listen, we're all on this earth temporarily, but none of us likes to admit it, even in old age. It's the human way of looking at life, I'm afraid. And *not* looking at death. We all tend to deny our mortality, but we're nonetheless mortal."

Carver limped outside into the sun and left Dr. Pauly to his housework. Dust to dust.

17

Carver returned to Edwina's and found she was away on the job. The echoing house was silent except for the breathing of the ocean. This must be what it was like inside a seashell.

He made a few phone calls, then piled some of his clothes as neatly as possible on the backseat of the Olds. Hot work. Sticking his head inside the car was like poking it into an oven set on Bake. He hoped none of his polyester shirts would melt.

Damp with perspiration, he went back inside the house and got a can of Budweiser from the refrigerator, downed it quickly, then opened another can and carried it into the spare bedroom Edwina used as an office.

The blinds were closed and it was dim in there, so he switched on the desk lamp. It was one of those banker's lamps with a green glass shade and cast a sickly light. He rolled a sheet of blank paper into the Olympia portable Edwina used when she typed real-estate contracts. Between sips of beer, he used his forefingers to peck out a letter to her. He tucked the letter in a white business envelope, wrote her name on it in blue felt-tip pen, and returned to the living room.

After laying the letter on the table near the front door, where she couldn't miss seeing it, he girded himself against the heat and limped back outside. He made sure he locked the door behind him.

Birdie Reeves was behind her receptionist's desk in Sunhaven's bright pastel lobby. She was engrossed in one of her checkout-counter tabloids and didn't pay much attention to the *tap*, *tap* of his cane; plenty of canes and aluminum walkers at Sunhaven. When she did glance up and see him, she smiled, then the country sweetness of the smile was clouded over by worry.

"I'm s'posed to tell Nurse Rule if you show up here, Mr. Carver."

"I didn't show up," Carver said. "You were busy with your work and must not have seen me pass."

"Mr. Carver—"

"It'll be all right, Birdie." He patted the hand that held the headline about a New England fishing village invaded by porpoises with legs, and sidled away to head for Amos Burrel's room.

A completely bald old man in a pink vinyl chair beamed at Carver and said, "Wha'cha know, young fella?"

Good question, Carver thought. He shrugged and said, "Not much," and moved on.

He knocked on Amos's door. No answer. He rotated the knob and pushed the door open. There was a minty, medicinal scent in the room.

Amos didn't look scared. Didn't look angry. Looked disinterested. He was wearing blue-and-gray-striped pajamas, sitting in a severe, straight-backed wooden chair that might have been made by Shakers to punish themselves for sins real or imagined. He was staring out his window at the slope of sun-browned grass that led to the parking lot. His long face seemed to sag even more, loose skin draping to the wattles beneath his jaw. It was as if the bone structure beneath the flesh were gradually disintegrating and soon there would be nothing to hold form. Amos's face, his entire body, would melt away like tallow.

Carver said hello and sat down on the edge of the bed. The springs squeaked; the mattress was surprisingly soft.

"Hot outside?" Amos asked.

"Hot."

"Looks hot."

"Kearny Williams died last night," Carver said.

Amos nodded, still staring at the bright sunlight outside the window. A jay fluttered down on the brown grass, decided it was too hot to strut around searching for nonexistent worms, and took to the air again.

"What do you think about it?" Carver asked.

"Think I ought not to talk to you," Amos said.

"Why not? Nurse Rule?"

Amos's scrawny chest rose and fell beneath the striped pajamas. "You gotta understand, Carver. Game I'm in here, I ain't got a lotta cards to play."

"Point is," Carver said, "you're in the game to stay. You don't have any choice about it."

"Yeah." Amos drew out the word as if it tasted bad sliding over his tongue.

"You hear anything last night?" Carver asked.

Amos pursed his lips. Regular Sphinx.

"Sooner you tell me, sooner I'll get outta here," Carver said.

There was logic in that. Amos wrung his narrow, withered hands. They were dry and Carver could actually hear them rubbing together. He didn't like the spot he'd put the old man in, but he was in a spot himself. The world seemed to work that way too often, robbing us of the best part of ourselves little by little.

"Heard nothing," Amos said. "I was hung over this morning. Still hung over. I think they mighta put something in my food to make me sleep through whatever happened. I sniffed an odd smell through the vent this morning, though. Like something had been burned. Like somebody'd struck a match maybe to smoke a cigarette."

"You mentioned a burned smell after Jim Harrison died," Carver pointed out.

"Did I?"

"Did Kearny Williams smoke?"

"Hell, no! Damn near nobody smokes in Sunhaven, Carver. Not the staff. Not any of the residents except them so desperate for tobacco they can't help themselves, and so rich they can't be tossed outta here. Think I ain't wanted to fire up a pipe now and again? Had a collection of meerschaum pipes. Gone now."

"Is it a strict rule? No smoking at Sunhaven?"

"Strict as that kinda rule can be. Straight from the top. Dr. Macklin figures smoking's the greatest evil in the world since sex. She don't do neither, way I figure it."

Carver remembered the Medallion Motel and the cigarette lighter inside Dr. Macklin's glove compartment. He wondered about the wisdom that was supposed to come with age. "Any of the staff smoke on the sly?"

"Not as I know of. One of the things they ask here before hiring attendants or anyone else is whether they smoke. Discrimination, you ask me. People like that, they look for a wisp of smoke the way censors keep an eye skinned for a snippet of pornography so they can fly into a righteous rage. Zealots, is what they are. Zealots is what's got the world screwed up. Radicals. Extremists. Oughta stand 'em all up against a wall and shoot 'em!"

Carver could see that Amos was torn. On the one hand he didn't want Carver in his room, but on the other it was so nice to have an ear to bitch into.

Worry won out over loneliness. "What I told you, Carver, that's all I know. Period. Jane was right. We had a long talk, and she convinced me that even if there is something bad going on here I oughta mind my own business unless I got facts and proof of what I think. It's my best interest she's got at heart.

121

She's an angel of mercy come late into my life, that woman."

"What exactly did she tell you?"

"I'm sorry, but she made me agree not to say what we talked about. It's private, between me and Jane. She don't want to be part of spreading rumors, she said. I think she's right about that, Carver. Right about a lotta things. Makes me wonder how my life woulda been if I'd met her years ago."

"Everybody wonders those kinds of things," Carver said.

"I wish you'd go now. Really do wish that."

"Okay, Amos, I understand. Thanks." Carver stood up and took the necessary two steps to the door. "You need anything, phone me. All right?"

Amos looked away from the window and smiled at Carver. "Okay." The smile suggested he was grateful for the invitation but probably wouldn't call.

On his way back through the lobby, Carver stopped at the receptionist's desk long enough to ask Birdie if any of Sunhaven's staff smoked.

"That's like strictly forbidden here, Mr. Carver." Her eyes roamed from side to side as if she and Carver were talking about political assassination.

"What about socially?" Carver asked. "Away from Sunhaven?"

"I don't see many of the staff away from here," Birdie said. "None of them smokes, far as I know."

"Isn't that sort of unusual?"

"Getting less and less. And I'm sure a few of them are sneaking a puff now and then, but I don't know which."

Carver thanked her and moved toward the door. A bent, gray woman in a wicker rocker gave him a lustrous if broken-toothed smile and said, "Beautiful day, eh?"

Carver agreed that it was.

"Don't rain all the time here in Florida the way it does in Seattle," the woman observed.

"Guess not," Carver said.

"Seattle was nice, but this here is lovely."

Carver wished he could stay for a moment and chat with the woman, but he knew he shouldn't. Miles to go and promises to keep.

He listened to the rhythmic creaking of the rocker's runners as he limped the rest of the way to the door. It was an oddly reassuring sound that suggested there was some simplicity and goodness in the world.

Nurse Rule was waiting for him outside.

She was standing in the sun near his car. She'd been there for a while; her white-and-blue uniform was damp with perspiration. A mustache of moisture glistened above her upper lip, which at the moment was contemptuously curled in reaction to Carver. Her feet were planted wide and her sturdy body looked immovable; her breasts swelled with firm assurance beneath her blouse. For an instant Carver thought about her with Dr. Macklin at the motel.

"Were you considering moving into Sunhaven?" she asked, motioning with her head toward the clothes piled on the backseat of the Olds. The car might have belonged to a gypsy.

"Maybe in the fullness of time," Carver said. "How come you object to my presence?"

"You're causing unease among the residents."

"It's *because* of unease among the residents that I'm here."

"I have the authority to have you forcibly removed from the premises, if that becomes necessary."

Carver looked beyond her to see two burly attendants standing side by side with their arms crossed. As if Mr. Clean had been cloned.

"Were you here last night when Kearny Williams died?" he asked.

"Mr. Williams's death doesn't concern you."

"But it does," Carver said. "And apparently it concerns Raffy Ortiz."

She glared coldly and directly at him, as if she were diagnosing cataracts. Carver understood how she'd sapped the fight from Amos Burrel. She said, "Just how's Kearny Williams of any interest to Mr. Ortiz?"

"I'll eventually be able to answer that question," Carver said. He adjusted the position of his cane and opened the car door. He patted his pockets. "Spare a cigarette?"

"I don't smoke, Mr. Carver. Smoking blackens the lungs with tar and causes death by cancer. If I had a cigarette, I'd give it to you. But you wouldn't smoke it here at Sunhaven. It's absolutely forbidden."

"You seem to live in a world of absolutes," Carver said.

"It's the kind of world I prefer. I'd also prefer that you weren't part of it."

Carver lowered himself behind the steering wheel and shut the door. The window was cranked down. He started the engine, then looked up at Nurse Rule. "If anything happens to Amos Burrel," he said, "I won't rest till I learn everything about it."

"Mr. Burrel suffers from paranoid delusions, which is why I want you to stay away from him."

Carver said, "Uh-huh." He slipped the Olds's shift lever to Drive and pulled out of the lot. In the rearview mirror he saw that the two attendants, disciplined as harem eunuchs, hadn't changed position in the searing sun. If they ever left Sunhaven, they could always find work as gateposts.

As soon as he was half a mile down the highway, he fished his pack of Swisher Sweet cigars from the glove compartment and fired one up.

He couldn't remember enjoying a cigar more. Might have something to do with Nurse Rule. *Puff! Puff!*

18

From Sunhaven Carver drove to Del Moray police headquarters to keep the appointment he'd made by phone with McGregor.

Going to see McGregor was never an act that lifted the spirit. Carver found himself driving a few miles per hour under the speed limit. The Olds was passed by tractor-trailers and motor homes. By vans and station wagons loaded with children Disney World–bound. Tires sang on the highway as miles and minutes ticked away; despite Disney, the children would find themselves in the real world all too soon.

McGregor was sitting behind his gray steel desk, thoughtfully rolling the eraser of a pencil over his chin, when Carver entered. The lieutenant pretended he was still alone. His visitor was scarcely worth acknowledging. That was how McGregor saw life; he was three-dimensional and everyone else was cardboard.

Carver sat down in the chair near the desk and held his cane loosely with both hands. Since the central air conditioner did a poor job of cooling the tiny office, McGregor had improvised. There was now a portable unit in the one window; it chugged away with an irritating clinking sound and didn't seem to do much to provide relief from the heat. McGregor was sweating. He had on a short-sleeved shirt and wasn't aware of the scrap of paper sticking to his left elbow as he sat rolling the pencil and putting on a show of deep thinking. It really was a crummy office; Carver could see why McGregor wanted to move up in the department.

"You decide it was time to include me in your plans?" McGregor finally asked.

"That's it," Carver said.

"So there's something the law should know about, hey?"

"Why I'm here."

McGregor let the pencil drop on the desk, where it bounced three or four times with a rattling sound before rolling onto the floor. Carver sat quietly and let the lieutenant find his way to where he was going. McGregor was looking at him now. That was a start.

"Let's agree I'm the only representative of Del Moray law you confide in," McGregor said. "For the sake of efficiency and containment of knowledge. After all, there could be leaks to the media; innocent people might be put in jeopardy. How 'bout it? I painting the situation correctly?"

Carver smiled. "Let's say a trade might be worked out."

McGregor leaned his long body way, way back in his chair and laced his fingers behind his neck. The odor of perspiration and days-old underarm deodorant wafted to Carver and hit him hard in the stomach. "Didn't think you came here to give away something for free, Carver. Comes right down to it, you ain't so different from me."

"What if I lie to you?" Carver asked. "What if we make an agreement and I break it?"

McGregor flashed his lurid grin and played the tip of his tongue behind the space between his front teeth. "Here's what, fuckhead: I'll drop on you like a forty-story building."

"We're no different in that respect," Carver told him. "Don't cross me."

126

"You threatening the law, shit-for-brains? Actually threatening the law?"

"Sounds that way."

"Now you made that point," McGregor said, his grin twisting into a sneer, "tell me your information and *I'll* tell *you* if it's worth what you want in return."

"We'll talk about what I want first," Carver said.

"Selfish, selfish. But go ahead; if you didn't have your balls in a wringer you wouldn't be here."

"Protection for Edwina," Carver said.

McGregor pulled his hands out from behind his long neck and dropped forward in his chair. He propped his bony elbows on the desk; the paper that had been struck to his damp left arm peeled away and fluttered unnoticed to the floor to land near the pencil. The lukewarm air from the window unit caught it and skittered it away beneath the desk. McGregor said, "She in some kinda danger because of her hero?"

"Can you assign some manpower to keep a watch on her?"

"With her knowing it?"

"Without. It'd be easier that way. She might object to being watched over."

McGregor ran his tongue around the inside of his cheek, pretending to think about what Carver had requested while he luxuriated in his authority. He was such a prick.

"This is sure a crappy little office," Carver observed, motioning in a sweeping gesture with his cane.

"I got the clout to give you what you want, Carver; you know that. Thing is, what you give me better make it worthwhile, or your ass is grass and I'm the lawnmower. Edwina's safe soon as I pick up that phone."

"You gonna pick it up or not?"

McGregor made a nodding gesture of acceptance, not just with his head but with his entire upper body. Only a very tall man could have managed it. "We got a deal. Now spill your guts."

Carver told him everything. Almost. He didn't mention the lesbian relationship between Dr. Macklin and Nurse Rule. And he omitted the fact that Birdie Reeves was a runaway. McGregor was the type to blackmail the two women and adopt Birdie for illicit purposes.

"It ain't much," McGregor said when Carver was finished talking. "Lotta circumstantial evidence, really. Mostly smoke without any guarantee of fire."

"More than smoke," Carver said. "You can feel the heat and see the red glare of the flames."

"That's opinion."

"Most everything is, including a jury verdict."

"So what's your plan now?" McGregor asked.

"I'm flying to New Orleans to talk to Kearny Williams's family."

"New Orleans, hey?" He was obviously thinking about Raffy Ortiz's recent trip to the city. "That's why you want Edwina protected; you're gonna be outta town for a while."

"That's it," Carver said. "And I'm moving back into my cottage until this thing's resolved. No sense having Raffy Ortiz visit me at her place when she's there."

"Or visit *her* when *you're* not there. Ortiz does very imaginative things to women, way I understand it. Abuses everything they got every which way. Maybe some ancient Oriental shit he picked up with all that martial arts training. Got it from the folks who gave us the Chinese water torture and the death of a thousand cuts."

Carver felt himself flush with rage, and he fought not to slash his cane up and across the desk and smash McGregor's long face. "That's what you're supposed to prevent. That's what this is about."

"Aw, she'll be okay. Safe as the fucking queen of England. Even if I gotta assign six men to subdue bad-ass Ortiz. Long as you and me keep this matter strictly between ourselves for the time being. Remember, we're partners, old buddy."

"We made an agreement. I'll keep it and you'd better take care of your end of it."

"What about Desoto?"

"I phoned him this morning; he won't say anything without telling you first. Police protocol."

"Glad he finally remembered it," McGregor said huffily.

Carver planted the tip of his cane on the smooth linoleum and stood up. His lower back was beginning to ache. It felt good to get out of the rigid chair. It would feel even better to get away from McGregor.

"Something for you to think about," McGregor said when Carver was leaving. "You're worried about Edwina here in Florida, but there's nothing to prevent Raffy Ortiz from taking another trip to New Orleans."

Carver didn't answer. He'd already thought about that. It was why he was making no secret about leaving. Even supernaturally tough Raffy Ortiz couldn't be in both cities at the same time. If Raffy had to be one place or the other, Carver preferred New Orleans.

He drove out of Del Moray and then north along the coast highway to his cottage. A few puffy white clouds kept pace with the car.

The inside of the place was hot and stale. A mud dauber droned around the dead potted plants suspended on chains before the wide window that looked out on the secluded beach and the sun-shot ocean. Waves were charging in high and wide against the beach, then withdrawing to leave creamy surf spilling over the sand.

The cottage was one large room, with a folding screen that partitioned off where Carver slept. Out of habit, he limped into the tiny kitchen area behind a breakfast counter to get something cool to drink.

He'd forgotten he'd switched off the main circuit and the cottage was without electricity. The little refrigerator stood with its door hanging open. It contained only two warm cans of Budweiser, left from when Edwina helped him load the last of his portable belongings into her car and the Olds. It was as if he'd taken up residence in her house bit by bit, one piece of him at a time.

He made his way to the circuit box in the corner and threw the main breaker. A lamp flickered on. The refrigerator clicked and gurgled and began to hum.

Carver switched on the air conditioner, then went to the refrigerator and shoved the door shut with his cane.

It didn't take him long to carry his clothes from the back of the Olds into the cottage. Didn't take more than ten minutes to pack what he'd need for his brief journey.

He had several hours before his turboprop commuter flight took off from the Del Moray airport for the short hop to Orlando, where he'd make the connection to New Orleans. Remotely, he considered driving down the highway and getting some lunch. But the heat had ruined his appetite and he decided against it.

He slumped in the webbed aluminum lounge chair on the cottage's shaded plank porch, his stiff leg stuck out in front of him at a sideways angle, his good leg propped up on the porch rail.

He watched the ocean rolling beyond the toe of his shoe and waited for the beer to get cold.

19

Carver carried his scuffed leather suitcase to the cabstand at the New Orleans International Airport and took a taxi into the city.

It was as hot here as in central Florida. As the cab drove through the poorer section of town, he saw that most of the women wore shorts or skimpy, loose-fitting housedresses of flimsy material. The men had on sports shirts or sleeveless T-shirts if they wore shirts at all. Quite a few people were out sitting on porches or concrete stoops, trying to take advantage of the somewhat cooler early evening air and get free of ovenlike, stifling apartments that heated up and stayed hot. An obese woman, patiently fanning herself with a folded newspaper, was slumped on a porch glider, surrounded by writhing, half-naked children and grandchildren. Poverty required endurance. The price of oil was low and Louisiana's unemployment was high. The city was economically depressed. It showed.

The kind of hotel Carver checked into didn't require a reservation. The Belle Grande was on Belton Avenue near Canal Street, in an old, mostly commercial neighborhood. It was small and retained a certain miniature faded elegance while it did battle to keep time at a standstill. Time would keep moving. The hotel was hanging onto respectability by a fingernail; in five years it would be a flophouse, if it still existed. Unless the neighborhood went the other way, in which case it would probably be an exclusive *concierge* hotel. It was downtown and within easy walking distance of the French Quarter. It suited Carver. He was paying for this trip.

His room was small and the furniture and carpet were threadbare, but everything seemed clean. The walls were papered in a busy fleur-de-lis pattern. Sound strategy; it would be tough to spot a roach crawling on them. Carver wondered if that was the sort of thing they taught in hotel management school. Probably.

He didn't really unpack. Hung a few shirts and a pair of pants in the closet. Tossed his shaving kit on the chipped porcelain washbasin in the bathroom. The rest of what he'd require he'd take directly from the suitcase as he needed it. Life on the move.

He wrestled open the dirt-streaked window and checked the view from his tenth-floor room. Beyond the old office buildings across Belton, he could barely see Canal Street sweltering in the summer haze. A man and woman were holding hands and standing in the wide median, both staring raptly at a red light, waiting for electronic permission to cross the street. Even the traffic seemed to be moving slowly, almost dreamlike. Carver turned away from the window and sat down in the room's one chair to read the *Times-Picayune* he'd bought in the lobby.

He'd had a reason, in addition to protection for Edwina, for making his arrangement with McGregor. Now he could invoke McGregor's name and gain the cooperation of the New Orleans police if it became necessary. He might do that to help him stave off the legendary samurai-sadist Raffy Ortiz, or to aid him in finding out what he needed to know about Kearny Williams. He hoped he wouldn't have to do it for either reason.

He learned from the newspaper's obituary page that Kearny Williams was laid out at King's Crown Mortuary before interment tomorrow morning. The death notice listed names of surviving relatives. The New Orleans phone directory contained the addresses and numbers of those relatives, and the address of the mortuary. Carver smiled. Who needed two healthy knees to do legwork?

He decided to postpone supper and shrugged back into the lightweight tan sport coat he'd worn on the plane. Briefly he thought about putting on the tie that he'd brought, then with open collar he limped from the room.

He had to walk all the way over to Canal Street to get a cab to take him to King's Crown Mortuary.

The cab hadn't been air-conditioned. Carver smoothed his hair back behind his ears, dabbed at his forehead with the sleeve of his sport coat, and made his way up the wide, shallow concrete steps toward the mortuary's ornate entrance.

King's Crown was a fortress of marble, brass, and black wrought iron. It reminded Carver of a bank with a select number of wealthy depositors. Sort of place that routinely turned down small business loans. He was surprised by its opulence.

A solemn man in a dark suit directed him to the "Williams suite," and Carver walked down a carpeted hall to a large room furnished in expensive and subdued French provincial. There were sofas and chairs in pale blue with cream-colored wood trim. Long, royal blue drapes matched the carpet. About half a dozen people sat around the room talking in soft tones. At the far end was an open casket surrounded by floral sprays and wreaths. The coffin was obviously expensive; it was made of polished mahogany and had fancy brass trim and handles. The propped-open lid was lined with buttoned white satin. The latest in underground luxury.

Carver avoided the registration book, which lay open and softly lighted on its wooden stand, walked to the coffin and gazed down at what had been Kearny Williams.

The undertaker had done expert work. Kearny appeared much

as he had the last time he'd talked with Carver. Carver almost expected the corpse to part its rouged lips and speak. Wished it could.

The walk back to the opposite end of the room gave him a chance to look over the various mourners.

There were four men and two women. Two of the men seemed ill at ease. The other two wore expensive suits and looked bored. One of the women was wearing a simple and elegant black dress and sat with one of the well-dressed men on a small sofa. They were staring at the coffin, not talking. As if they were in some sort of suspended animation that allowed only limited movement. The other woman, elderly and black, had on an ill-fitting gray dress with a blue flower design. She was very thin and sat hunched over with her bony hands folded in her lap. Though there was a quiet, subservient air about her, she looked angry. Angry at death? Or maybe something else? Carver changed direction and set course toward her.

She had a lean, seamed face with watery almond-shaped eyes. Her gray hair was carefully combed but thinning and without enough body to stay in place. It flew like wisps of cloud in unplanned directions. She looked as if she'd just stepped in out of a high wind. Carver tried to guess her age but couldn't. Somewhere between sixty and eighty was the best he could do. Narrowed it down to this century.

He stood near her and said, "Damned shame about Kearny."

She looked up at him with her large, dark eyes, which seemed to peer into his thoughts. He noticed that her dress smelled like mothballs. "He was of an age to go."

"Guess that's some solace," Carver said. "But I think he'd have preferred a few more years, don't you?"

She didn't comment. Her eyes stayed fixed on him.

"Like most of us," he added.

"Where'd you know Kearny from?"

"He and I drove a lumber truck together a long time ago."

"Out in California?"

"That's right." Carver smiled down at the woman. "My name's Frank Carter. I suppose you and Kearny go back a long while."

"Quite some years. I'm Wanda Pichet. My mother used to be the Williams's maid over on Naval Avenue. Knowed Kearny since he was twelve. Used to throw rocks at each other, hide out when it was bedtime. I guess that's goin' back a long while, wouldn't you say?"

"I'd say." Carver stooped down as low as he could with his stiff knee, leaning most of his weight on his cane. "I don't know any of the family; wanna help me out?"

Wanda Pichet studied him with sad speculation. Then she said, "Them two is Kearny's son Lawrence an' his son-in-law Jack Lipp. The other two men's names I ain't sure of, but they used to drive with Kearny, too. They's from the union, I think. That's Kearny's daughter Melba. She's Jack's wife." Wanda's voice had grown strained when she spoke of Melba Lipp.

"Kearny never talked much about his kids," he said.

Wanda shook her head slowly. "Ain't much to brag on there," she said. "Lawrence got hisself messed up with drugs an' still ain't straightened out, though he's workin' steady now at some sales job. Melba, she's got even less of a mind than Lawrence; does what that husband of hers wants an' nothin' else."

Carver looked more closely at Melba. She was a mousy brunette with a knife-thin humped nose, an underslung chin, and a superb figure. Hers was a dichotomy of beauty that intrigued some men. "I get the impression you don't care much for Melba."

"You think that's any of your concern?" She asked it gently, as if inquiring whether he thought it was going to rain.

"It might be," Carver said. "If Kearny was your friend."

"Hmm." Wanda shifted her frail body in her chair. She seemed out of place in the palatial mortuary, a beggar in the royal court. "Melba's got no morals nor willpower whatsoever. That's all there's to her, Mr. Carter. Clay to be molded by the devil."

"And her husband?"

"He owns a jazz club down in the Quarter. Melba's Place. He's the one did the latest molding."

"How long they been married?"

" 'Bout five years. He got her from a trumpet player she was living with over in Metairie. They passed her down like she was so much baggage—not that she didn't ask for that kinda treatment."

"Was she married to the trumpet player?"

Wanda's face puckered with distaste. "Thought she was married to the whole band, but none of 'em seen a wedding ring nor man of God all the time they was spending her money and taking advantage of her."

"Didn't Lawrence try to talk sense to her?"

"Ain't you been listenin'? Lawrence got no sense hisself."

"How about the mother? Kearny's wife?"

"Died givin' birth to Melba. You oughta know that, 'less you forgot."

"No, Kearny never mentioned it. Never talked a lot about any of his family. Too much pain, I guess."

"Whole Williams family knowed pain. They was well-to-do when my mother worked for them in the big house on Naval. Financial affairs went all to seed, though. Somethin' about the commodity market. I don't know what an' I don't wanna know. It caused Kearny's father to let his health go downhill so he died a few years later. 'Nother five years, then old Mrs. Williams went. She was a fine woman, way I recall. Kept her good spirits right up till the cancer took her. After that's when they called in workmen and divided up most of the house, 'cept for the wing where my mother and me lived. Kearny made sure we could stay on long as we wanted, sorta kept an eye on the place for him."

"You live in the house now?"

"Just me alone in the north wing. My mother passed on twenty years ago. Guess I'll have to find someplace else now, though. Half a dozen roomers live in the other part of the house, come an' go as they please."

"Why don't any of the Williams children live there?"

"Too run-down for 'em. Too expensive to keep decent. Big place like that's a cross to bear. Kearny left it to be run by Kemper Management, where I send my rent check to. But they couldn't spend much on it neither an' still use the income to help keep Kearny at that old-age home in Florida. That an' the money he borrowed on the house is all he had, way I hear. He was born too late to enjoy any of the family wealth as a man, was poor Kearny."

Carver's good leg was cramped and beginning to tremble. Losing feeling. He had to straighten up or he'd need help in order to stand.

He made it with effort, and felt circulation returning to the leg. Pins and needles.

"Goin' to the funeral tomorrow?" Wanda asked.

"I don't think I'll be able."

"Me neither. Not that I got other matters at hand. Just don't like to see the end of things. Me and Kearny, we was best of friends." She fixed those dark, almond-shaped eyes on Carver. "*Best* of friends."

Carver dug the tip of his cane into the plush carpet. "Mind if we talk again sometime? About Kearny?"

She looked away. "I mind. Kearny's over an' done with. What's up there in that coffin ain't him, and even that'll soon enough be dust. What's gone is gone."

Carver started to say good-bye to her, but she seemed to be in a trance, absorbed by the echoes and visions of long-ago summers. Throwing rocks and running through shadows. She was wrong. What she thought was gone would never be completely over as long as she drew breath.

"It'd really be a big help to me if we talked again," Carver said. "Be honest, I didn't really know Kearny all that well."

Wanda Pichet sniffled. He thought she might begin to cry, but she was an old woman years past tears. She might even have smiled. "Think I don't know that? Kearny never drove no lumber truck in California nor anyplace else."

137

"Then why'd you go along with our conversation?" Carver asked.

She slipped back into her memories. Into a kinder world. She wasn't going to answer.

He took a last, long look at Kearny Williams's mourners and limped from the mortuary.

Into heat and life.

20

The next morning Carver phoned from the Belle Grande lobby and had Hertz deliver a rental Ford to him. He assured the woman who brought the car that, despite his bad leg, he could drive a vehicle if it had an automatic transmission. She was dubious, but she filled out the paperwork and he signed for the car. It was a blue, medium-sized Taurus model he'd be able to wriggle in and out of okay with the cane.

He called Kemper Management and got the address of the Williams house on Naval by pretending to be a potential buyer of the property. Kemper Management also sold real estate, Carver was told, and would have the listing on the Williams house when and if the heirs decided to put it on the market.

The agent asked if he could meet Carver at the house, but Carver told him he wanted only to drive past and look the place over from the outside before thinking more about an offer. The agent didn't ask Carver how he knew the property was managed by Kemper and might soon be for sale; he must have assumed Carver was a speculator with a running knowledge of such things who used the obituary pages as guides to potential cheap property purchases from heirs who usually didn't mind taking several thousand dollars under market value. The difference in sale and asking price was divided evenly among the heirs and made little difference to them individually, and it eliminated the problem of keeping the property on the market for months while it ate up maintenance and interest money. Edwina had swung some deals like that for sellers in much the same position as the Williams heirs.

The Kemper agent had said the house was half a block off Saint Charles, a wide street upon which a streetcar line ran. Most of the homes in the vicinity of Naval Avenue and Saint Charles looked like plantation manor houses in their reincarnations of sumptuousness. Only a few were what might be described as run-down. After what had apparently been a period of decline, this was again one of the better addresses in New Orleans.

Carver waited for a green-and-red trolley to sway and clank past, then made a left turn onto Naval and drove slowly.

The houses on Naval Avenue were somewhat smaller than on Saint Charles, but still impressive and expensive. Several of them were being refurbished and had skeletal, crude scaffolding erected beside them. Two homes in the middle of the block were in terrible disrepair. The nearest of these was the Williams house.

Carver parked the Ford across the street, left the engine and air conditioner running, and looked closely at the house. It had to contain at least twenty rooms. The vast slate roof was broken by dormers and cupolas, and there was a wide, once elegant gallery porch that wrapped around the front and east side. Many of the spokes in the porch's railing were missing or broken, and several separate entrances had been placed on the face of the house when it was divided into rental areas, without regard to architectural balance. The clapboard siding had been painted white long ago, but it was a mottled gray now and cracked and peeling.

Most of the windows had yellow shades pulled all the way

140

down against the heat. It gave the impression that there was no one inside, though Carver knew there probably was. Wanda Pichet might be home, in the corner of her past that Kearny had given her and that Kearny's children would now force her to leave.

The house was set well back from the street, and the grounds were overgrown with weeds. About twenty feet from the porch steps was a huge magnolia tree that shaded the front yard. It had to have been there when Kearny Williams and Wanda Pichet were children. Carver wondered if they'd played in its branches, hidden there together from the world.

He'd seen enough. He put the Ford in gear and drove toward Kemper Management on Maitland Avenue.

Carver explained to the receptionist at Kemper that he might be interested in a preliminary way in the Williams property; he wanted to talk to someone to get more information.

The receptionist was a young man with a toned-down punk hairdo and a gold stud in his ear, wearing a white shirt and tie. He referred Carver to a Mr. Clyde Arlan, who appeared within a few minutes and smiled and shook hands and ushered Carver into a small, square office without a window. Carver again used the name Frank Carter.

There was a brown-enameled steel desk with a glass top in the office, and two padded green chairs. On the wall was a large map of New Orleans with red dots plastered all over it. The dots were plastic or metal and stuck to the map in some way Carver couldn't fathom; not pinned or taped. Glue, maybe? Magnetism? He assumed each dot represented property managed or listed by Kemper. On the opposite wall was a framed photo of Clyde Arlan posed formally with a pleasant-faced, plump woman and two preschool children who had blond hair and looked like identical twins.

"Nice family," Carver said, lowering himself into one of the padded chairs.

Arlan grinned. He was in his mid-thirties, skinny, and had

thinning sandy hair that had probably started off blond like his kids'. "Thanks. Those husky twins are almost four now." He sounded especially proud to have fathered twins, as if it made him twice the man. "You the fella I talked to earlier on the phone about the Williams place?" He had a syrupy southern accent and made *place* two syllables.

"Me," Carver said. "I heard it'll be on the market soon and wanted some information."

"Uh-huh. You an agent?"

"Not actually. An agent here would handle the transaction if I decided to buy. Mind you, I'm not anywhere near making a decision. I mean, the property isn't even on the market."

"It'll be soon, though," Clyde Arlan said. "Owner just died down in Florida and the heirs plan on selling it. It's one of those rare old fine homes been in the same family for decades."

Rare old fine homes. Carver liked that. "You sure about them planning to sell?"

"Uh-huh. One of them told me so just yesterday. We've got instructions to contract some work on the place to make it presentable for market, bring it up to code, then list it soon as the will's probated."

"How long will that take?"

Arlan shrugged. "Depends on the will."

"*Is* there a will?"

"Well, nobody seems quite sure. But one way or another, the family'll inherit and they do intend to sell. We've managed the property for the last ten years. Some of the rent money went to support the owner at a retirement home down in Florida. The rest of it went into upkeep."

"Any liens against the place?"

"There's a second mortgage of twenty-five thousand, but that's minuscule compared to how much the property's worth. Woulda been sold a long time ago, only it had sentimental value for the owner."

"What'll the asking price be?"

Arlan flashed a cagey smile. He was trying to grow a mustache, Carver noticed. Just a shadow on his upper lip now. "Price hasn't been talked about yet. But in that area, half a block off Saint Charles, and with that big lot, it won't be cheap. It's prime property. You know that, I'm sure."

"Last thing I want is to seem nosy," Carver said, "but which of the heirs will be handling the sale? I mean, which of them contacted you? I'd like to talk to him myself, just to be assured that when the time comes they'll be open to an offer. Save everybody some wheel spinning."

Arlan wasn't sure he should give out that information. On the other hand, there was no point in sabotaging a possible deal. The wife and twins stared trustingly at him from the framed photograph.

"The heirs' names were in the paper," Carver pointed out. "All I'm asking is you save me some time. I'll wait a decent interval, then go to the executor or the one handling matters and we'll talk."

"Guess there wouldn't be any harm," Arlan said. "The one that came here yesterday wasn't a man, though, it was Mrs. Melba Lipp, the deceased's daughter. There's two kids, a son and a daughter. The mother's dead."

"How come they're so eager to sell?" Carver asked.

"Don't know that they are all *that* eager." Salesman talk. Mrs. Lipp mighta just been in the neighborhood, figured she'd drop in and let us know the plans for the house."

"I mean, the father isn't even buried yet."

"They got a need for the money, I suppose. Mrs. Lipp and her husband own a lounge down in the Quarter, Melba's Place, and she's been here before trying to borrow money against the property to put into the business. We had to explain we couldn't do that, even if we would like to help them get into the black." Arlan stared at his fingertips for a few seconds and tapped them on the desk, as if to make sure they still worked. "It's not exactly right I should be telling you this, but I don't want you going

143

and putting your investment dollars elsewhere thinking the Williams place might not really be listed. It'll be for sale and I'll be the listing agent."

"You know for a fact the lounge is in financial trouble?"

Arlan frowned. "I'd better not say any more about that. You want to leave me your card or phone number, so I can reach you when the property goes on the market?"

"I'll get in touch with you, Mr. Arlan." Carver stood up and they shook hands. "Thanks for your help. Everything you told me about the Williams family will stay confidential, and I promise if I do decide to make an offer you'll be the sales agent."

When an agent both listed and sold a property, it meant he didn't split the commission. The frown left Arlan's face and he was smiling when he showed Carver out. It was the same smile as when he'd ushered him into the office.

As he drove away in the Ford, Carver congratulated himself on being convincing. If he'd fooled Arlan as thoroughly as he thought, he owed his success to Edwina, who liked to talk about her work.

He glanced at his watch and saw that it was ten o'clock. They'd he holding a service and interring Kearny Williams in the family crypt about now. Carver knew they didn't bury people in New Orleans, because of the swampy soil and grisly lessons learned long ago.

Jack and Melba Lipp would be at Kearny's funeral, which meant Carver could go to their lounge in the French Quarter and not worry about being recognized by anyone from last night at the mortuary.

The lounge might be open, but it was too early for serious drinking. Too early to listen to jazz.

Maybe a cup of coffee and some answers.

21

Melba's Place in the French Quarter was on Dumaine, incon-
gruously tucked between a musty-looking used-book store and
an antiques shop. It wasn't a jazz club, as Carver had been told;
it was a narrow lounge with no room for a band to set up and
play. There was a long bar running front to back along one
wall, and space for only a single row of small tables opposite.
Behind the bar and shelves of bottles on the wall was a mirror
that extended to the ceiling. Carver guessed the idea was to
make Melba's Place seem more spacious. All of this he had to
observe through the front window, because Melba's Place was
closed and the lettering on the door said it wouldn't open until
five that evening. The Vieux Carré, as the French Quarter was
sometimes known, and Melba's customers, thrived on night air.

There was shade on the narrow streets of the Quarter, providing a modicum of shelter from the glare and heat, so Carver
walked around for a while, until he found a restaurant at the
corner of Royal and Saint Philip.

He had an early lunch of blackened redfish and Dixie beer
while he listened to a street musician play beautiful clarinet.

Not a bad way to spend an afternoon. Maybe this was why they called New Orleans the Big Easy.

Finally the clarinet player moved on. Carver had a second cup of rich black coffee, then made his way back to the Belle Grande.

He was tired. He hadn't walked all that far, but the cane had been tricky on the Quarter's roughly paved streets and sidewalks, and the day was heating up fast.

When he reached his room, he lay down for a while on the bed, then he got restless and went into the bathroom and ran cold water over his wrists. The tanned face in the mirror above the basin looked back at him grimly and admonishingly, as if to say there was no point in wasting time until Melba's Place opened; you're a detective, so detect. Face had a point.

Carver rode one of the rickety elevators downstairs and walked through the lobby to the street, then down the block to where he'd parked the Ford.

He drove to the Williams house and limped up on the porch. No one objected but some crickets concealed in the weeds.

The house was in even worse shape than it had seemed from across the street. It probably hadn't been painted in decades, and some of the planks in the porch floor were rotted all the way through. A fetid odor of decay lay in the shadows beneath the sagging roof. Carver watched a large black waterbug drag itself across the porch, seeking shelter and shadow, and disappear into the darkness of one of the rotted fissures.

Wanda Pichet's name wasn't on any of the mailboxes, but a painted wooden arrow read "Pichet Residence" and pointed toward the near side of the house.

Carver went back down the hollow-sounding porch steps, cut across the hard lawn, and found a stepping-stone path to a door beneath a rusted metal awning.

Wanda's name was crudely printed with red marking pen on a black metal mailbox. Carver rang the doorbell but got no answer. He knocked loudly, waited almost five minutes, then knocked again.

He was sure he'd heard someone moving inside the house—a shuffling noise and the faint groan of a floorboard. Furtive sounds. Wanda Pichet was home but chose not to come to the door. Judicious noninvolvement was the only control she had in life.

Finally Carver decided there was nothing he could do about that, and he went back across the street to the Ford. As he was driving away he was sure he glimpsed a pinched, dark face at one of the upstairs windows.

He braked the car suddenly and looked more carefully, straining his neck to peer upward from the low seat.

The yellowed shade was back in place, though swaying ever so slightly. The face was gone. Wanda had said she was done talking about Kearny Williams and apparently she'd meant it. Everything about her suggested she always meant what she said.

Back in his room at the Belle Grande, Carver sat on the edge of the bed and dialed long-distance to Orlando. Desoto was in his office and got on the phone immediately.

Carver told him where he was and why.

"You learn anything other than Kearny Williams been put in the ground, *amigo*?"

"Above the ground," Carver corrected. "They don't bury people here."

"Figure of speech. McGregor phoned me a couple hours ago."

"Pissed off, I guess."

"No, he was very friendly. Like a rattlesnake without a rattle. Said he'd keep me tapped in as he was informed. What a guy, eh?"

"Yeah, he's sure to be governor one of these days."

"*Sacro Dios*, Carver!" They both knew it was impossible. McGregor had a nose for other people's weaknesses, and there was no ceiling on his ambition.

"There's an old black woman here," Carver said. "She was the daughter of the Williams's maid and sort of grew up with

Kearny. She could give me a better slant on the situation before Kearny's death, only she won't talk."

"Maid? Kearny Williams drove a truck. Didn't figure to be from the kinda family had a maid."

"Old southern wealth," Carver said. "The family lost most of it when Kearny was a kid, but the homestead's still here in a prime area of New Orleans and worth a small fortune. Kearny was the owner of record, though he didn't hold clear title. He'd borrowed against the place to foot the bill at Sunhaven, but the net value's still up in six figures."

"So what's it all mean, *amigo*?"

"Can't tell at this point. The money'll go to Kearny's two kids, a son and a daughter, who seem the kind that'll diddle it away in no time." Carver hesitated, then said, "Any family members profit big from Sam Cusanelli's death?"

Desoto answered in his detached cop's voice. "I don't think so. It's something I'll check."

"In a little while I'm going to a lounge owned by Kearny's daughter and son-in-law; maybe I can get a better feel for things. Meantime, can you use your police contacts in Indianapolis and get me an address on a Linda Redmond? She was the social worker who handled Birdie Reeves's case two years ago. Probably still with one of the agencies there."

Desoto said he could do that, and Carver gave him the Belle Grande phone number and his room extension. Said he'd be there later that evening.

"This hotel where you're staying—is it expensive?"

"Expense is relative."

"You got a bathroom with running water?"

"Sure; place even has windows that go up and down."

"I put a money order in the mail for you this morning."

"Not necessary."

"Tell 'em that at the desk when you go to check out, *amigo*. I hired you. You need anything, you let me know."

Carver said, "Just Linda Redmond's address," and hung up.

22

Though Melba's Place didn't feature a live band, it had a ferocious sound system. Huge box speakers were mounted on all four walls, and B. B. King was plucking up a storm through them when Carver limped to the bar.

It was only five-thirty, and there was one other customer, a skinny guy in Levi's and one of those athlete's shirts made of net from the chest down. There was a big red number 22 stenciled on the front of the shirt, which looked brand-new. Number 22 was seated at one of the tables near the back, reading a paperbound book.

Carver mounted a stool near the front end of the long bar and watched the bartender amble toward him.

He was a short man with military-cropped blond hair, a barrel chest, and crescent-shaped, friendly eyes. He had a beefy face with a reckless half smile pasted on it that Carver suspected was always there as a sort of mild defense. No matter what he was doing, he was having a hell of a good time, the smile proclaimed. It probably helped him to slip through life with a minimum of confrontation. Hard to imagine the man with that smile being duplicitous or angry; hard to imagine him without the smile. A tough marine drill instructor gone hopelessly good. Nice guy no matter what.

"Not much happening here," Carver remarked over the music.

"Early yet. What can I getcha?"

"Scotch. You Melba?" Carver was smiling as he asked.

"Not me," the bartender said. "I'm Jerry. But there's a sure enough Melba owns Melba's Place." He poured some Usher's into a glass.

"You're shittin' me," Carver said. "Al's Lounge, Mom's Diner, Cal's Used Cars—there's never an Al, Mom, or Cal."

"Well, there's a Melba. Want water or ice in this?"

"Straight-up's fine." Jerry set the pebbled glass on the bar in front of Carver on a round cork coaster with "Melba's Place" lettered on it in black. Carver took a sip and put the glass back down carefully on the coaster, centering it as if that were important. He said, "Hard to believe there's actually a Melba owns Melba's Place. Usually it's a big syndicate or something, and if there was a Melba she's been dead for ten years or she's retired someplace down in Florida."

The bartender chuckled. "It's that way a lot, but not here. I'd show you our Melba only she ain't in. Her father died and the funeral was just this morning."

"That's a shame."

"Kinda thing always is, but she and the old man weren't that close."

"She own the place herself, or she got partners?"

"Got a husband's what she's got." Jerry said it as if he didn't like Jack Lipp. "He's the actual owner, only it was Melba's money got 'em in here."

"Rent must be high, right in the Quarter."

"Eat you up alive. Come winter, though, the place might be bigger. Hear talk of taking over the bookstore next door, knocking out that wall. Make the place twice as big."

"Make the rent twice as much, too, wouldn't it?"

The bartender shrugged. "Sometimes it costs money to make money. The main thing is to turn this joint from a hole-in-the-wall into a place where tourists'll come and listen to live music. That's what they want here in the Quarter. Hell, they can play tapes at home, that's what they feel like hearing. Drink at home, too, for that matter."

"You got a point," Carver said, and took another sip of scotch. It tasted good; he must have needed a drink and not known it.

B. B. King wrapped up his number. Winton Marsalis took over.

Another customer came in and sat at the opposite end of the bar. He had on a tropical-print shirt and broad red suspenders and needed a shave. The numbed look on his face suggested that life had been kicking him around.

Jerry wiped his hands on a towel tucked in his belt, though his hands were perfectly dry. As if he'd seen too many reruns of old Jackie Gleason shows where Gleason does his friendly-bartender routine. He wandered down to take the new guy's order. Number 22 got up and left.

Carver downed the rest of his scotch in one gulp, felt it sear the back of his throat and warm his stomach, and swiveled down off his stool. He caught the bartender looking at him in the back-bar mirror and lifted a hand in a parting wave. Jerry widened his jaunty grin and turned away to talk to the customer in the wild shirt and suspenders.

When Carver stepped outside, he didn't see Melba Lipp staring at him from behind the window of the pastry shop across the street. She stopped there often to pick up cream *beignets* and coffee before going into Melba's Place. Her figure was one thing she didn't have to worry about, and she'd long indulged an incurable sweet tooth.

Her mouth hung open and her eyes bulged with surprise. She'd recognized Carver almost instantly, as soon as she'd seen the cane and stiff leg. No doubt who he was. The cruel-looking guy who'd been talking with Wanda Pichet last night at the mortuary.

The evening was cooling off. Carver stopped in a restaurant with tables outside on the sidewalk and ordered a cheeseburger and a Coke.

When he was finished eating he sat and watched the Quarter residents and tourists wandering by. It was easy to tell who was who. When that got stale, he paid his check and enjoyed the walk back to the Belle Grande.

There was a new man behind the desk, young and sharp-looking. He had on a neat blue suit and wore a gold watch that looked like an imitation Rolex, a big maybe-diamond tie tack. He'd splashed on just the right amount of cologne, which gave off a crisp spearmint scent. Women who liked money and chewing gum would find him irresistible.

Carver gave his room number and asked if there were any messages, and the sharp young guy checked the boxes and said no, there was nothing for him. He hoped Carver was enjoying his stay at the hotel, he said, as if they were in the lobby of the Royal Orleans.

Carver coaxed a newspaper from the battered vending machine and went upstairs to read it while he waited for Desoto to call.

He stretched out on the bed and had barely opened the paper when he dozed off. The booze and dinner, and then the walk back to the hotel, had made him feel doped and drowsy.

The room was dark when he abruptly woke up.

What the hell? Something was wrong. His arms were stretched over his head and he couldn't move his hands. Worse than that, he was having a terrible time breathing.

Something—somebody—as heavy as a building was sitting on his chest.

23

The dark, bulky shape looming over Carver reached out a thick arm to the bedside lamp and switched it on. Yellow light flooded the room.

Raffy Ortiz smiled down at Carver. The lamp was reflected as tiny oblong slashes of brilliance in his narrowed eyes, lending him the look of a feral cat about to relish a kill.

Raffy was straddling his chest. Must have slipped the lock on the door, or forced it without Carver hearing. Carver writhed desperately, twisted his neck, and saw that the tie he'd draped over the chair had been knotted around his wrists to bind them to the old iron headboard. He tested all his strength against the knots. The silk tie drew tighter around his wrists, cutting off circulation in his hands. Panic welled cold and black in his bowels. He wriggled his fingers and could barely feel them.

Raffy said, "No use you struggling, *compadre*." Still grinning, he used his thumb and middle finger and nimbly flicked the tip of Carver's nose. Hard. It stung, causing Carver to toss his head from side to side in a futile attempt to protect himself. He threw back his good leg and tried to hook it around Raffy's neck. He couldn't quite make it. Raffy expertly flicked the tip of his nose again. Damn, that hurt!

"I told you," Raffy said in his Cuban accent, "you gotta stop talking to people down in Florida. You didn't hear me, I guess, huh?" *Flick!* went the finger. Tears spilled from Carver's eyes.

"Bastard!" Carver spat. But even through his rage he felt a chilling fear. He was completely helpless. And Raffy was enjoying this; he was in control of where it was going. In total control.

Flick! "I dunno, Carver, maybe if your other leg was broke in eight or ten places that'd slow you down. Have to do your asking around over the phone, wouldn't you, asshole?"

The idea of both legs ruined, of complete immobility, made Carver frantic with fear. He strained against his bonds and thrashed futilely with his good leg, his breath hissing and his body heaving. Raffy whooped and waved an arm, as if he were riding a rodeo bronco. This was sport to him.

When Carver finally lay quiet again, Raffy chuckled. It was a high, nasty sound, like something brittle breaking. His eyes got dreamy. *Flick!* More tears. Warm. Tickling Carver's neck as they tracked down to the sweat-soaked pillow.

Slowly Raffy dismounted Carver's chest. Carver sucked in a rasping breath of air and tried to blink the tears from his eyes. It helped, but his vision was blurred.

Raffy said, "Somebody tells you something, fucker, you oughta listen or you might be making a major mistake. You agree?"

Carver lay silently with his chest working like a bellows. God, it was good to be able to breathe! The warm air was like sweet liquid.

Raffy chuckled again. He reached beneath Carver's shirt and pinched his right nipple and then twisted it brutally. Carver's body writhed in pain. "Hear me ask if you agree?"

"I heard," Carver groaned through his agony and anger. And he felt something else: humiliation. He knew he shouldn't feel that, but he did.

"You're just like a bitch, Carver. Do what you're fucking told." Raffy walked over to the old easy chair, whirled neatly in the air, and kicked a hole in the backrest. Chair didn't stand a chance. White upholstery batting bulged from the rip. Raffy had on a sleeveless black T-shirt and painted-tight Levi's. The Levi's didn't seem to restrict his range of motion. He swaggered over to the floor lamp near the window and chopped it in half with the callused edge of his right hand, grunting in an explosion of air as he struck. The upper half of the lamp dropped to the floor, dangling from the lower, the two pieces held together only by insulated wiring. "Hey, I could do that to your good leg, Carver. Snap that fucker easy as shit, you know?" He slashed the air with his hand. "Eee-yow! Nothing to me."

He moved lithely toward the foot of the bed, incredibly graceful for such a wide and muscular man. He was getting high on domination now, the dreamy grin fixed firmly to go with an unblinking hardness in his gleaming dark eyes. Like a kid engrossed in pulling the legs off an insect. "What you'd do then, Carver, is sit in a wheelchair or drag yourself around like a fucking snail. Wouldn't be no problem to me or anybody else." He leaped like an oversized ballet dancer to the bathroom door. The wall jutted out there; he side-shuffled gracefully and with another primal, explosive grunt slammed his fist into it. His hammerlike hand, chalked white with plaster dust, emerged inside the bathroom. He laughed and wriggled his fingers. "Punched right through the goddamn wall, *compadre!* Know anybody else can do that? You're a strong fucker—bet you can't do it, huh? Well, maybe that ain't a fair thing to say. 'Cause maybe you won't get the chance."

He pulled his arm and hand back through the wall. Brushing white powder from himself and his clothes, he said, "Tied up like that, Carver, with your worthless leg, I could walk over there and pull your pants down and shove it to you. Stretch your bunghole nine directions. You're lucky I ain't that way. I mean, I might cut your dick off and shove it down your throat,

155

but I ain't a goddamn fag. You oughta be glad, you know? You glad?"

"Glad," Carver said.

Raffy whooped again and suddenly leaped onto the bed, standing and straddling Carver. One of the bed slats gave and a corner of the mattress dropped. Didn't bother Raffy with his feline balance.

He unzipped his Levi's, held his penis with both hands, and urinated on Carver.

At first Carver couldn't believe it.

This couldn't be happening.

Then he did believe it and rage overcame reason. He yanked desperately at the knotted tie, roaring, kicking up at Raffy with his free leg. Raffy ignored his efforts. Carver felt warm urine spatter over his chest and neck, then his face. He spat and cursed. Gagged. The ammonia stench of the urine was sickening him. He was clenching his fists so tightly that feeling was returning to his numbed fingers.

Raffy grinned and said, "You can make noise if you want. Nobody hear you in this old hotel. If they did hear, they wouldn't do nothing anyway."

Carver knew he was right.

When Raffy's bladder was emptied he casually zipped his pants back up and hopped down off the bed. Then he drew a switchblade knife from his pocket. The spring had been removed and the blade was balanced so it could be scissored out and locked into position with a quick wrist motion. Carver barely saw Raffy's arm move as the long, gleaming blade leaped from its bone handle and snapped into place with a firm, metallic click. It was polished steel and finely honed, and it gave back the light from the lamp by the bed. Moving as if his muscular mass weighed about ten pounds, Raffy walked around to stand near Carver's head.

"I oughta slice off a few of your fingers, you think? Or maybe the tip of your nose. Be really ugly then. Or how 'bout I cut the big tendons in your elbows so you flop around like a goddamn chicken? Now, that's something to see, all right. Look like you're trying to fucking fly. Or maybe you'd rather I cut off your dick, huh? Naw, don't wanna do that. How 'bout we just pry out an eyeball?" He moved the glinting point of the blade slowly to within a thousandth of an inch of Carver's right eye. "You got two eyes, you can spare one."

Keeping his head perfectly still, Carver began to tremble. He could feel his body vibrating from the neck down. It was such a violent motion that the bedsprings whined.

Raffy gave his brittle chuckle again and slowly moved the knife away.

Then he stopped smiling and put on a serious expression. "Thing for you to know, Carver, is if I make up my mind you're dead, then you're dead. Oh, you might not stop breathing and lay down right away, but you're dead all right. Understand that?"

"I get what you mean," Carver told him. He couldn't keep his body still. His hands were cold above the knotted tie.

"It's good you understand." Raffy leaned over and very deliberately used the edge of his free hand to chop at Carver's elbows. He was an expert. On the first try each time, he struck what's sometimes known as the crazy bone. Something like electrical shock jolted along both of Carver's arms. He felt a painful kind of lameness in them as Raffy cut through the knots binding them and then straightened up.

Raffy deftly folded the knife and slipped it back in his pocket, pushing it all the way in with his thumb because the Levi's were so tight.

Carver tried to roll away, off the other side of the bed, but his arms were useless. He kicked at the soggy mattress with his good leg but couldn't even turn his body.

Raffy said, "Hey, you're a real man. Didn't even shit in your pants."

Laughing, he swaggered from the room, closing the door behind him softly, with an odd gentleness.

Carver lay quietly in the stench of urine and fear. And with an anger so deep and volcanic it scared him. Right now he'd do anything destructive to Raffy Ortiz and love doing it.

He didn't move for about ten minutes. Then he sat up, located his cane, and limped into the bathroom. He ignored the jagged hole at eye level in the wall.

He turned the shower on full blast, peeled off his wet clothes, and climbed in beneath the hot needles of water with a fresh bar of the Belle Grande's bargain soap.

Carver stood there for a long time, scrubbing himself over and over with the soap—his face, his chest, everywhere—until the bar had melted to a knife-edged sliver that slipped from his hand.

Then he twisted the cracked porcelain faucet handles to turn off the shower. Nude, clean, he returned to the room with the broken bed.

He slowly got dressed. The shower had helped, but emotion, rage, was returning to him full force. Every few minutes he literally shuddered with revulsion and fury.

When he was dressed, he sat in the chair Raffy had kicked, feeling the protruding wad of batting lumped between his shoulder blades.

The phone jangled.

He could easily reach it from where he sat, but he waited five rings before lifting the receiver and holding it to his ear.

He heard himself mumble a hoarse hello.

"Wake you up, *amigo*?" Desoto.

"No. I just had a talk with Raffy Ortiz. He's sick. Even sicker than we thought. And more dangerous."

Desoto said nothing. He must have heard something in Carver's voice.

"Another very physical warning to stay away from the Sunhaven thing," Carver said. "He could have killed me but it wasn't on his agenda tonight."

"What'd he do?"

"Never mind."

"You okay?"

"Yeah. Not happy, but okay. No lasting injuries."

"He's toying with you." Desoto sounded angry. Then a resigned sigh came over the phone. "That's the way of him," Desoto said. "He's a sadistic bastard. Doesn't kill anybody right out unless he has to. Gets his jollies watching people suffer deeply and die slow. Not a nice man, Raffy Ortiz."

"Not one of my favorites."

"What now, *amigo*?"

"Find that Indianapolis address?"

About ten seconds passed with only static and oceanlike whispers on the connection. Then Desoto said softly, "Maybe you should listen to Ortiz."

"I am listening to him. I'm on to something live or he wouldn't be taking all this trouble with me."

"It isn't trouble to him, my friend, it's his amusement."

"He won't know I'm in Indianapolis."

"He found out you were in New Orleans."

"That's because he knew I might come here to dig into Kearny Williams's death."

Carver watched the shadows on the far wall while he waited for Desoto to say something. The intermittent sounds of traffic over on Canal drifted to him. Jesus, the room stank!

"You don't have to do this, *amigo*."

"Yeah, I do," Carver told him.

"I figured you'd say that. You're fucked up in such a way you can't let it drop, eh? Not 'won't'—'can't.' Seen it in you before. Tough guy. So fucked up. Still, I feel responsible for you this time."

"That doesn't change where we are now."

"Thing I'm afraid of," Desoto said, "isn't where we are now. It's where you might be going."

But he told Carver Linda Redmond's address in Indianapolis. What friends were for.

24

Linda Redmond was in the phone directory, along with the address Desoto had given Carver. Carver phoned her from the Indianapolis airport. She was home. In a weary, cynical voice, she tried to brush him off, treated him like a siding salesman—until he mentioned Beatrice Reeves. Then she agreed to talk with him. He told her he didn't have a lot of time, and she said there was none like the present.

Since Carver wasn't going to be in town more than a few hours, instead of renting a car he took a cab to Linda Redmond's address.

She lived in an old brick apartment building on Meridian, in a neighborhood that lay in hot and despairing limbo while it waited for demolition.

Carver limped into the graffiti-marked vestibule. There was a three-speed Schwinn bicycle leaning against the wall, near a bank of tarnished brass mailboxes beneath round black holes where doorbell buttons used to be. The bike's front wheel had been removed and the frame was chained to a floor-to-ceiling steam pipe. A large padlock dangled from the chain, and the pipe had nicks and dents in it where the chain looped around it, as if the bike had been secured there countless times. The floor was littered with trash, some of which had probably been there so long it would take an archaeologist to fix the dates. In a far corner, near steep wooden steps, sat a rusty baby stroller with three wheels. Nobody figured to steal that. The vestibule smelled like humidity-dampened varnish and stale urine, and rage and nausea welled up in Carver for a moment as he flashed back to the Belle Grande and Raffy Ortiz. Then he whacked aside a crumpled McDonald's bag with the tip of his cane, found Linda Redmond's apartment number on the mailboxes, and began climbing the stairs.

She'd heard the clatter of his cane on the wooden steps. When he reached the third floor she had her door open and was standing waiting for him.

Linda Redmond was in her late thirties. She'd been pretty once, possibly beautiful. Time had taken care of that, worked on her lean face and frame as it worked on ancient artifacts; it hadn't left a major mark, but in a myriad of minor ways it had exacted its toll. Her straight blond hair was thinned and lank, her blue eyes faded, her pale cheeks too sunken even for the gauntest of fashion models. Carver wondered if she'd lost most of her molars to disease or violence. She was wearing an untucked white blouse above raggedy cutoff jeans that reminded him of Dr. Pauly's. But her legs were thinner and better-looking than Pauly's, even though there were scars around her knobby knees, as if she'd done a lot of kneeling on rough surfaces.

Slightly unnerved by his appraising stare, she said, "Mr. Carver?"

He said he was. She smiled. It was a placid, attractive smile. All her teeth were there, but they were badly yellowed. A fine network of lines, like those seen on old folding money, spread around her eyes and the corners of her lips. Carver immediately liked her, felt almost as if he knew her, but he wasn't sure why.

She stepped aside to let him pass and then closed the door

behind him. She was out in front of him again, moving with loping strides that suggested surprising strength. She had on rubber thongs that flopped softly, loose at the heels but held tight on her feet by toes like talons. "Sit down, please. Get you some tea or coffee?"

Carver declined the offer of something to drink as he lowered himself into a round, wicker basket chair; he hadn't seen one of those in years. Now that he'd heard the word *coffee* he noticed the scent of it, pungent, as if it had been freshly brewed. He crossed his good leg over his bad and laid his cane sideways in his lap, looked around.

The apartment had bare hardwood floors and was cheaply and sparsely furnished. The windows had venetian blinds with missing slats and no curtains. There was a bookcase stuffed with paperbacks on one wall. Updike, Bellow, James Baldwin, a Flannery O'Connor short-story collection. One of the windows held a gray box fan that was ticking away and creating a cool breeze through the warm apartment. Stapled to the wall near the window was an unframed museum print of pastel water lilies on a foggy pond, an idealistic rendering of reality. Near the door to the kitchen a bicycle's front wheel leaned against the wall; the bike chained in the vestibule was Linda Redmond's.

She crossed thin arms and stood with her weight on one leg. One of her rubber thongs had slipped half off her foot. "You mentioned Beatrice Reeves on the phone."

"Birdie Reeves, actually. That's what she calls herself now."

Linda lowered her chin and fixed a frank and studious blue gaze on Carver. "What's your interest in Beatrice?"

"I'm not searching for her," Carver said truthfully.

"You said on the phone you were a private investigator. You working for the welfare authorities?"

"No. Birdie—or Beatrice—is only incidentally involved in what I'm working on."

"Then why should I talk to you, Mr. Carver? Why should you want to talk to me?"

"I know where Birdie is."

Linda's arms came uncrossed and dangled at her sides. Then she sat down on a low, green sofa and absently caressed one bony hand with the other. She knew she had little choice about talking to Carver, if she didn't want Birdie's whereabouts revealed. She leaned forward and said, "She all right?"

"Yeah, I suppose you could say she is. But there might be trouble at the place where she works."

"Trouble's in everybody's life. Think she'll come out of it okay?"

"Possibly unemployed. And the law might delve into her past and find out who she really is."

"She's never had any trouble with the police. That what she's got now?"

"No, not the kind you mean. You still a social worker?"

Linda laughed and tilted her head in a practiced way. Probably a sexy little move long ago. Sunlight glinting off golden locks. Now her lank blond hair swayed without the body or bounce so often mentioned in shampoo commercials. "I haven't had anything but temporary office work for six months. Laid off because of government funding cutbacks. Instead of me, the taxpayers get another guided missile."

"You must have handled a lot of cases, though. Got to know plenty of hard-luck kids. How come you seem to regard Birdie as special?"

Linda clasped her hands over one of her knees and rocked back. "There *is* something special about Beatrice, a kind of spirit I didn't often see in the sad cases I handled. Despite the fact that fate kept shitting on her, she kept fighting. She has intelligence and courage, but at the same time a kind of innocence and vulnerability it seems a sacrilege to have violated. Things were bad for her, and they kept getting worse. Finally she broke and ran, but I can't blame her."

Carver shifted his weight. Wicker creaked. "What about her family?"

"Her father, Clement Reeves, is dead—which strikes me as justice. He should burn in hell for two eternities for what he did to her. The mother's a sometime waitress, sometime prostitute out in Waverly. She's a fulltime boozer."

"How about the foster father who molested Birdie?"

"That bastard? He'd have been tried and convicted if she'd stayed around to testify against him. He and his wife moved out of town not long after Beatrice disappeared. They went to Cincinnati, I think. The prosecuting attorney, with his usual perseverance in such cases, was content to let him leave."

"Hard to get a guilty verdict without a victim," Carver said.

"People know that and take advantage of it with children. See to it that they're afraid to testify, or too confused to be believed." There was a rush of feeling behind the words. It was obvious that Linda loved underdogs and identified with victims.

Carver said, "Who'd want Birdie back here in Indianapolis?"

"The state. She's officially a ward of Indiana and a runaway child. Until she's eighteen."

"That's a few years away," Carver said. "What if she turned up at your door?"

"Well, what if she did?"

"Ever think about that happening? What you might do?"

"Yeah, I've thought. Look around this place. Look at me. Figure out how much I could help her." The tendons in Linda's lean neck worked like cables as she swallowed.

"And you'd be sheltering a fugitive," Carver pointed out.

"I know the law."

"Would you break the law for Birdie?"

"If I thought it'd help her. But it wouldn't. Don't you understand, Carver? The other side's got me. I'm one of the hard-luck cases I used to be able to help."

Carver knew she was right. Linda Redmond had enough problems, and little to offer Birdie other than moral support. And there was always the possibility that the authorities would find out she was illegally sheltering Birdie.

"Where *is* Beatrice, Mr. Carver?"

164

"I'll tell her you asked, give her your phone number."

"Fair enough."

Carver stood up out of the basket chair. *Creeeak!*

"Everything wrong that can happen to a child," Linda said, "happened to Beatrice. A man can't possibly understand what it means when a girl's father molests her over a period of years. Then, she was supposed to have been granted sanctuary, another molestation. That bastard poured gasoline over her legs and threatened to set her on fire if she didn't do exactly what he wanted."

"I didn't know that," Carver said.

Linda tucked her chin into her scrawny neck again and shook her head, as if shaking off a mood. "She's had a crappy life. She deserves a break or two."

Carver started toward the door, but Linda got up and stood next to him, her fingertips lightly touching his shoulder. "Why'd you come here to talk to me about Beatrice?" she asked. "I mean, really."

"I see the storm coming. It bothers me what I should do about her."

"She has layers and strengths not many people know about. What she's gone through's given her that, along with the nightmares."

He looked into Linda's weary, faded eyes. They had no depth, as if they were mere reflections of the crushing world about them.

"I want to do what'll turn out all right for her," he said. "She might be cut from her moorings again, partly because of me. Nowhere's going to be easy for her. At least in Indianapolis she knows people, you among them. Has some support. I don't know, should I let her be sent back here?"

"No, Mr. Carver. Anyplace but here."

She turned away from him.

Carver left her that way, standing and staring out her window at the drab buildings across the street. The woman who'd been traded for a guided missile.

25

He was leaning hard on the cane, trudging toward his cottage by the sea, his carry-on leather suitcase slung by its shoulder strap and jostling against his hip, when he stopped and stood in the heat, staring. Behind him the ocean pounded like a heartbeat.

Someone had been digging. Carver could see the edge of what appeared to be a mound of dirt alongside the cottage, toward the back and almost out of sight.

After depositing the suitcase on the porch, he walked around the side of the cottage to where he'd seen the dirt.

He stood quietly, looking down. There was a mound of loose, sandy earth heaped next to a freshly dug hole. Stuck in the mound was a new shovel, shiny through the dirt on its blade and with a price sticker still affixed to its wooden handle. The hole was rectangular, about three feet wide, six feet long, and six feet deep. Very neat and symmetrical. Carver knew immediately that it was a grave. Knew who'd dug it, and who was meant to lie in it. *If I make up my mind you're dead, then you're dead.*

Fear he tried to deny came to life in Carver's brain. He pushed the cold, quiet scream of it to a corner of his mind and went back around the cottage to the porch and inside.

He dropped the suitcase just inside the door, turned the air conditioner on high, and thumped with his cane into the kitchen. A clear drinking glass rested upside down on the sink. He rinsed it and filled it with cold tap water, then hurriedly drank it empty. He filled the glass again and drank deeply from it. As if he were trying to drown something within himself. Then he splashed the rest of the water down the drain, replaced the glass too hard, upside down again, with a loud *clink!*, and pushed himself away from his leaning position on the sink.

Carver limped into the main room and sat down next to the phone. He didn't think, didn't move, until the window unit had stirred enough stale air to make it reasonably cool in the cottage.

Then he phoned Dr. Lee Macklin and made an appointment to see her late that afternoon at Sunhaven.

Dr. Macklin saw Carver not in her office but in her home on Sunhaven's grounds. It was a flat-roofed extension of one of the garish Plexiglas cubes, out of sight from the highway. Built of cedar, it was rather plain from the outside but opened up inside into spacious and surprisingly luxurious quarters. There was a living room, furnished modern with a lot of polished steel and glass, carpeted in dove gray and containing matching charcoal gray sofa sections in a sunken area—what used to be called a conversation pit. A white concert-grand piano looked right at home near the powder blue drapes that lined the back windows. The lid was down on the piano, and there was a vase of fresh-cut flowers on it. White and yellow roses.

Beyond the living room was a slightly raised level bordered by a natural wood railing. Several doors led from that area to what Carver assumed was the kitchen, dining room, and bed-rooms. In one corner of the vast living room there was actually a small, round pond bordered by mosaic tile and groupings of lush potted tropical plants. Light streaming in through the wide front windows was transformed by the pond into a gently wavering luminescence that played over the room and was oddly restful. Oil paintings lined the walls, mostly psychedelic seascapes, with oversized suns rising or setting for color. The ocean was there in all its moods, from placid to stormy, but in no particular order. And looking like something dreamed by Van Gogh after a bout with a bottle.

Dr. Macklin stepped down ahead of Carver into the sunken area of the living room and motioned elegantly for him to have a seat on one of the sofa sections that were arranged more or less in a square around a low, glass-topped table with chromed legs. She was out of her work mode, apparently, wearing a graceful blue silk dress. Her long dark hair was combed back sleekly and then slung forward over her right shoulder, its feathery edges resting lightly just above her breast. She was slender and beautiful, with cover-girl features and complexion. Her dark eyes were made up skillfully to appear even larger than they were.

Yet at the same time there was a businesslike air about her, a crispness and economy of movement that suggested authority, and that somehow reminded Carver of Edwina. A woman of contrasts, obviously.

As she sat down opposite Carver, a man about sixty stepped through one of the doors beyond the wood railing and smiled at them both. He was short and had a stomach paunch, and wore baggy khaki slacks and a wrinkled but expensive yellow cotton shirt with flaps on the pockets and with epaulettes. A pair of gold-rimmed glasses protruded perilously far from one of the shirt's breast pockets, as if the exposed round lens were chancing a wondrous peek at the world.

He said, "I'm going to drive down to Vanessa's and take advantage of the marvelous light."

Carver realized he meant the soft early evening light favored by painters and photographers.

Dr. Macklin seemed compelled to make introductions. "This is my husband, Brian, Mr. Carver. Brian, Fred Carver."

"Nice meeting you, Mr. Carver, but I'm afraid I have to run. Someone's waiting for me to pick them up."

"Your work?" Carver asked, motioning with his cane to take in the numerous wild oil paintings on the walls.

" 'Fraid so," Brian Macklin said, strangely apologetic.

"Very nice," Carver said.

Brian nodded his thanks.

"Don't let Brian's modesty fool you," Dr. Macklin said. "His work's been displayed all over the South. He sells his paintings regularly and has his own show in Miami next month."

"Which I'd better get to work on now, if I expect to be prepared." Brian grinned almost impishly. He had a round, scrubbed-looking face with even features. An aged, gone-to-seed cherub. His gray hair was cut short on the sides, but it was longer and still thick on top, so it lay in a mass of loose curls. It was the hairstyle of a much younger man, say one about his wife's age.

"Remember to be home by nine, dear."

"Not to worry," Brian said. *"Ciao."* He went back through the door. Carver heard movement in another room, and what sounded like furniture being shoved around. Then he heard the front door close. Felt a stirring of air.

"My husband's studio's behind that wall," Dr. Macklin said, gesturing vaguely with a red-nailed hand. She sounded genuinely proud of whatever success Brian enjoyed. Florida was full of would-be artists, most of whom had never sold a canvas or had their paintings displayed publicly.

"He does excellent work," Carver said.

"Do you know art?"

"No."

"Neither do I." She crossed her magnificent legs; Carver heard the swish of nylon against nylon and felt a tightening in the core of him. He remembered Dr. Macklin with Nurse Rule at

169

the Medallion Motel, how they'd kissed. The unmistakable possession and passion. Nurse Rule! Jesus! "Why did you set up this appointment, Mr. Carver?"

"I think you know I'm looking into a matter concerning Sunhaven."

"Let's not be cute or evasive. You're looking into Sunhaven itself. Why?"

"Some of the residents feel there's something wrong here."

"I won't ask which residents. I will ask what they think is wrong."

"They're not sure. Which is why I was hired."

"By one of the residents?"

"Not exactly."

"Be exact, Mr. Carver."

"All right. Some people think there's something wrong with the deaths that have occurred here in the past several months."

"This is an old-folks' home, Mr. Carver. Old people live to get a little older, and then they die. Death's part of the package, I'm afraid. Unless you believe in earthly immortality. Old people imagine things. Sometimes they get unreasonable, even paranoid. Don't you have a grasp of that?"

"I'm not old, not paranoid."

"Ah, and what have you seen here that disturbs you?"

"Raffy Ortiz."

The beautiful, intelligent face was blank for a moment. "That man who comes here occasionally to see Dr. Pauly?"

"That one," Carver said.

"He's Dr. Pauly's patient."

"He needs another kind of doctor. He's a sicko who's dealt in drugs and death all his life."

"That might well be, but it's no concern of mine."

"Isn't it?"

She leaned back on the sofa and set one of her black high-heeled shoes bobbing rhythmically. It caused the muscle in her smooth calf to flex in the same tempo. Sexy. "I'm not interested

170

in the histories of my staff physician's patients," she said. "Dr. Pauly might have his problems, but he's quite competent and discreet. If he thought Mr. Ortiz's presence constituted some sort of danger or disturbance, he'd drop him as a patient or see him elsewhere, I'm sure."

"What kinds of problems does Dr. Pauly have?" Carver asked.

"The usual. But you figure it out. You seem to see problems everywhere—you might as well assign some to him."

"How about Nurse Rule? She have problems?"

No change in Dr. Macklin's mascaraed eyes. "None that I know of. No one at Sunhaven has personal problems of such magnitude that they affect their work. That's the pertinent point."

"Then you don't mind cooperating with me."

"But I do mind. You see, I know more about Sunhaven than you or anyone else possibly could. I'm sure I can't convince you there's nothing here to investigate, but I can do what's possible to see that you don't interfere with the care and well-being of our residents. That, Mr. Carver, is an important part of my job." She stood up and smoothed her skirt over her lean thighs, slipped a nyloned foot all the way back into the high-heeled shoe that had been dangling from her toes while she pumped her leg. "It's a job that requires a great deal of late afternoon and evening work. So please, if you don't mind . . ."

Carver stood up and, with the aid of his cane, climbed out of the carpeted conversation pit. A clear path to the door now.

He said, "I notice your husband's quite a bit older than you. It's nice to see a May-December marriage that's working."

"I'm more like July, Mr. Carver."

She strode ahead of him on those long, fine legs and opened the door. The room temperature rose a few degrees immediately with the influx of outside air. Heat inundating like water.

Carver said, "I came here on the off-chance you'd help me clear away whatever misconceptions there are about Sunhaven. Instead you've only added to my suspicions."

"I think you carry your suspicions with you like building

171

blocks, and place one atop the other whenever you want, no matter what you see or hear."

No common ground here, Carver decided, and pushed past the perfumed, feminine warmth of Dr. Macklin and out into the diffused evening light so coveted by her husband.

"Please leave Sunhaven alone, Mr. Carver," she said behind him. It was a plea for mercy, and it was a warning.

"I can't," he told her, and limped to his car through the soft sunlight that made everything seem unreal.

Or at Sunhaven, maybe it *was* unreal.

Instead of driving out of the parking lot, he circled around to the main building, parked, and went inside.

The lobby was deserted except for an old woman in a robe who was shuffling toward him on her way to a door at the far end of the building.

When she noticed Carver's cane, she flashed him a sunken smile of kinship and for a moment raised her own cane. It had a rubber tip and made no sound, but her leather-soled slippers scuffed loudly on the smooth floor.

"Here for supper?" she asked. "Chicken casserole."

"Another evening, thanks," Carver said.

So it was dinnertime at Sunhaven. He remembered Desoto describing the dining room as a mess hall.

"Got no bones in it," the woman assured him.

"Sorry, I'm not hungry."

"Suit yourself," the old woman said. She sounded somewhat insulted, as if he'd turned down an invitation for a meal she'd prepared. She shuffled back up to speed and moved away from him.

A white-uniformed attendant charged into the lobby and asked if he could help Carver. He was a tall, slender man with black wavy hair and the kind of pencil-thin mustache Errol Flynn used to wear. Deeply etched lines from the corners of his lips to the wings of his nose gave his age away. He was closing fast on the half-century mark.

Carver hadn't seen the man before and wasn't afraid of being recognized, so he asked if Birdie Reeves was around. The attendant told him Birdie had finished her day and left Sunhaven a little after five o'clock. Carver thanked him and went back outside to his car, aware the attendant was watching him.

He hoped no one else was watching.

When he got back to his cottage, he phoned Birdie at home.

She didn't seem pleased to hear from him.

"I need a favor," he told her.

"Well, if I can do it, Mr. Carver." *But not if it sounds too difficult.*

"I need copies of the files of residents who died at Sunhaven during the past year."

After a long pause she said, "I dunno about that." She sounded somehow unnatural. Distraught. Her voice dragging.

"It's very important. Will you get them for me?"

"It makes me scared, that kinda sneaking around."

"*Can* you do it? I mean, do you have access to the files?"

"No."

"Birdie?"

"What you're asking would be awful hard to do."

"But possible?"

"Well, barely so."

"Think about it, Birdie. If you can get file copies, mail them to me. Or phone me if you'd rather, and I'll meet you somewhere or drive over to your apartment to get them."

He made sure she had a pencil, then gave her his address slowly while she wrote it down. He hoped she was writing as he dictated. It would be hard to blame her if she wasn't paying attention to him and was reading one of her supermarket tabloids while he talked.

The truth was he felt a little guilty. He was using Birdie, imposing his will on her to get what he wanted, as had other men in her life. She had no real choice but to try to get the files. Not if she didn't want to run the risk of being sent back to Indiana. Ends justifying means, Carver told himself, but he wasn't so sure. Maybe ends and means were one and the same.

"I'll do my darndest," Birdie assured him, still sounding frightened. She hung up, leaving him feeling low enough to crawl under the phone.

He replaced the receiver and sat there in the quiet, darkening cottage. It was as if he could see through the wall to the open grave only twenty feet from him. His grave. His own personal eternal resting place. He noticed the broken pieces of his cane propped now in the corner where he'd set them after McGregor returned them to him at Edwina's. Carver didn't want Edwina to see them and had tossed them into the Olds. Driven here with them. The ends were sharp and would poke holes in a plastic trash bag; he'd put them out next week when the bulk refuse pickup was scheduled. The cane had been snapped in half simply by the force of abruptly checked momentum. Carver could imagine the strength and ability that must take. His own upper body was unusually powerful, but he possessed only a fraction of Raffy Ortiz's conditioning and quickness.

He stared at the broken pieces of cane until the cottage was almost completely dark. Then he picked up the phone again and pecked out Desoto's number. To get an address on Raffy Ortiz.

Carver wasn't superstitious or easily influenced by the power of suggestion. He also wasn't out of time. The grave on the other side of the wall wasn't yet occupied.

26

In the morning Carver drove down the heat-shimmering highway into Del Moray. On his left, the ocean rolled blue-green and too sluggish for whitecaps, as if it felt the burden of the heat and was lulled to lethargy. Gulls circled lazily above the waves, and in the gray haze of the horizon white sails seemed to hang by invisible threads attached to their points, like triangular pieces of a mobile. The fish-rot smell of the sea clung like a fog to the shore.

He went by Edwina's house, but she wasn't home. In the bedroom, he removed his old Colt .38 automatic from where it was taped behind the top dresser drawer. He didn't like carrying a gun, and he'd decided to leave the Colt here rather than go through the aggravation of dealing with airport security on his trip to New Orleans. A gun wouldn't have been much use to him there anyway. He tucked the Colt into his waistband beneath his shirt. From Edwina's, he drove to police headquarters.

McGregor was in his shoebox-sized office, seated behind his desk with a disgruntled look, tugging heavily at his long face. He might have been very tired. Ever the genial host, he glanced up and said, "I ain't got time for you today."

Carver went in anyway and sat down in the chair by the desk. He began tapping his cane gently on the floor, as if in time with silent music. Or with the varying hum of the air conditioner fighting the good fight against the heat.

"You ain't got ears?" McGregor said.

"Got ears. Got questions, too."

"Too bad. Chief's been on my ass, Carver."

"I'm sure you don't deserve it."

"You got that right. I'll take care of the little bastard when the time comes."

Carver knew McGregor well enough to feel sorry for the chief, who probably thought he was dealing with something human.

McGregor gnawed at his right index fingernail, detached part of it, and began working it between his eyeteeth. He liked to chew on minute objects. A nervous habit, Carver supposed.

McGregor stopped clicking his teeth and said, "Well, state your business so you can get the fuck outta here."

"I want to know if anything happened concerning Edwina while I was gone."

"A lotta gasoline and shoe leather was used, is all. Your lady gets around. I was hoping I'd be able to tell you she's seeing somebody else, but no such luck. What she does is shows property, works on real-estate deals. Some go-getter. Made herself well-off and she might even make herself goddamn rich. I can understand what a guy like you sees in her. I was you, I'd grab two handfuls of that and never let go."

"Raffy Ortiz was in New Orleans," Carver said.

McGregor spat out the sliver of fingernail and leaned back to his chair. "Was he now?"

"He came to my hotel room. We had a chat."

"Bet you did."

"He might be even more screwed up in the head than you are."

"Oh, doubtless he is. What'd he have to say?"

"Told me to drop the Sunhaven case. But I don't think he really believes I will."

"I don't think he wants you to," McGregor said. "I know how shitheads like him see shitheads like you. He's taking his time, is all, getting his kicks playing with you before he decides to do whatever it is he's leading up to. Foreplay, you might call it. To say Raffy Ortiz is a sadist is to say flies like sugar."

"That's more or less how Desoto reads it."

"Hey, I ain't surprised. Desoto's a bright guy. How he got mixed up with a downhill roller like you is beyond me."

"What *shouldn't* be beyond you is that something more than watered-down Geritol is happening at Sunhaven. Otherwise Raffy Ortiz wouldn't be commuting between here and New Orleans around the time of Kearny Williams's death and funeral."

"His second trip might have been just to see why you went there."

Carver had to admit that was possible. But in the room at the Belle Grande, Raffy didn't ask him what he was doing in New Orleans. Which suggested he already knew. He'd been watching Carver.

"Was Raffy doped up when he talked to you in New Orleans?" McGregor asked.

"I'd say so, but I couldn't be sure."

"I hear he's on drugs more and more these days. And he's losing control and falling toward bottoming out. Guy like that can be especially dangerous. As if he ain't dangerous enough already."

"If the law knows that much about him, why can't he be nailed for possession?"

"That'd be kinda like nailing a great white shark for swimming in the wrong end of the pool. The guy's not your ordinary dopehead. He's got some heavy-duty connections, people who turn white and shit in their pants if he looks hard at them. Believe me, Raffy Ortiz wouldn't take some short fall for carrying a little coke. He'd bounce right back onto the street meaner than ever."

"That his drug of choice? Cocaine?"

"I couldn't guess. Right now, I'd say you're his drug of choice, what's giving him his ongoing high. Sorta the way a cat gets a rush outta toying with a mouse."

"You know him so well," Carver said in disgust, "but you can't get it through your dense bureaucratic head he's into something out at Sunhaven."

"Don't get your blood boiling," McGregor said. "Happens I agree with you. That's why I lowered myself to entering into a kind of agreement with you. That's why I got one of my men trailing around after Edwina Talbot like she was a bitch in heat and he was a hound with a hard-on." He rested both huge palms flat on his desk, as if he were getting ready to compress the poor piece of furniture against the floor. "Edwina's still breathing and bouncing around unbruised, Carver. That was my end of the deal. Now, what've you learned about Sunhaven?"

"What I've been trying to get across to you. I'm surer than ever something's wrong when residents are dying out there. I talked to Dr. Macklin yesterday."

"I talked to her, too. While you were in New Orleans. Used the subject of you as an excuse. She doesn't like you coming around. Says everything's hunky-dory at Sunhaven and you oughta go back to peeking through motel keyholes."

"She said that? About motel keyholes?"

"Not exactly," McGregor admitted, raising a pale eyebrow. "I'm paraphrasing. But the intent was there."

"She used the same attitude on me. You meet her husband?"

"Nope, I saw her when she was alone in her office. Great legs for a doctor, hey?"

"Know anything about Brian Macklin?"

"The hubby?"

"Yeah. He's a painter."

"Oh? Houses or sunsets?"

"Sunsets. He's supposed to be good. Actually sold some canvases. He's getting ready to have a one-man show in Miami." Miami again, Carver thought. But he didn't mention to Mc-

178

Gregor the frequency of the city's name popping up. It could merely be coincidence. Miami was the large cosmopolitan area where somebody like Brian Macklin might be most likely to have his work shown.

"I'll see what I can find out about hubby Brian," McGregor said. "Guy must be crazy, out painting pictures instead of running up the miles on that wife of his. Being a doctor, I bet she knows some moves. Meantime, you better do what you can to stay away from Raffy Ortiz."

Carver knew McGregor wasn't expressing concern for him. He didn't want Carver's corpse to turn up somewhere and prompt a lot of questions he might have to lie about or play dumb on. Danger either way.

"I'll try to avoid him," Carver said. "But if I do see him, I'll mention you know what I know."

He was a little surprised, and unsettled, when McGregor looked genuinely frightened.

He wondered what McGregor would think if he knew Carver's next stop was Raffy Ortiz's condominium.

27

The white Cadillac was parked in a slot in the ground-level garage beneath the building. Painted in luminescent pink on the raw concrete wall behind it was "6-D," apparently Raffy's condo unit number.

The harsh glass-and-stone structure was called Executive Tower and was on the ocean side of Ponce de Leon Drive. It didn't have a doorman but it featured a wide private beach. There were Keep Out and No Trespassing signs in every direction. Very exclusive. An expensive place to hang your hat and proud of it.

Carver limped to a low wooden fence and stood beneath a blue-and-yellow umbrella to look out at the stretch of sand, some colorful striped cabanas, and the surf reaching gentle white fingers up the beach. About a dozen people lounged on the beach, some on towels, some in chairs, a few sitting where the sand was damp and dark and letting the waves lick at their bare feet. There were no children; Carver supposed Executive Tower was one of those condo developments whose bylaws prohibited residents with young offspring. Kept the place neat and quiet for solid citizens like Raffy Ortiz.

Carver didn't see Raffy's formidable form among the bodies on the beach, and at the moment there was no one bobbing in the swells or swimming out beyond the surf.

Across the street from Executive Tower was a strip retail center that contained the usual assortment of beachside shops and tourist traps. At the end of the low, L-shaped building's short leg was an ice cream parlor called Frosty Frieda's. Carver crossed the street, went inside, and sat at a table by the window.

It was appropriately cool in Frosty Frieda's. The tables were round and cutesy, with bentwood legs. A teen-age waitress with chocolate stains down the blouse of her yellow uniform wandered over and introduced herself as if they were going out on a date.

Carver looked at the menu and ordered something called a Chunky Chill. It sounded as if it would take a long time to consume, and he could have a cup of coffee afterward and sit at the table and watch Executive Tower without arousing suspicion as other customers came and went.

The Chunky Chill turned out to be a concoction of frozen custard, chocolate syrup, whipped cream, and peanuts. It was topped with a maraschino cherry. Carver didn't like maraschino cherries; if cherries died and were embalmed, they would come out maraschino. He plucked the garish red glob from the whipped cream with his thumb and forefinger and deposited it in the ashtray. There it would shrivel and stick like chewed gum and have to be chipped away by whoever cleaned the ashtrays. Teach Frieda to sell the nasty things here.

The rest of the Chunky Chill was delicious, and probably less than thirty thousand calories. He had to force himself to spoon it into his mouth slowly while he watched the Executive Tower garage exit.

He was on his second foam cup of coffee when Raffy's white Caddie inched its nose out of the shadowed exit like a cautious shark, saw a break in the traffic, and glided out into a smooth left turn and drove away. Raffy was behind the steering wheel and alone in the car. His dark hair was pomaded and slicked back neatly, and he had on a cream-colored sport coat or suitcoat with a blue shirt open at the collar. He was also wearing a contented expression on his broad, tanned face, as if his life were free of worry. And maybe it was at that. Maybe he was the lion in the jungle, just as he thought.

Hoping Raffy wasn't merely driving to the corner for a six-pack of beer, Carver paid for his coffee, left the iciness of Frosty Frieda's for the oven outside, and crossed the street to Executive Tower.

He limped through a large, glitzy lobby and rode an elevator to the sixth floor. The hall carpeting was thick and spongy and caused his cane to sink deep and drag, so he had to walk more slowly than he wanted to the fancy white door marked "6-D" an inch below its round glass peephole.

He knocked three times, to be on the safe side in case Raffy had left a friend behind in the condo. When there was no answer he tried the brass doorknob and wasn't surprised to find it locked. Carver had picked locks before, but it was a damned sight harder than it seemed in movies and detective novels, so he glanced around to make sure there was no one else in the hall and then rocked back on his cane and stiff leg and used his good leg to kick the door.

The lock held but the doorjamb gave, and without a great deal of noise. The door swung open. There was an ugly dark smudge from the sole of Carver's moccasin on its white surface.

Noting with satisfaction that the damage wouldn't be notice-able at a glance from the hall, he went in and closed the door behind him.

He saw that there were two locks on it beside the cheap mechanism in the knob. One was a thick chain lock that hadn't been engaged. The other was a Schlage dead bolt, half of which still clung by its screws above the section of wood frame that had been split away and now lay on the floor with shiny brass hardware attached.

Raffy would be pissed off mightily when he saw the damage.

Know who'd been here. Carver smiled and went on about his business. The best defense was a good you-know-what.

The condo was furnished even more garishly than Desoto's. Deep red-orange carpet. Dramatic furniture with lots of glass and metal and pale green leather. On the wall over the marble mantel there was actually a large framed painting of a clown on black velvet. Didn't look like a Renoir. The scent of recently fried onion permeated the place; Raffy must have eaten a snack or an early lunch.

Carver made his way across the living room to the hall. He almost gagged. Arranged on the hall walls was a series of graphic color photographs apparently taken at a slaughterhouse. Close-ups of the panic in the eyes of the doomed cattle, huge carcasses dangling from steel hooks while workers in bloodstained aprons dispassionately hacked away with long knives. The last shot was a tight one of a cow's head, with most of the flesh stripped away and the eye sockets empty but for clotted blood. Raffy's idea of humor, maybe. Or, worse still, something he enjoyed without humor. Carver thought he wouldn't eat steak for a while.

The centerpiece of the bedroom was a large round water bed with a mirrored canopy. On the walls were framed prints of virginal-looking blond women in flowing white dresses, some of them romping through idyllic fields of wild flowers.

Carver rooted through dresser drawers and found only the expected assortment of socks, underwear, and shirts. Quality material. Expensive labels.

There were more good labels on the coats and slacks in the closet. On the closet shelf was a stack of bondage magazines with photos of women in various stages of agony or ecstasy while constricted by ropes or leather bindings. Some of them looked underage. Next to the magazines were some Polaroid photographs of a slender blond woman, nude except for high heels and held fast to a chair with adhesive tape and suffering various indignities at the hands of a man. Only the man's arms and hands were visible in the photos. He had his sleeves rolled up a few turns and was wearing a wristwatch with an expansion band. The woman had a rubber ball stuck halfway in her mouth and held by tape, and her eyes had a dazed quality as if she might be on drugs.

The condo's second bedroom was Raffy's office. It had the same red carpeting and rough white plaster walls. Also a white leather couch and chair, and a massive cherrywood desk with curved legs. The top of the desk was bare except for a ceramic lamp in the shape of a nude woman with her hands joined above her head, as if she were diving straight up. On a table sat a black push-button phone and a small gray portable electric type-writer. The walls were lined with wooden bookshelves, but instead of books contained a complex stereo system, a portable TV with a video recorder, and stacks of cassettes. Carver looked over the cassettes. Raffy's taste ran to X-rated movies and Arnold Schwarzenegger. Propped at one end of a shelf was even a signed eight-by-ten publicity photo of Schwarzenegger stripped to the waist and wielding a machine gun. He was wearing a stoic expression and perspiring heavily after a hard day on the set.

Carver returned to the desk and searched through the drawers one by one, not bothering to put things back the way he found them. The two bottom drawers were stuffed with martial arts magazines, and in the back of one drawer was a jumble of Oriental weaponry: the obligatory chain with a wooden handle at each end, some star-shaped steel throwing disks for death from a distance, a lead-weighted leather sap that resembled an ordinary blackjack.

The upper drawers were reserved for papers. Raffy usually waited until he'd received a warning notice before paying his electric bill, but he was too smart to leave anything more incriminating than that lying around. There was a small Rolodex but it contained only the phone numbers of local merchants, so if there was an address book that meant something it probably stayed with Raffy.

In the desk's wide, shallow top drawer was a typed note from Raffy to Raffy, reminding him to pick up cleaning on Wednesday. There were similar typed reminders crumpled and discarded in the wastebasket. Raffy was one of those organized and orderly people who were in the habit of typing themselves messages. A man of compulsions.

Carver felt toward the back of one of the drawers where he'd seen a stack of small boxes. As he'd hoped: spare typewriter ribbon.

The typewriter was the kind that used one-time ribbon on a cartridge. Carver removed the cartridge and slipped in a fresh one. He typed some dots and random letters so the exposed part of the ribbon was used, slipped the old cartridge into his pocket, and was about to leave the room when he heard a soft sound in the front of the apartment.

Fear leaped to his throat and formed a lump there.

Moving silently with the cane, he crept to the office door and peered down the hall into the living room. Blood beat like a drum in his ears.

He saw no one, but again he heard the sound. A soft scuffing noise with something tentative about it. There was no denying what it was—someone walking around in the living room.

Carver was about to turn and look for a place to hide, when a tall blond woman in nothing but a red bikini strutted into view, stood with her hands on her hips near the broken door to the hall, and said in a loud voice, "Jesus H. Christ!" She moved her head from side to side to stare around her, as if in disbelief that someone had entered the condo in such a blatant manner.

Carver stayed perfectly still and she didn't seem to notice him. But if she moved farther into the apartment there was no way he could avoid being seen by her.

He saw fear cross her beauty-pageant features as she realized whoever had broken in might still be there.

She did a quick deep-knee bend and snatched up a red beach towel from the floor where she'd dropped it. Then she wrapped the towel tightly around herself, as if for the magical protection of terrycloth, and backed out into the hall.

Carver suddenly realized who she was: the blond woman in the Polaroid photos.

She must have been down on the beach.

Now she was probably bustling toward the nearest phone to call the police. Or, more likely, to call Raffy.

Past time for Carver to leave.

He made his way quickly through the living room, poked his head out to make sure the hall was empty, and limped with exaggerated casualness to the elevators. Just a visitor, or maybe one of the new tenants. He longed to toss his cane aside and run. Bolt to safety like a twenty-year-old. He had to remind himself that was impossible.

It seemed an hour before an elevator reached the sixth floor. It start-and-stop rumbled in its shaft as it sought floor level, then was silent. Carver swallowed hard and heard his throat crack.

When the doors hissed open he half expected to see the blond woman in the bikini, perhaps with a security guard at her side.

But she hadn't had that much time to organize her thoughts and efforts. The elevator was empty.

Carver rode the plush little cubicle down to the lobby. Dropping from danger, or into it.

No one seemed to pay much attention to him as he limped outside onto the sun-washed sidewalk.

28

Beneath the bright glare of the lamp he'd set up, Carver sat at the breakfast counter in his cottage, carefully unwinding and studying the ribbon from the cartridge he'd removed from Raffy Ortiz's typewriter. He played the ribbon gingerly through his smudged fingers and tried to imagine spaces between words so he could decipher the steady stream of typing. It was more difficult than he'd imagined to make sense of the impressions on the flimsy ribbon.

After a while it became grinding work that made Carver's back ache and his vision swim. Raffy used his typewriter to send routine household correspondence and countless of his terse reminders to himself. There were dozens of addresses with zip codes. Also a few phone numbers, but a check of Carver's Del Moray cross-directory showed them to be numbers of merchants in the vicinity of Executive Tower.

His own phone rang, causing his body to jerk and his mind to bob up from the depths of concentration. He pinched a slight kink in the ribbon to indicate where he left off, then grabbed his cane and crossed the cottage to snatch up the phone on the

187

fifth ring. He said hello and stared through the wide front window at the glimmering Atlantic and at distant sails leaning against the wall of a stiff easterly breeze. A few high, white clouds were racing each other out to sea.

"McGregor here, Carver," came the assertive voice over the line. "Thought you oughta know we got a call about a break-in over in Executive Tower on Ponce de Leon."

"That the tall, ritzy condo looks like an office building?"

"Looks like all the other beachside condos in Florida," McGregor said.

"Right across the street from a shopping center?"

"Now you got it. Somebody was in there prowling around Raffy Ortiz's unit."

"No kidding?"

"Uh-hm. His girlfriend phoned us. Blond cunt name of Melanie Star. Real name, too, though she said it used to have two *r*'s in it."

"So Raffy's place was burglarized. Couldn't happen to a more deserving victim."

"When I heard the squeal," McGregor said, "I got myself over there like a good public servant while the uniforms were still making the prelim and taking information. Raffy was there, all angry and ugly with his muscles bunched up and fire in his eye."

"Well, can't blame him. Somebody break in and steal your whips and chains, you'd feel the same way."

"Oh, nothing was taken. I could tell that what Raffy was actually sore about was two things. First, that somebody'd been nervy—and stupid—enough to B and E his condo. Second, that the Star bitch was dumb enough to phone the police."

"He's got an aversion to the law, that guy."

"Like so many. Hey, Carver, what were you doing late this morning, say about eleven or quarter after?"

"Vacuuming dust balls behind my sofa. You sure nothing was taken from Raffy's?"

"I'm sure 'cause he's sure. He looked around very, very carefully. Whoever broke in there didn't try to disguise the fact. Smashed the shit outta the door. Then left things in mild but unmistakable disarray, you might say. I mean, didn't really tear up the place, but left it just messy enough so Raffy'd know somebody'd been there rooting around. Almost like the guy that busted in didn't mind if Raffy got pissed off. Mighta even wanted it. Got some kinda death wish, I guess, not to leave poison like Raffy alone. Our housebreaker oughta know better, huh? Always a chance the victim'll come up with a name and inflict great bodily harm on whoever it was broke in the place. Wouldn't be surprised what Raffy'd do. For that matter, I wouldn't wanna be in that Melanie Star's shoes."

"I doubt they'd fit," Carver said. He noticed, far out at sea, a huge oil tanker. It was fixed on the horizon like a motionless gray island, but he knew it was making its way south along the coast. It was like a different world passing by, without the problems of this one. He wondered if the residents at Sunhaven could see it.

"Real reason I phoned," McGregor said, "was to tell you I saw a few people, made a few phone calls about Brian Macklin. He's a painter, all right. Supposed to be real talented and gets his stuff displayed all over the state. He's sixty-four and got an arrest record from back in the sixties and seventies when he was mixed up in the peace movement."

"Anything interesting on the record?"

"Yes and no. Fucking commie sympathizer's what he was. Maybe still is. Usual garbage on his sheet: resisting arrest, destruction of government property, that kinda thing."

"What sort of government property?"

"Hah! Everything from a fence around a missile site to his tax form. He was one of them longhairs that stirred up so much shit back then. Now they're artists and lawyers and whatever. Got secret drug habits and live in expensive condos with their wives, who used to wear love beads and fuck everything had pants with a zipper in front. Sophisticated, they call themselves these days. Junkies is what I call 'em."

"I heard he had a drug problem."

"Word I get is he does, but not a big one. Mostly pot. A little crystal meth. What the hell you expect, Carver, guy's an arteest. Makes me wonder, too, what a used-up ex-hippie like that's doing with a young goodie like the Macklin cunt."

"You mean Dr. Lee Macklin."

"Yeah. Sure as hell he ain't hitting it like he should. Old pothead probably can't even get his dong up anymore. Way I see it, theirs is a marriage for appearances only and hubby's actually a closet fruit wants a sharp wife to show off to the world and help him financially with his career. I mean, hey, she's a doctor; she's busy looking down throats and up assholes and ain't interested in sex anyway, so it works out nice for both of them."

"Sound reasoning," Carver said. He rolled his eyes. "Give me a call if you find out anything else about Brian."

"Sure. And *you* call *me* if you find out anything about anything. But I guess you ain't interested if we catch the guy broke into Raffy's condo."

"Only if it's Brian," Carver said, and hung up.

He plucked a Budweiser from the refrigerator and sat down again at the counter, where the ribbon from Raffy Ortiz's typewriter was unfurled and draped onto the floor. He took up where he'd left off.

Near the end—or what to Raffy would have been the beginning—of the ribbon, his attention was heightened by a series of numerals, one of which had a slash typed through it: 50З4543-9876.

It didn't take Carver long to figure out he was looking at a phone number preceded by an area code. The "3" key had been mistakenly struck instead of the "4" and then crossed out. The area code was 504.

Carver phoned the long-distance operator and was told the

504 area code included the city of New Orleans. He depressed the cradle button, then direct-dialed the area code and phone number.

The phone at the other end of the connection in New Orleans rang six times.

When it was answered there was music in the background, a trumpet solo. And voices. A shout, a woman's laughter.

Then a vaguely familiar male voice said, "Melba's Place in the Quarter."

Carver said, "Oops, wrong number," and hung up.

But his harsh features wore a predator's smile. It hadn't been a wrong number at all.

It couldn't have been more right.

There was a subtle change of light in the cottage, the faintest of sounds from the front porch.

Carver grabbed his cane, went as quietly as possible to his dresser, and removed the Colt .38 from where he'd placed it beneath his socks in the top drawer. He worked the action and there was a solid metallic double click as a round was fed from the clip into the chamber, then he moved toward the front of the cottage.

For an instant he caught a glimpse of someone peering through a window, then the image was gone.

Footsteps on the porch.

The doorknob rotated.

The door opened.

Edwina.

"I've been trying to catch you here," she said. She noticed the gun but didn't change expression. Always so cool.

"You and maybe somebody else," Carver said.

"You're in a shitty line of work," she told him. She'd been working her own job; she was wearing a tailored gray business suit with a white blouse and oversized black bow tie. The skirt was short and slit up one side, showing off the fullness of her calves and a neat turn of nyloned ankle. In her right hand was

191

her blue leather attaché case. No doubt stuffed with hot contracts.

Carver said, "Maybe we both work too hard."

Edwina smiled. "Not tonight, though, okay? We go have a quiet dinner someplace, then we go home—to my place."

"I'm staying here because I don't want to be seen at your place," Carver explained. It sounded lame. He suddenly felt as if he'd been caught by a grown-up while playing a child's game. It seemed absurd and adolescent. He was scared of a bully and didn't want his girlfriend hurt if there was a showdown. Very dramatic.

But he knew that Raffy Ortiz and whoever else was involved in the Sunhaven deaths were more than mere bullies playing schoolyard games. Something other than a bloody nose was at stake.

"A motel, then," Edwina suggested.

No child's game there. Carver looked at Edwina and she looked back with those direct gray eyes that saw to the pit of his soul. They were two people closer to each other than either of them might have preferred. She knew what he was thinking. He could see the material of her white blouse, taut between her breasts, quake faintly with her breathing.

She said, "Trying to make up your mind?"

He imagined her breasts, her thighs, the soft and secret places of her body. Her flesh would be damp from the heat and humidity, smooth and yielding and the slightest bit sticky beneath his fingertips. She would taste like butterscotch and salt. She would be eager.

She *was* eager.

It was contagious.

He put the gun back in the drawer and went with her.

29

Carver slowed the Olds on the coast highway and turned onto the secondary road leading to his cottage. The car's canvas top was up, but the morning sun beating through the windshield heated up the interior even though all the windows were cranked down. The warm, whirling air made the Olds a mobile blast furnace.

They'd taken separate cars to the restaurant, but only Edwina's Mercedes to the Howard Johnson's motel where they'd spent the night. She'd driven him to pick up his car only half an hour ago, then gone on to her place.

Carver shook his mind from the motion and warmth of last night and watched alertly as he approached the cottage.

The small, flat-roofed structure was still there; Raffy hadn't burned it down or bulldozed it into the sea. It occurred to Carver that Raffy might not be sure who'd broken into his condo. No shortage of enemies for a guy like that.

But a scarcity of enemies with enough nerve to walk right into the beast's lair and deliberately leave tracks.

Did Ortiz recognize that kind of nerve in him? Is that what

there was about Carver that amused him and provided entertainment? Prey that might make for sport?

It was an unsettling thought.

Though everything about the cottage looked reassuringly normal, Carver decided to play it cautious. He parked the Olds in its usual spot, but instead of walking up on the porch, he used his cane to move quickly in a hobbling gait toward the back of the cottage. The surf breaking on the beach seemed to be telling him *Hush! Hush!* No noise, or whatever he feared most might happen.

He took a quick look through a side window and saw no sign that anyone had been inside. A mosquito the size of a Cessna buzzed around his face and made him blink. He took a swipe at it and didn't hit it, but the rush of air from his open hand drove it away. Careful not to stumble into the grave Raffy had prepared, he continued to the back and peered through another window.

No one. Nothing suspicious. He knew every inch of the cottage had been covered by his surveillance; unless Raffy had known which window Carver was going to look in next and figured out where to hide, the cottage was unoccupied. Raffy wasn't psychic, even if he was a three-nutter.

Carver went in through the back door and locked it behind him. Still cautious, he limped through the cottage and was satisfied that everything was in place before he relaxed and switched on the air conditioner.

He decided to let some fresh air in the place while waiting for the window unit to take over. The breeze from the blower was stirring icily around his ankles, but he knew it would take a while before it spread and built high and filled hot space.

When he opened the front door he saw the penciled note that had been slipped halfway under it and picked it up off the threshold. It was written on paper ripped from a spiral notebook:

Mr. Carver,
I came by to see you about the things we talked

about but you weren't here. Meet me at my place
soon as you can. Please.

Birdie

Carver crumpled the sheet of lined paper with the raggedly
torn edge, slammed the door, and said, "Shit!"

He wasn't sure if Birdie had left the note last night or this
morning. What if somebody else had come here *after* her visit
and seen the note? Whoever the person might be, he or she
might want answers from Birdie, and God knew what ways
might be used to persuade the young runaway to talk. Images
flashed on the screen of Carver's mind. He shivered and forced
the screen to go blank. Some things you didn't want to imagine,
suspecting that reality might be worse.

He called Sunhaven and was told Birdie wasn't there—she'd
phoned in sick. Then he called her apartment and got no answer.

As he dropped the receiver into its cradle he noticed the back
of his hand was glistening with perspiration. It was still hot in
the cottage, making it difficult to breathe. Summer, with its
humid Florida air that it was almost possible to drown in.

He made sure the cottage was locked. The Olds was waiting
for him, ticking like a bomb in the heat.

He got in and drove.

The old apartment building on West Palm Drive sat glaring in
the sun. Its curlicued wrought iron showed it needed paint badly
in the cruel slanted light. Its cracked tile and patched stucco
were lent beauty by the red-blossomed bougainvillea and rose
vines writhing up the walls. Nature was trying to reclaim the
ruin before developers and yuppies moved in. Nature didn't
have much chance.

Carver had parked around the corner on Newport and walked
back. Noting with satisfaction that the inquisitive and combative
Mrs. Horton didn't seem to be around, he limped with care
over the uneven walk, through the gate and beneath the iron-

arch trellis overgrown with roses. He pushed the button next to Birdie's door. He heard the faint, faltering sputter from inside the apartment, as if the buzzer were thirsty for more electricity. The sun pressed hot against his back and shoulders like the confining embrace of an unwelcome lover.

Holding his breath, he thumbed the push button several times in succession, as if he were grinding a tiny insect into a smear. Time and silence were accumulating. So was concern. He didn't want to force his way in, or rouse Mrs. Horton and talk her into using her passkey. Didn't want to look at what might be inside.

But there was a metallic snick on the other side of the shiny new dead-bolt lock and the door opened on a chain. A wary blue eye appeared in the crack between door and frame. The eye brightened and sprang wide.

"Mr. Carver!" Birdie breathed his name with relief.

The door closed, the chain clattered, and she swept the door open and motioned for him to come in, while her gaze darted about behind him.

When he was all the way inside she closed the door and dramatically reattached the chain lock. Checked the dead bolt. The child in her was enjoying what she perceived as an adventure, but at the same time real fear glinted like underwater diamonds in her eyes.

The apartment was still a mess; he could see into the bedroom, where clothes and a towel were heaped on the floor. A show-biz magazine that promised to reveal how Elvis Presley's spirit possessed Sean Penn was spread out on the sofa. It was hot in the apartment. Carver couldn't imagine what Presley would want with Penn.

On the carpet near the sofa was a dog-eared paperback romance novel with a cover illustration of a knight leaning low from a charging horse to scoop up a woman whose breasts threatened to spill out of her bodice. Carver couldn't be sure if the woman wanted to be scooped up by the knight or was trying to flee from him, but he thought the artist had done a dandy job.

Birdie lifted a corner of the painted crate that was her coffee table and withdrew a red spiral notebook. There were ink doodles all over the cover, mostly crude flowers and what looked like English castles. The TV was tuned without sound to a soap opera. A handsome guy with an engineered hairdo was moving his lips in silent earnestness while another with a black patch over his eye was listening and frowning. Two beautiful women observed them gravely. The guy doing the talking had on a sharp dark sport coat. The listener was wearing a shirt with a turned-up collar, unbuttoned so a gold chain was visible. A macho guy, all right. Everybody had perfect teeth and wore new-looking clothes. It was as if department-store mannequins had sprung to life and developed big problems.

Birdie tore the first page out of the notebook and handed it to Carver. It was the same kind of lined paper that had been tucked under the front door of his cottage. There were some names scrawled on it in the same pale shade of pencil.

"When did you come by my place to give me this?" Carver asked.

Her eyes got shallow and guilty, as if he might accuse her of having done something naughty and of course he'd be right. "This morning, about eight o'clock." A little girl's voice.

"What about your job?"

"It's okay, I phoned Sunhaven and said I had a dentist appointment."

"I don't want to scare you, Birdie, but you oughta be more careful."

"About the dentist story?"

"The note. Somebody looking for me might have seen it and figured you were involved. They might have taken it without me ever finding it and be here now instead of me."

Her mouth fell open for a moment and then she clamped it shut. Just a glimpse of white teeth and pink gums. "Yeow! I never thought about that! It's okay, though, isn't it? I mean, like you got the note and nobody else saw it, did they? You suppose?"

"I think it's all right," Carver said. But he couldn't be sure. No way to be sure. He looked down at the notepaper, not carefully yet, not reading it.

"I couldn't get actual filed information, Mr. Carver. I only got you the names. Otherwise I think I mighta got caught where I shouldn't of been. I mean, it woulda been my butt for sure."

"Caught by Nurse Rule?"

"Yeah. She can come right outta the walls sometimes. Anyway, those are the names of all the Sunhaven residents that died the past year."

Carver looked at the list. Nine names. Less than he'd expected. Two of them were female. Sam Cusanelli's name was there. So was Kearny Williams's. "Why so many more men than women?" he asked.

"It's just that way, I guess. They say women live longer. Must be some truth in it."

"This about an average number of deaths for a nursing home the size of Sunhaven?"

"Retirement home, they like to call it."

"Okay, we'll call it that, too."

Birdie's frail shoulders rose and fell in an exaggerated shrug. She looked about twelve years old. "I dunno, tell you the truth. I expect it depends on the kinda home it is. Some of the old folks out at Sunhaven are sick, and some of them are just old and like can't make it on the outside. A home where the people are all sick'd have more deaths every year, don't you think?"

Carver said he thought so.

"I really don't wanna get into any trouble over this," Birdie said. "I mean, with my job and all."

"Nobody'll learn from me where I got this information," Carver said, waving the notepaper. "Should we take a blood oath of secrecy?"

She looked too pale even to contain any blood. She smiled. That made Carver feel good. "Guess not."

"Birdie, you scared?"

"Yeah, I am."

"Of losing your job, or of something else?"

"I'm not sure. I wonder what might be going on out there. It's creepy to think people you know might be mixed up in . . . whatever. I mean, it's like folks live in two worlds. There's one we see, and another one nobody talks about."

Like the one in Indianapolis.

Carver said, "Birdie, I saw Linda Redmond. She sends her love and wants you to call her sometime."

Birdie winced; she'd been kicked hard in the psyche. "You went to Indianapolis? You saw Linda? You talked to her?"

"Want her phone number?"

Birdie swallowed. Carver actually heard her Adam's apple work. "Tell you, Mr. Carver, I got Linda's number. Had it since I left that place. But I never called her."

"Why not?"

"Well, let's just say she's done enough for me. More'n she had to. I was trouble for her and I don't wanna be again."

"She doesn't see you as trouble. Though she says you shouldn't go back to Indianapolis, and she's probably right. But if you ask me, it wouldn't hurt to call her and talk."

Birdie's lower lip did a tremulous dance. She dug her front teeth into it and said nothing. She stood that way for a while. Wasn't going to talk. Not about back home in Indiana. Finally the teeth loosened their pressure and the lip stayed steady. She had hold of her emotions.

Carver said, "As long as you got these names without being seen, I think you'll be safe enough out at Sunhaven. You might attract more suspicion if you don't go in this afternoon."

"Oh, I'm gonna go to work. No other reason, I need the money bad. I'll say my mouth's still sore from the dentist."

"That'd be my advice," Carver told her. He leaned nearer with the cane, reached out with his free hand and patted her arm. "Thanks, Birdie. You've been a big help. I really appreciate it."

She couldn't meet his eyes; she turned her face away sharply, as if he'd struck her. Not many adults had thanked her or given her words of approval. Not when it counted. She had a hunger for it and she wouldn't—and probably couldn't—admit it, except maybe only to herself momentarily in the dim, dawn hang-point between sleep and wakefulness.

At that moment, though he'd never met the man and never would, Carver hated Clement Reeves.

30

Carver stopped at Sanderson's Drugstore on Ocean Drive, which had old-fashioned enclosed phone booths in the back where he knew he could talk confidentially and without interruption. The rows of stationery supplies, motor oil, hardware, and everything else other than drugs were laid out neat and orderly and cool. He limped toward the back of the drugstore, past a middle-aged woman with frizzy red hair who was trying to decide what kind of home perm to buy. There was a tiny prescription counter just before you got to the phones, but there was no pharmacist in sight.

Of the four booths along the back wall, one was occupied by a young black girl grinning and chomping gum as she gabbed. She gave Carver a look as if he'd interfered with her constitutional right to privacy and yanked the booth's accordian door shut so he couldn't overhear. He squeezed into the booth at the other end, propped his cane in the corner, and called Desoto.

"So where we at, *amigo*?" Desoto asked. There was tango music in the background. In Desoto's soul.

"We got a link." Carver told him about finding the phone

201

number of Melba's Place impressed on ribbon from Raffy Ortiz's typewriter.

"You didn't mention how you got that ribbon," Desoto said.

"That's right, I didn't. Thing is, Ortiz is mixed up with Kearny Williams's family, mixed up with Sunhaven, and if there's anything wrong with how Kearny died he's mixed up with that, too."

Desoto said, "Yeah, and mixed up with Dr. Pauly."

Carver was puzzled. "Sure. He sees him every once in a while—supposed to be a patient."

"I mean before that, a few years ago in Miami." Carver caught the hard edge in Desoto's voice and knew he had something. Desoto said, "Word I got is Pauly was the one who supplied Raffy and some of his friends with designer drugs. Didn't have much choice, because he's an addict himself and Raffy knew it."

Carver said, "Lots of doctors do drugs."

"Um-hm. Too true, *amigo*. But Ortiz somehow found out Pauly was hooked, or maybe he even got something else on him. He's an industrious guy for a killing machine, that Raffy. And the people he ran with down there, ones who use drugs, they're always on the watch for a doctor they can bend. Nobody can supply like a medical man."

"Or medical woman," Carver said.

"A thought. Point is, he got Pauly to supply him with drugs to sell, and once that started Pauly was on the pin forever. Understand, my friend, when the operation went bust in Miami, Pauly wasn't brought in or even mentioned. He's clean on the deal far as the law's concerned."

"How good's your source of information?"

"Top grade. Somebody I know in Miami leaned on one of Raffy's old running mates, a guy looking at a life stretch in Raiford. He's informed before and it's always turned out true, and his ass is really in the wringer this time. A murder charge that'll stick. He knows whatever he tells the law better pan out as gold. They were striking a plea-bargain deal, so I had my friend ask hard about Raffy. The informer isn't brave or stupid enough to give us anything solid on Raffy, but the Dr. Pauly thing came out. Curiouser and curiouser, eh?"

"Sure is," Carver said. Faintly, he could hear the girl in the other end booth screech and giggle. He said, "You should know I got a list."

"Now I do know," Desoto said. "List of what?"

"The deaths out at Sunhaven the last year."

"Hmm. At this point, McGregor could have obtained that for you. You should have asked him. Why not let the bastard earn the taxpayers' money he pockets twice a month?"

"This way McGregor doesn't know I have the list. Neither does Sunhaven."

"See your point. Should I ask how you obtained such a list?"

"You could say I got an ally, leave it at that."

Desoto said, "It's left."

Carver told Desoto he'd keep him posted and then hung up. The girl in the other booth was screeching again, enjoying life. Enjoying youth and not knowing it.

He found an aisle where no one was browsing and stood next to a display of window shades and narrow plastic blinds and looked more closely at the list Birdie had given him.

She'd copied not only names from the files, but the cities the deceased residents were from. Four of the nine, including Sam Cusanelli, were from Florida, one of the women from right here in Del Moray. The dead men had found their way into Sunhaven from a variety of places but, except for one from Iowa, all of their hometowns were in the south: Dallas, Texas; Morristown, Tennessee; Rome, Georgia. Two of the men were from Miami, Florida. Miami again. And of course there was Kearny Williams from New Orleans.

Before leaving the drugstore, Carver bought a pack of Swisher

Sweet cigars at the front counter, where a couple of teenage girls were studiously taking some kind of inventory of Kodak film. One of the girls had a phone tucked between her jaw and shoulder. She giggled. He wondered if she might be talking with the girl back in the phone booth.

He smoked a cigar on the drive out to Sunhaven.

Birdie hadn't made it in to work yet. The attendant with the Errol Flynn mustache was behind the reception counter. There were bags under his eyes today and he looked haggard, maybe hung over; ten years older than he'd appeared last time Carver had seen him. No more leading-man roles. Carver told him he wanted to see Dr. Pauly.

"Not in today," the attendant said. He tapped a pencil point rapidly on the desk, as if impatiently wishing he were someplace else. Carver didn't blame him.

Across the lounge, the old checker player with the hawk nose was locked in a serious game with an obese old guy Carver hadn't seen before. The game was down to kings and hatchet face had four black ones to his opponent's two red. The outcome was easy to predict but the fat guy, a scrapper, kept fighting, moving toward opposite corners of the board to engage in a holding action.

"Maybe they'll let you sit and watch the next game," the attendant said to Carver. Might have been sarcastic, but Carver wasn't sure.

"You expect Dr. Pauly in later today?"

The attendant said, "Expected him here by now. He was due early this morning."

"He call in?"

"No, sir. Not while I been on the desk. Wanna leave your phone number, I can tell him you were by."

The hatchet-faced player shouted "Gotcha!"

Carver said, "No, nevermind," and went out.

Nurse Rule, vigilant as ever, was standing with her arms

crossed and her buttocks pressed against a front fender of the Olds. The sun's glare made her broad features appear harsh and vaguely mongoloid, but the combative glint in her eye would have been there even in shadow.

When Carver got close to her he stopped and leaned with both hands on his cane. He didn't say anything. The drone of insects was loud from the grass beyond the lot.

She said, "May I ask your business here?"

"I suppose so; you're in charge."

"I'm surprised to hear you acknowledge that, Mr. Carver. Doesn't answer my question, though, does it?"

"I came to see Dr. Pauly. He isn't here."

She stared at him, still with her arms crossed, her blocky body motionless as a rock and firmly rooted as an oak. "Why'd you want to see him?"

"Can't tell you," Carver said. "Patient-client stuff."

"You're sure you didn't come here to see Amos Burrel? Or Birdie Reeves?"

"I told you—Dr. Pauly. Know where he is?"

"No. He didn't phone."

"Maybe he's with Raffy Ortiz."

She shifted away from the car. Lowered her arms to her sides. She was bulky but balanced, ready to move in any direction. "Why do you say that?"

"They know each other, that's all. How come you object to my talking to Birdie, if there's nothing outside the rules going on here?"

"It's for Birdie's sake."

"I got a good idea why you might say that. But I don't believe it."

"She's an innocent young girl."

"One you were all over until you got warned away."

Nurse Rule stood straighter and inhaled. Stomach in, chest out, like a soldier at attention. A speech that would have made Oliver North proud was coming, Carver could sense it. "I'm not ashamed of my sexuality, Mr. Carver. When I found out Birdie was fifteen instead of eighteen I backed off. My private life's no business of a shit-disturber like you, but for what it's worth, I don't molest children. And I don't like seeing them taken advantage of, which is why I object to you and Raffy Ortiz sniffing around Birdie."

"Raffy Ortiz bothered Birdie?"

"He did. I had a talk with him in his car and warned him about it. Warned him sternly. Since then he's stayed away from her when he's come to see Dr. Pauly. You damn well better follow suit."

Carver remembered the blond woman, Melanie Star, in the Polaroid shots. The adhesive tape over her mouth, some of it over her hair. The drugged, gloomy expression in her eyes. He didn't want to think about what Raffy might have had in mind for Birdie.

Nurse Rule said, "I mean it. Stay clear of Birdie. Don't see her here or anyplace else."

"What if I told you I was trying to help her?"

"I wouldn't believe you. I can tell the type of man you are. Like the rest of your kind, like Raffy Ortiz. You think with your crotch; it's a male trait."

Carver said, "Well, sometimes it works out as if I did."

"I'll just bet." She shifted her weight in a way that conveyed menace. "Time to leave, Mr. Carver."

He smiled, squinting into the bright sun, and nodded. Then he limped toward the car door. No sense arguing with Nurse Rule while she was protecting her territory. And God it was miserably hot, standing here in the parking lot! Though she didn't seem to be in any discomfort. She wasn't even perspiring.

As he was lowering himself in behind the steering wheel, Nurse Rule, seeming a little surprised by his sudden compliance, walked around to stand near him and said, "What do you know about Raffy Ortiz?"

206

"More than you wish I knew." Carver closed the door. He twisted the key to start the engine. Tapped the accelerator so the car roared and vibrated with throaty power. Nurse Rule glared at him and didn't move.

She watched him back the Olds out of its parking slot and drive away, the expression on her face unchanging.

31

Carver drove to a restaurant on Marina Drive, where he sat at the bar and had a dozen oysters on the half shell with lemon while he sipped beer. His kind of lunch.

Outside the wide window the bright white hulls of pleasure boats belonging to Del Moray's wealthier citizens bobbed gently at their moorings in unison, as if doing a slow and lazy dance. The brilliant sunlight seemed to purify the air and gave objects a dazzling clarity. People in expensive sportswear and flashing gold and silver jewelry wandered along the dock. Lots of stomach paunches and white shoes, white belts, and white hair. In the past few years Del Moray had become essentially a rich retirement community. It was what enabled Edwina to make so much money turning real estate. It was what had raised the median age of the small city on the coast well up into the bracket of graying hair and growing waistlines. And what made "retirement homes" like Sunhaven such lucrative operations.

After lunch Carver phoned Sunhaven and was told by Birdie that Dr. Pauly hadn't arrived to make his regular rounds, and that he still hadn't phoned in. The restaurant phone was in the open, at the far end of the bar, and the mingled sounds of conversation, ice clinking in glasses, and occasional loud laughter made hearing Birdie's small voice difficult. It was like listening to someone from another, distant universe.

"Everything okay there?" Carver asked.

"Just fine," Birdie said.

"I mean, about the toothache."

"That? It'll be okay."

"You sure?"

"Sure."

She seemed hesitant to talk, and Carver didn't feel like forcing her.

He told her good-bye and hung up, then left the restaurant to drive to Pauly's house on Verde Avenue. It was good to get away from the crowded bar and inane cocktail chatter.

The sun hadn't let up at all. He could still taste the oysters and beer and felt a little queasy in the heat.

Verde was an old street, one of the first in Del Moray, and was lined with tall, gracefully bent palm trees and spreading sugar oaks. The houses were of varying size and architecture and set on large lots. Dr. Pauly's little house with its window flower boxes looked cool recessed in the deep shade of its overgrown yard.

As soon as Carver stepped up on the low concrete porch he saw that the door was open a crack.

He sounded the door chimes, but no one came. Birds were nattering like crazy in the backyard. An orange-striped cat emerged from beneath an azalea bush, gazed with disinterest at Carver, then slunk in the direction of the birds like a minitiger on the hunt.

Because the foliage was so thick, Carver wasn't very noticeable from the street. That was fine with him. He left the porch, found some firm ground with the tip of his cane, and limped to the attached one-car garage. It had a wooden overhead door with a line of small windows in it. He moved close, raised himself up slightly with a push on the cane, and peered inside.

Sunlight slanted into the garage at a sharp angle, swirling with dust and fractioning the dimness. He saw a power lawn-mower with a drooping grass bag attached, metal shelves against the back wall that seemed to contain assorted junk and lawn-care tools. A few loose, unfinished boards and what looked like a length of pipe were laid crookedly overhead on the rafters. A paint-spattered aluminum extension ladder rested horizontally on hooks along the side wall away from the house. No car.

Maybe Dr. Pauly, realizing he'd overslept, had left the house in such a hurry he'd neglected to close the front door all the way. Hustling healer, late for his rounds. Could have happened.

Carver made his way back onto the porch, pushed the door all the way open, and walked inside. Called, "Dr. Pauly? Man losing blood here!"

Silence and heat.

He shut the door behind him and noticed that a mahogany plant stand near the door had been knocked over. An orange ceramic pot lay shattered and dirt had been scattered to expose the roots of a green viny plant. Someone, in their haste to get out of the house, might have struck the plant stand and kept on going.

Carver moved farther inside. He looked around the living room but saw no disorder. As he went down the short hall, he glanced into the kitchen. There was a plastic milk jug and a half-full glass of milk on the sink counter. Next to them, on a white paper towel, lay a wheat-bread sandwich with only a couple of bites out of it. Someone had been interrupted during their snack, or had simply lost all appetite. Shaken by startling news? A phone call? A visitor?

The bedroom was still a mess. Clothes and shoes were scat-tered on the floor and the bed was unmade, the sheets twisted. The room smelled of stale sweat and desperate emotion. As if it were the scene of recent sexual coupling.

Carver moved carefully, noting the areas of the room blocked from his sight by furniture. Slowly he shifted position until he could see the floor on the other side of the disheveled bed, the space in the corner beside the tall chest of drawers. Everywhere that might shield a body from view.

Satisfied that he'd covered the bedroom itself, he limped to the closet and slid open its tall doors on their growling rollers.

There were gaps where Dr. Pauly's clothes were draped on wire hangers from the smooth metal closet rod. Half a dozen hangers lay tangled on the floor.

Among the boxes and folded clothes stacked on the closet's crowded shelf was a space large enough to have accommodated a suitcase.

Carver ran his hand over the shelf there and examined his fingertips. No dust.

He went into the bathroom. A half-used, dry bar of soap lay on the tile floor. None of the towels on the racks was damp. No toothbrush, toothpaste, shaving lotion, or deodorant. No razor, either blade or electric. Not even a comb.

Dr. Pauly had packed and left home in a hurry, not worrying about leaving a mess behind.

Again Carver realized how warm the little house was. Pauly had either gone this morning before the sun had gotten brutal, or been out of the house at least long enough for the air-conditioned atmosphere to have been displaced by heat.

Carver limped into the kitchen and touched the backs of his knuckles to the half-full glass of milk. It was room-temperature. So was the milk in the plastic jug. A tiny brown roach scurried out of sight beneath the lunchmeat-on-wheat sandwich on the paper towel.

There was a wall phone in the kitchen, a beige push-button job with a long, coiled cord that touched the floor. Carver used it to call McGregor.

"Time to share," he said when McGregor had come to the phone. "I've got some information for you."

McGregor said, "My ear's all tuned."

"Dr. Dan Pauly's disappeared. Didn't show up at Sunhaven to make his rounds this morning. I went by his house to talk to him; front door was open and it looks like he packed and left in a hurry."

"Packed, did you say?"

"I said. I'd also say he's been gone for a while. Several hours at least."

"I'll be damned. Your detective training tell you that, or what?"

"My police training. Same training you got, only I didn't forget mine."

"That where you're calling from, Pauly's house over on Verde?"

"I'm standing in his kitchen."

"Some more breaking and entering, huh?"

"I told you the front door was open."

"Got any idea where the good doctor ran off to, Carver? Could it have been some humanitarian mission came up suddenly? Maybe a guy having a heart attack? Or some fruit just realized he got AIDS?"

"No idea," Carver said.

"Well, I think I might know something about it. 'Cause Raffy Ortiz has disappeared, too."

Uh-oh! "Disappeared how?"

"I had a man watching him, and it seems Raffy knew about it but didn't let on till he was ready. Early this morning he did some fancy maneuvering and breaking of the speed limit in that white caddie of his and shook my guy. Raffy's on the loose now and unsupervised. Running away, it looks like. Same as Dr. Pauly."

"You saying Raffy and Dr. Pauly were partners and decided it was time to leave the scene?"

"Looks that way. They been partners before. Hey, you know how I found that out? I know about that plea-bargain deal in Miami. We weren't gonna talk about that one, though, were we, fuckhead?"

"Sure we were. You didn't give me a chance."

"Yeah, I shouldn't butt in the way I do. With you just bubbling over to spill everything to me. My bad manners cause me to miss a lot in life. Tell you, Carver, you keep your ass right where it is, and I'm coming over to look at whatever it is you seen at Pauly's. Don't dick around with the evidence or you got trouble."

"Why would I do that?"

"Why's a loose cannon like you do anything? You're just a bit smarter than a parking meter, I guess."

"I'll be here," Carver said. "Help yourself to a beer from the fridge while I wait."

"Only one," McGregor said. "You ain't gonna make sense when I get there, I'm sure, but I'd like it to be in your usual way."

He plonked down the receiver. Unnecessarily hard, Carver thought.

Ah, the doctor drank Budweiser.

McGregor was accompanied by the uniform who'd been at Edwina's, but he left him sitting in the patrol car parked out on Verde and entered Dr. Pauly's house alone. He made the place seem even smaller.

He nodded to Carver, who was sitting on the sofa holding a beer can. Then he glanced around. "High-rent neighborhood, but not such a hot-shit house for a medical doctor, hey?"

"He probably still has an expensive habit. Even doctors have to pay something for drugs. Pauly's not exactly at the apex of the medical profession, and who knows how much he's been paying Raffy Ortiz, if Raffy's been bleeding him for the past couple years?"

"That's a point. Guy with three nuts, he'd probably be worse'n the IRS. But maybe not."

McGregor took his time. He walked around, looked things over, touched things, came to the same conclusions Carver had reached.

213

"He's been gone for a while," McGregor said. "No telling for sure how long."

"He's with Raffy, like you said."

"Maybe. Or maybe he ran off on a Caribbean cruise with some hot nurse he knows. Doctors do that kinda thing, just like anybody else."

"He left in a hurry," Carver reminded McGregor.

"Coulda been one fine nurse. Didn't wanna be kept waiting to spread her legs on board ship." He squinted from up high, down at the beer can in Carver's fist. "There more of that stuff on ice?"

Carver said there was.

He watched McGregor stride into the kitchen, then return with his own can of beer.

McGregor wiped his big hand on his pants, leaving a damp spot from the condensation on the can. He tapped the side of the can with a fingernail. "Doc wouldn't care if he was here, I'm sure, seeing it's such a hot day."

He sectioned his long body down into a chair opposite Carver and sighed. His cheap cologne was hard to endure in the warm house. He said, "Tell me what you been doing this morning."

Carver told him, but he didn't mention the list Birdie had given him. Only said he'd driven to her apartment and talked to her before she'd left to go to the dentist.

"You didn't go by her place to give her your own kinda root-canal treatment, did you?" McGregor asked. "There ain't nothing wrong with that undernourished kinda cunt; put her on your prick and spin her like a propeller, hey?"

Carver said, "You're sick as Raffy Ortiz."

McGregor grinned, showing the pink tip of his tongue between his widely spaced front teeth. "Sure, and you're as up-right a guy as Jerry Falwell. I mean, girl young enough to be your daughter and all that. Is that what you're gonna tell me? Don't mean diddly, Carver. Birdie's not *that* young. She was probably popped years ago. You could have good sex with her and then lay around and talk about the new Whitney Houston album."

"Maybe you're even *more* messed up in the head than Raffy."

"You don't like Whitney Houston? Fine black stuff. Like to put it to her and listen to her sing her best."

"You know my meaning."

"Yeah. I know something else, too. Your cock's got no conscience. Not really. You're no exception to the human race."

"I am to the human race the way you see it."

McGregor took a long pull of beer. Some of it spilled sideways out of the can and dribbled down his chin onto his shirt. "Naw. Difference is I *do* see it and you don't." He grinned again and stretched out his long, workable legs and crossed them at the ankles, wriggling both feet, as if rubbing it in that he could walk and Carver needed the cane. Actually stared hard at the cane leaning on the cushion beside Carver; still grinning, trying to get to Carver. No mistaking what he was thinking. Doing. Some guy.

He said, "Tell me again about this morning, Carver. Lay it all out for me. And yesterday, too. Sure. What the fuck, why not yesterday?"

It was three-thirty before Carver finally got out of there and drove toward the coast highway and then north.

When he opened the door of his cottage the phone was ringing.

32

Amos Burrel's voice on the phone sounded faint but vibrant with frustration. "He snatched her right away from here, Carver! Drove right up and dragged her into his car and screeched to hell and gone outta here with her! Damn!"

Something inside Carver grew cold and sank. "Slow down and tell me the who and what of it, Amos."

"Nurse Rule'd have a cow if she knew I phoned you," Amos said. "But there comes a time for a man not to give a shit—I believe that, Carver."

"And maybe you're right, Amos. What happened?" Carver wanted to get the story out of the old man before he was discovered on the phone at Sunhaven and the conversation was terminated.

"I seen it only five minutes ago. That Latin thug in the white Cadillac; he's the one talked to Nurse Rule that night. He drove up and parked right near the front entrance. Little later I seen him walk back out with Birdie at his side. At first I thought the poor little thing was going with him willingly, though that sure didn't strike me as right. Then I seen that as they got closer to the car she started trying to hang back, dragging her feet. He had her tight by the elbow then. When he had the car door open she tried to jerk away but he laughed and wouldn't let her. Laughed, goddamn him! Having himself a good time!" Amos began to cluck his tongue; Carver could imagine him shaking his head.

"Go on, Amos. Then what?"

"She tried to kick him but he shoved her into the car on the driver's side, then across the front seat while he climbed in himself. I think she tried to open the door on the other side and jump out, but it looked like he slapped her one and yanked her over close to him while he started the car. Slapped her hard! Then he gunned the motor and sped outta the lot. Nurse Rule, along with one of the attendants, came running out after him, but all they did was stand and watch him drive away with Birdie. Useless as tits on a boar hog. Jesus, Carver, it ain't right, what happened. You shoulda seen it!"

Carver stared out the window at the vast blue plain of the ocean and the gulls circling above it, wings flashing white in the sun. "Anybody out there call the police?"

"I guess so, but hell, I dunno! I ain't the only one seen what went on. What they're mostly doing here's running around trying to convince people nothing outta the ordinary happened. Like they think they can smooth things over and nobody'll get upset and their heart give out. But I tell you, Carver, it won't take them long to see that won't wash. Birdie didn't leave here of her own free will, and I don't give a hot damn who says otherwise."

The old guy had his fighting blood up, all right. Carver was glad to hear the spirit back in the cracking voice. "I'll call the police, Amos. You did the right thing, but you better get back to your room. Keep a low profile, you understand?"

"I don't feel like keeping no low profile. Feel like grabbing that Cuban punk by the throat and giving him a shake. Teach him some civility. Goddamn, that's what I'd do if he was here now!"

Carver said, "Don't grab anybody's throat, Amos. Go on back to your room. Okay?"

"I'll do that knowing you're calling the police," Amos said reluctantly. "And that's the only way I will."

Carver understood why he didn't want to return to his room and a nonactive role. Big things were happening and he wanted to be part of them. Fuel that fed life.

"I can't call the police while I'm talking to you, Amos. Now, don't start anything else out there; wait for the law."

Amos slammed the phone down. Hurt Carver's ear.

Carver depressed the cradle button, then called McGregor at Del Moray police headquarters.

There was a lot of hissing and crackling on the switchboard, and then half a minute of the Muzak version of "Lucy in the Sky with Diamonds" before the phone rang in McGregor's office.

"No time to talk," McGregor said, as soon as he learned it was Carver. "Squeal just came in about an abduction at Sunhaven. Your little twist Birdie. Sounds like Raffy Ortiz took her."

"Who called?"

"Sergeant said it was Nurse Nora Rule. He checked the call for authenticity before he had a unit dispatched."

"You going to Sunhaven now?"

"Not actually. Instead I'm wasting my time talking to the jerkoff mighta caused all this."

Carver said, "I'll see you there," and hung up.

There were four Del Moray squad cars parked at haphazard angles near Sunhaven's main entrance. Red and blue roof-bar lights still rotated and flashed on two of them, but weren't making much of a showing in the bright early evening sun. A door was hanging open on one of the cars, and a radio was squawking loudly and intermittently. Just outside Sunhaven's tinted-glass entrance, a uniform stood slouched with his arms crossed, talking to a bespectacled blond man in a brown suit. Another uniform stood with his foot propped on the front bumper of the nearest patrol car. His head was bowed, as if he were thinking deeply. Or maybe the heat had gotten to him.

When he heard Carver approaching he looked up. His face was flushed and shiny with perspiration, but his marksman-blue eyes were calm and alert. He said, "Yes, sir?" in a neutral tone that meant who the hell are you and what are you doing here.

The plainclothesman in the brown suit heard the uniform and swiveled his head to stare blankly. He was a small man with a narrow, wise face. Studious-looking. The kind of guy who years ago had learned devious ways of dealing with the class bully. "You Fred Carver?"

Carver said he was.

"Lieutenant said a bald guy with a cane'd be out here," brown suit said. He smiled, shifting position slightly. The round lenses of his glasses blazed as twin reflected suns. "Said he'd be a little younger than the others. Go on in."

Carver didn't return the smile as he limped inside.

The bright lobby had been cleared of residents. The checkerboard on the table across from the desk held half a dozen checkers, including three red kings. A game had been interrupted. Black was probably glad. In a far corner was a line of chrome-spoked wheelchairs, collapsed in on themselves and stacked neatly against one another. They looked too frail to support the burden of years and human experience.

McGregor stood leaning with one giant palm flat on the reception desk. His dark suitcoat was unbuttoned and draped from his shoulders awkwardly. The butt of his Police Special peeked from its shoulder holster, only partly concealed by his lapel. Part of a crescent of underarm perspiration stain on his white shirt was visible, too.

Nurse Rule stood next to him with her feet planted wide and her fists on her hips. Dr. Macklin, wearing a tailored beige blazer and skirt, was cupping her elbows in her palms and rocking back and forth slightly on her high heels, as if she were cold. Maybe she was, in the spacious, air-conditioned lobby. Behind the curved desk, the attendant with the pencil-thin mustache was manning the phones. The two women looked concerned, angry, and somewhat dazed, as if events had caught up with them and then run over them. McGregor had on his cop face and appeared remotely interested and in calm and complete control. Carver knew better.

When he saw Carver, McGregor said something to Dr. Macklin and walked away from her and Nurse Rule, so he could talk privately to Carver. Nurse Rule stared at Carver, then looked away as if she'd glimpsed something uniquely repulsive.

"Looka what you stirred up," McGregor said.

Carver said, "It was here before I touched it with a spoon. I didn't create it."

McGregor surprised him. "Guess you didn't."

"Get the story?" Carver asked.

"Sure. Simple enough. Raffy parked out front, came in and talked to Birdie Reeves for a few minutes, then they left together. Looked like she was going willingly with him, but when they got near the car she put up a struggle. Before anybody could do anything about it, he shoved her in the car and drove away. It wasn't neat, but it was quick. Sometimes that's better."

"Any doubt it was Ortiz?"

"Naw, none at all. He's been out here before and some of the people know his face. And he was driving his hotshot white Caddie."

"Why would he nab Birdie at all? And why would he take her in plain view of the staff and some of the residents?"

"Well, I'm sure he thought he could make it look like she was leaving with him of her own accord. For a while it did look that way, story I get. Probably scared the living shit outta her and it took her a while to realize what was really happening. As to why he wanted her, maybe he figured she was on to whatever's going down here at Sunhaven and she posed some kinda danger to him. Or maybe he just wanted her in case he might need a hostage for a bargaining chip. Could have been an impulsive thing, for that matter. The guy thinks that way, especially these days."

Carver's stomach tightened as he thought about Birdie rifling the files for the information he'd asked her to get for him. Possibly she'd been seen. Ortiz might have been told. Possibly Carver *had* caused her abduction. And whatever else would happen to her. Was happening to her now. Possibly. *Oh, Christ!*

"Way I see it," McGregor was saying, "Pauly and Ortiz are on the run, and they wanna clean up whatever mess they might leave behind."

"They got a bigger mess now, though," Carver said, "since Raffy was seen dragging Birdie away from here by force."

McGregor shrugged and held the pose. It made him look like a gaunt blond vulture. "Not necessarily. They go underground. Maybe head for another country. Raffy changes his name, hacks fucking sugarcane for a while in Brazil or someplace. Dr. Pauly treats lepers in some godforsaken jungle. Makes atonement and all that. Feels good about himself. Albert Schweitzer bullshit, hey? Who the hell knows? One thing they *ain't* gotta worry about is somebody here in Del Moray, Florida, U.S. of A., able to pin anything on them."

"Other than kidnapping."

"Hah! I tell you, Carver, the staff here, meaning one attendant and that butch-looking nurse, only saw Raffy walk out with Birdie, holding her arm like a perfect gentleman. Witnesses saw her struggle getting into the car are about four hundred years old, you add up their ages. Raffy and Pauly stay clear of here for about a year or so, anybody can do them any damage in court'll be looking on from some other world. Even if some witnesses *are* still among the living, who's gonna believe a couple of old feebs that drool when they make an identification?"

Carver said, "I hope I see you in about twenty-five years and remind you you said that."

"You're not the type to live that long," McGregor said.

"I'll outlive you."

"Asshole! You'll outlive me like a rabbit'll outlive a fox."

McGregor might be right, Carver thought. "At least you've got enough evidence to come down on what's happening at Sunhaven."

McGregor's blond eyebrows crawled high on his forehead. "Oh? And what evidence is that?"

"There's a link between Raffy and Kearny Williams's daughter, Melba, and her husband, Jack Lipp. The Lipps have got a business that's in trouble—they need money. That means motive. Raffy and Dr. Pauly are choosing convenient times for Sunhaven residents' deaths so the survivors will benefit. Raffy handles the business end and Pauly fakes the death certificate. No doubt they both get a cut of whatever their clients inherit."

"No doubt, huh? If you was a judge, would you issue warrants and exhumation orders on what you just said?"

"Damned right I would!"

"Shows why you ain't a judge. This is the day and age a defendant's gotta be standing there with the victim's blood on him, if you're thinking conviction. Evidence needs to be so strong some pansy-ass judge won't let a killer walk or let him spend a little time behind the walls where he can learn new techniques and come out a state-of-the-art criminal. We need more than we got, Carver. I know it. You know it. Come on back outta dreamland."

Carver knew it. He was back. "I'd like to talk to one of the residents here."

"A witness?"

"Maybe." Carver wasn't going to tell McGregor about Amos Burrel's phone call. It was McGregor himself who'd told Carver about Birdie's abduction, before Carver had had a chance to tell *him.*

"Nope. Sorry, the ones seen the perpetrator leave here with the victim are still making their statements."

McGregor didn't seem sorry. But he had the badge and the rank and knew how to use them. Felt like using them this evening.

Carver traced circles on the floor with the tip of his cane, sensed it was time to go. "Let me know soon as you hear anything on this," he said.

McGregor shot his nasty grin. "Oh, you betcha. You make sure your Radio Shack police scanner's tuned and I'll see you're posted right up to the minute. Won't make a move without you."

"I'll call you from time to time," Carver said.

As he limped out he noticed Nurse Rule and Dr. Macklin standing near each other and talking in low tones. They moved apart and stood silently when they saw McGregor walking back toward them, like a couple of conspiring schoolgirls.

Carver needed to talk to somebody about all this himself. So he could unburden his heart of some of the guilt he felt for placing Birdie in danger and making her a maniac's hostage. So he could get a perspective from someone who wasn't a twisted cop or a Sunhaven resident or a murder suspect.

Edwina fell into none of those categories.

He stopped the Olds at a phone booth on the coast highway and called her at Quill Realty. Reminded her of last night and asked her if she wanted to meet him again for dinner.

She did. She was as easy for him as he was for her.

33

They sat at a table in The Happy Lobster, a circular restaurant on the edge of the sea. They were next to the vast curved window that looked out on the Atlantic, dawdling over drinks before dinner and watching night creep in. The purple line of the horizon became indistinct and then disappeared. The sea became as black as the sky, and only whitecaps were visible, dancing like playful spirits on the water. Then they also disappeared, until a high wind swept the clouds from in front of a gold sliver of moon. Darkness, shimmers of white, distant low stars like a galaxy that had fallen. Some of the stars were very slowly moving. Ships' lights, far out at sea.

"Endless dark," Carver said, and sipped his scotch. It had too much bite.

Edwina said, "Don't be so exuberant. It takes my breath away."

Still gazing over his drink, out at the black ocean, Carver told her everything about his day. About how a murderous sadist had dragged a fifteen-year-old runaway into his car and driven off with her. Because of foolish and melodramatic cloak-and-dagger work that Carver had virtually forced the child to do. He gave Edwina the details, the eyewitness accounts. See how cheerful that'd make her.

She said, "You're feeling sorry for yourself. I find that disgusting in a man."

Carver was irritated. "What I feel," he said, "is guilt."

"Think there's a difference?"

He thought it over and said, "Not much, I guess."

Edwina stirred her martini with the olive impaled on a little plastic red sword, holding the sword's handle deftly between thumb and forefinger. "Well, you screwed up. You can sit there and loathe yourself, but that won't work you back in time so you can make things right. Besides, you don't *know* if your having Birdie go through the Sunhaven files has anything to do with why this Ortiz monster abducted her."

"Don't I? If I were a gambling man . . ."

"But you are," Edwina said. She stopped stirring. "Not with money, maybe, but you are." She was smiling at him. Popped the olive into her mouth and slowly withdrew the tiny red sword from between her pressed lips. Seductive, all right; apparently she approved of his gambling. "There are all kinds of currency. You'll keep gambling with whatever's being used and you'll figure things to their logical conclusion. And you'll find out that people do things for their own reasons and you're not to blame for the human condition."

"And what is that condition?"

"Totally fucked up."

"You wouldn't like it if I said who you sounded like."

"Okay, not totally. Nothing's totally. There's you and me. I mean, together."

She had a point. Seemed to right now, anyway.

He watched the flashing red and white lights of a high-flying aircraft, heading north. Out of Miami? Winging to Washington or New York? Carrying passengers and legitimate cargo? Or narcotics? He knew drug shipments were flown out of Mexico and even South America to points along the coast. Sometimes the planes landed at private airfields. Other times they dropped their cargoes in the sea with flotation devices, so the drugs could be picked up by small, fast boats and ferried to shore.

The waiter came with the food. Edwina had ordered crab legs. Carver had the stuffed flounder and asparagus. She asked for wine. He was drinking beer. The spiced scent of the seafood heightened his appetite and prodded him at least partly out of his gloom. Food, sleep, sex, shelter—maybe simple gratification was all there really was to life. Maybe McGregor was right.

After dinner they had ice cream and coffee. Carver was still thinking about Birdie Reeves, and halfway through dessert he realized something wasn't right.

He pulled the list of the past year's Sunhaven deaths from his shirt pocket and unfolded it. Scanned it twice. There was no James Harrison from Oregon on it, the resident whose death had prompted old Amos Burrel to call Carver after overhearing his conversation with Kearny Williams. An oversight by Birdie? Or had Harrison's file been removed before she'd searched the records?

"I think a repeat of last night is in order," Edwina said, finishing her ice cream and fastidiously licking the spoon. She sure was oral tonight.

Carver said, "You're talking to a middle-aged man."

"Middle-aged woman doing the talking. It's logical that something wonderful has to come from all that experience."

"I agree with your logic," Carver told her, "but the experience will have to be one night less, I'm afraid. I need to get back to the cottage. Somebody might try to get in touch with me about what happened."

She shrugged. "Okay, I'll go with you. We'll sleep there."

"Not a good idea."

"Dangerous, you mean?"

"Yeah. Maybe very dangerous."

"Then why do *you* have to be there?"

"Gambling," Carver said.

She smiled. "I'm your best bet. No way to lose."

"There's a way. For both of us."

She tried not to show she was aggravated, but she was. Finally she said calmly, "Damn you. I love you so much it makes me terrified of losing you. I hate that."

Carver knew exactly what she meant.

He also knew what it would do to him if he brought her the kind of harm that was possible, even likely, because of where the Sunhaven case had taken him.

He promised he'd make it up to her. Make it up to himself. She seemed unmoved. The earth had cooled. He resisted the urgings of his heart and groin to change his mind and tell her to come with him. Love, perhaps the most basic emotion in the world, could create the most wrenching complications. Could make people the victims of cosmic practical jokes.

When they left the restaurant, he sat in the Olds in the parking lot and watched the taillights of her Mercedes dwindle and disappear down the highway. Then he waited for a tractor-trailer with a hundred red and yellow running lights to roar past. He listened to its howl change to a diminishing high-pitched whine of rubber on pavement. When the sound had almost died, he drove from the lot and hit the accelerator hard.

He followed the wildly speeding truck all the way to the turnoff to his cottage. Warm air crashed and boomed through the car and flying insects bounced off the windshield like stray bullets.

He parked in his usual spot, not being as careful as he might have, still locked in gloom. Ortiz was running now, with Dr. Pauly, perhaps. And with a hostage. Anyway, Carver *hoped* Birdie was still a hostage and nothing worse had happened to her. Possibly Raffy realized her struggle at Sunhaven had been seen, and to decrease the intensity of the hunt for him he'd set her free.

But Carver knew better. Knew Raffy Ortiz well enough to

be sure he wouldn't simply turn Birdie loose on some deserted road and drive away. He would kill her, or he would kill everything in her. Cruelty lived in him like an animal.

Carver slammed the Olds's door and limped over to the dark porch.

The tide was high, and behind him the sea was giving the beach a beating. A warm breeze carried to him the smell of things alive and dead that the waves had washed onto the sand. He set the cane firmly on each step with a solid *thunk!* as he took the stairs.

On the top step he froze in surprise. His heart seemed to swell and began hammering ferociously. Thudding so powerfully he was sure he could hear it—or was that the pounding of the surf on the beach?

In the shadows at the end of the porch was the outline of a man sitting in the webbed lounge chair. Sitting almost casually, with an ankle crossed over a knee, dangling foot pumping rhythmically, nervously.

The dark figure's right arm rose slowly. The shape in its hand was unmistakable. A gun.

A voice as strained as taut wire said, "I've been waiting for you."

34

The figure got up from the lounge chair and stepped from shadow into moonlight. Dr. Pauly. He held the gun steady on Carver, held it as if he were familiar with firearms and knew how to use them as effective life-and-death instruments; part of his medical training.

The surf breathed in slow rhythm and frogs croaked behind the cottage, but Carver felt as if he and Dr. Pauly were somehow caught in silent suspension of time.

Until Dr. Pauly said, "I don't want to shoot you, Mr. Carver, but if you try to come near me, I will. I swear it!"

Carver folded his hands over the crook of his cane and leaned on it. Might as well stay where he was for a while.

Dr. Pauly's deep-set eyes were in shadow. His thin mouth was a tight line arced downward at the corners as if scrawled that way in a child's crude drawing. He glanced down at the automatic in his hand, back up at Carver. "I don't want anyone else killed," he said. "For God's sake, I'm a doctor! That's why I came here to warn you."

"Warn me about what?" But Carver knew what. Knew who.

"Raffy Ortiz. He's got it fixed in his mind to kill you. Kill us both. You don't know him the way I do, the things he's done. He's sick and vicious! More dangerous than you can imagine."

Carver tightened his grip on the cane. *Kill us both.* So that was why Dr. Pauly had bolted—not so much from the law as from Raffy Ortiz. Raffy had exercised an evil control over him, but that also meant the doctor knew some damaging information about Raffy. Which put Dr. Pauly in mortal danger.

"Is that why he snatched Birdie Reeves?" Carver asked. "Because she'd talked to me and gone through the Sunhaven files? Because she knew too much?"

Dr. Pauly appeared startled. Lowered the gun for a moment and gave a trembling, nervous smile that almost blurted into a laugh. Pressure had built in him close to the bursting point.

Then his mouth set again in its hard line, his jaw thrust forward. "Birdie knew too much, all right. She was in this all the way with Raffy and me."

Comprehension started to seep in on Carver, cold and unsettling.

"All the way in what?" he asked. He knew and dreaded the answer but he wanted to hear it from Dr. Pauly. Hear all of it at last.

Dr. Pauly planted his feet wider, to create a more stable firing stance in case he had to use the automatic. The front of his white shirt was stained with perspiration and plastered to his chest and upper arms.

"When a senior citizen takes up residence at an expensive nursing home like Sunhaven," he said, "there's almost always a considerable potential inheritance when that resident dies. Often that inheritance is being rapidly eroded by the cost of the nursing home itself. Now, in most families there's at least one member who'd profit enormously if the resident died, who might even be in immediate financial need and would like to see the resident expire somewhat sooner than nature intended."

Carver thought about Jack and Melba Lipp in New Orleans, and their foundering business in the French Quarter. "You'd supply Raffy Ortiz with names of the wealthiest Sunhaven residents with pressing medical problems," he said, "and it was Raffy's job to find those family members, feel them out, and proposition them."

"Exactly," Dr. Pauly said. "And when the time of the resident's death was moved to an earlier and more convenient date, we'd later receive a share of the inheritance for . . . expediting matters."

"Neither you or Birdie was living in luxury," Carver pointed out.

"I'm a former drug supplier and I have an expensive addiction," Dr. Pauly said. "Birdie's a chemically dependent fifteen-year-old runaway. Still, you'd be surprised by certain dollar amounts; only Raffy pulled the strings and he didn't want attention drawn to us if our life-styles improved dramatically. That was smart of him but tough on us. In a year or so, when we'd made enough money, we were going to stop what we were doing. That was the plan. Nobody would have any reason to suspect us, and Birdie and I would leave Sunhaven and collect our share of the proceeds."

"You hoped."

Dr. Pauly hefted the gun as if it weighed twenty pounds and shook his head sadly. "We had no choice but to hope. Raffy could reveal our backgrounds anytime. When he found out I'd gotten the position at Sunhaven, he brought Birdie up from Miami and made me wangle her the receptionist job. Neither of us had a say in the matter. Birdie had been part of Raffy's stable of prostitutes in Dade County, and I'd had a close brush with the law. There's evidence that I'm sure could reopen the case and result in an indictment against me. Raffy was keeping that evidence hidden, but he made it plain to me it might not remain hidden."

Carver was still trying to adjust his perception of Birdie.

Woman-child Birdie. "Raffy and Birdie knew each other in Miami?"

"You shouldn't be shocked," Dr. Pauly said. "It's the way a lot of runaways get money to survive. It's an indifferent world out there for them; they either sink or they swim. Some of the ones that sink drown, and some learn to live on the bottom of the ocean. Birdie was one of Raffy's personal favorites, and the favorite of a few of his wealthiest clients. The ones with predilections for very young girls." Dr. Pauly's features twisted into a grotesque visual plea for pity. Not for Birdie, for himself. "You've got to understand, Mr. Carver, some of us do what we have to in this life."

"And when Raffy gave you the signal, you had to murder Sunhaven residents and then sign phony death certificates. A flawless setup, with you being the attending physician."

"I knew the residents' medical histories," Dr. Pauly said, "and I'd simply extend what problems they had to the degree that they'd cause cessation of life. It was all plausible, really only a matter of altering the time schedule of mortality."

"It's murder," Carver said, "to give a patient you're supposed to be helping a lethal injection or the wrong kind of pills, or whatever methods you used. Blow all the smoke you want around it to disguise it, but it still shines through as murder."

Dr. Pauly moved nearer. He looked angry and injured. "Damn you, I'm a doctor! I save life, not take it. I was referring to the causes of death I listed on official documents. You've been made a fool of, Carver. It was Birdie who did it."

Carver stool paralyzed, not wanting to believe. Not wanting to listen to what Dr. Pauly was telling him.

But the doctor was persistent. Using the truth like a scalpel. "She was the one who agreed to kill them," he said. "That's why Raffy worked her into Sunhaven. For that precise purpose. She killed them all."

"Killed them how?" Carver asked.

"I honestly don't know. I'd be told when they were going to

expire, so I'd be present to handle the details. The corpse would always be without a mark on it to suggest unnatural death. I think only Birdie knows how she killed them. Raffy didn't care how it was done, as long as it was clean enough that I could make out the death certificate without raising questions and prompting some of the family members or the authorities to request an autopsy. That was no problem; remember, the victims were *expected* to die while at Sunhaven."

"Poison?"

"I don't think so. Most poisons leave some trace. Distinctive odors, or symptomatic signals in the deceased, that are evident even without an autopsy. I'm afraid only postmortem internal examination would reveal how Birdie did her work, and maybe even then it wouldn't be obvious. There are imaginative ways to do murder that only the most careful and detailed autopsy would reveal. Raffy might very well know those ways, and he might have given Birdie her choice of which method to use. All I know is, I was never told how the residents actually died. And as long as I could state a cause of death consistent with the condition of the corpse and the deceased's medical history, it didn't matter to me."

"You said Raffy was fond of Birdie in Miami."

"No, Mr. Carver, I said she was one of his favorites. That isn't good for her, it's bad. If Raffy has Birdie, there isn't any way she can be helped. She poses a danger to him. The way you and I do. He caught up with me in Del Moray and almost killed me. I got away only because I managed to reach my car before he got to me. He's a heavy abuser of drugs himself and he's high on something now. Methamphetamine and God knows what else. He's insane, like an enraged tiger. You can't reason with him."

"We get in my car and go to the police," Carver suggested.

"Not the police. Not for me. I need to get clear of the law and of Raffy and start over. I can do that."

"Sure. Live in the jungle and treat lepers."

233

Dr. Pauly cocked his head sharply to the side and stared at Carver. "It sounds farfetched but it's a possibility."

"You aren't talking good sense. Are *you* high on something, Dr. Pauly?"

"No games, please," Dr. Pauly said. "Not enough time for them. I came here to warn you, and I have. When I leave, phone the police, but don't try to come after me." He motioned with the gun. "Right now, get down off the porch and walk over toward your car."

"You going to steal it?"

"No, I've got my own car parked down near the highway." Another curt wave of the gun barrel. Somewhere this guy had become very familiar with guns. "I said right now, Mr. Carver. I just want to be assured you can't follow me when I leave."

Carver thumped down off the porch and crossed the sandy earth to where the Olds was parked. Dr. Pauly knew what he was doing with the gun, all right; he stayed about five feet from Carver all the way. Not so close that Carver could make a grab at the gun, but close enough so there'd be no doubt about accuracy if the trigger were squeezed. The frogs behind the cottage were croaking up a wild cacophony of protest; they were outraged by what was happening.

Keeping the gun leveled at Carver with one hand, Dr. Pauly stooped low and used the other to feel for the Olds's hood latch. The latch gave with a squeak and the hood sprang up a few inches in a crocodile smile.

The doctor raised it the rest of the way, reached into the engine compartment, and deftly withdrew the coil wire. All like a neat operation. Dr. Pauly made Mr. Goodwrench look like a klutz.

He hurled the short, rubber-insulated wire into the night. Now the Olds wouldn't start. Carver had no wheels.

Legs were next.

Dr. Pauly said, "Sit down on the ground and toss your cane aside. *Aside*, not at me!"

Carver did as he was told. Dust or sand worked up the pants cuff of his stiff leg, extended out in front of him, and found its gritty way under the elastic of his sock. The baked ground was hard and uncomfortable beneath his buttocks. He was sweating heavily and felt helpless without the cane.

Dr. Pauly slammed down the Olds's hood. The sudden collision of steel on steel hushed the frogs. No sound now but the surf. Sighing. Whispering.

The doctor walked over and picked up Carver's cane, then propped it against the left front tire and stamped on it until it snapped. He threw the two pieces in the direction of the cottage, into darkness. Carver heard one of them clatter off the porch or the front wall. The noise was lost in the night.

He didn't have another spare cane; he was surprised by how totally vulnerable he felt. He remembered the early days of his physical therapy. Fought down the old panic. *Jesus! This was how it was to be crippled! Really crippled!*

"You won't be able to drive, or to come after me on foot now," Dr. Pauly said. He stared down at Carver with a measure of pity and chewed nervously on the inside of his cheek. His face gleamed white as bone in the moonlight. "Listen, all I want's a fair head start."

"Fair?" Carver said. "What the hell are you talking about, *fair*?"

Dr. Pauly said, "Well, as fair as possible. There aren't any choices in some lives. None at all. I'm sorry. Good luck."

He tucked the gun in his waistband, beneath his shirt, then turned and jogged away in the direction of the highway. He held a steady, moderate pace, like a health buff running to take off a few pounds.

Carver watched the wavering signal of his white shirt until it was absorbed by the night.

Then he crawled toward the cottage.

235

35

The cottage's front door had been forced open. The lock appeared intact, but the interior mechanism had been sprung and the bolt was sheared, as if someone had rammed his shoulder hard into the door. Carver had assumed Dr. Pauly was sitting on the front porch because he hadn't been able to get in the cottage, but maybe that was wrong. Or maybe someone other than Dr. Pauly had been inside.

Carver supported himself by leaning on the doorjamb. He ran his fingertips over rough plaster, feeling for the wall switch. He found smooth plastic, worked the switch, and the lamp by the sofa winked on.

A glance around told him things were out of place. Whoever had broken the lock had gone through the cottage, either looking for something in particular or merely making an idle search.

Carver stood as straight as he could, balancing with just his fingertips touching the doorjamb. Then he lurched across the room to the chair where he customarily sat after his morning swims. He clutched the back of the chair, swayed this way and that, but managed to stay standing. Using furniture and the walls for handholds, he made his way to where the umbrella he'd used as a makeshift cane was leaning in the corner, near the pieces of the walnut cane Raffy had snapped in half in Del Moray.

When he'd gripped it by its curved plastic handle he felt immeasurably more secure, but he couldn't put his entire weight on the umbrella or it would bend. He moved gingerly taking short, uneven steps, being very careful where he placed its slender metal tip.

There hadn't been much attempt to conceal the fact that the cottage had been searched. Carver made his way behind the folding screen that partitioned off the sleeping area. He saw that the mattress had been lifted so someone could check to see if there was anything concealed between it and the bedsprings. The pillow had been tossed to the side against the wall. None of the dresser drawers had been shut all the way after they'd been rummaged through. It looked like a teenager's room.

With a sudden foreboding he limped to the dresser and yanked the top drawer open all the way. Rooted through its contents.

The Colt .38 automatic was gone from beneath his socks.

Carver closed his eyes and pictured Dr. Pauly holding the gun leveled at him waist-high. An automatic. In the darkness he hadn't recognized it, but it must have been the Colt. One automatic handgun looked much like another. Dr. Pauly had been in the cottage and taken the gun from the drawer before Carver arrived. Not surprising. His life had been in danger, and it figured that a private investigator would keep weapons in the house. His search had paid off.

The doctor wasn't to be trusted, but he *had* given sound advice. If Raffy was hyped on drugs and on a homicidal rampage, he'd be just the person to avoid.

Carver tried to remember where he'd last put his flashlight. Wished he were more of a place-for-everything kind of guy. The air conditioner had overloaded the cottage's wiring last month, and he'd used the flashlight to locate the blown fuse and screw in a replacement. He thought it was in the cabinet beneath the sink.

He wielded the umbrella with vigor and purpose and hobbled toward the kitchen area. He'd use the flashlight to try to find the coil wire Dr. Pauly had hurled into the darkness. Then he could get the Olds started and drive to safety.

His first stop would be Sanderson's Drugstore on Ocean Drive, where he remembered the rack of aluminum and wooden canes and crutches between the prescription counter and the display of condoms and Ace bandages. He needed mobility more than he cared to admit.

He sat on the floor and used both hands to pull everything out of the cabinet under the sink. Bug spray, dishwashing detergent, spot remover, scrub brush, steel-wool pads.

Everything but a flashlight.

The phone rang. Made Carver drop the spray can of glass cleaner he was holding. The yellow plastic lid popped off, bounced, and wobbled back into the cabinet.

Dragging the unopened umbrella behind him, he crawled to the phone and pulled it down on the floor. Held it in his lap and lifted the receiver. Gave a cautious hello.

A faint voice said, "He's on his way, Carver."

Carver's heart danced against his ribs. "Who's on his way? Who is this?"

"It's Dr. Pauly. Raffy's on his way to your place. Right now. He thought he killed me . . . maybe he did. I had to warn you. God, the blood! It'll take him about ten minutes to get there. Understand? Ten minutes!"

"Where are you?" Carver asked levelly.

"It's not like somebody else's blood," Dr. Pauly said weakly. Almost a horrified moan. "Not at all. My own blood. So much of it! It won't stop. No matter what. Won't . . ."

"Where are you?"

"Ten minutes. Ticking away. Save yourself!"

"Listen! Dr. Pauly!"

There was a clatter, then a steady buzzing,

The connection was broken.

Carver sat on the floor gripping the droning phone in both hands and staring down at it, as if it held the fascination toys hold for infants.

Ten minutes!

He knew it would take the police at least fifteen minutes to reach the isolated cottage. And he hadn't called them yet!

He dialed 911.

"I'm a private detective," he told the operator. "I've just been told someone's on his way to my home to try to kill me." He gave the emergency operator his name and address, even directions to the cottage.

"You say you're a detective?"

"Yes!"

"With what department?"

"Private! I'm a licensed private investigator!"

"Will you give me your full name and your phone number, sir?" She didn't seem excited. Other people's desperation was routine. Death threats were all in a night's work.

"He'll be here in ten minutes!" Carver said.

"I need your name and phone number, sir. Then I'll call you back and get more information concerning the emergency. It won't take long."

Christ! She thought this might be a hoax. Didn't she know what it was to be terrified?

Ten minutes! And he was bogged down in bureaucracy land! Fear stuck like a jagged lump of metal in his throat—he could taste it.

Carver pressed down the cradle button and punched out the number of the sheriff's office.

Better luck there. He told a switchboard operator what the problem was and she assured him a car was on the way.

"On the way" might not be good enough. Carver thought about the fire station on the coast highway. He knew the fire department could reach the cottage in about fifteen minutes, maybe in slightly less time if the highway wasn't congested. It could take them longer if there was traffic.

He called in and reported that the cottage was on fire.

Then he sat sweating and staring at the phone, wondering how to defend himself against Raffy Ortiz. If he simply tried to crawl into the night and hide, Raffy would easily track him, perhaps with a flashlight, and kill him. If he called someone near enough to arrive before Raffy, he might only be providing Raffy with another victim. Besides, this was a comparatively desolate area of the coast, and there might not be anyone near enough to beat Raffy to the cottage. An enraged tiger on drugs, Dr. Pauly had said. Dr. Pauly, who was himself probably dead or dying because of Raffy.

Carver glanced around the cottage from his seated position on the floor. A different, lower perspective that lent a disturbing strangeness to familiar surroundings.

He stood up slowly and carefully with the umbrella and lurched into the kitchen.

From the clutter in the sink drawer he lifted a carving knife, then he hurried to the front door. Cicadas were trilling and the moon's reflection lay like a sad smile on the sea. He used the knife to cut the wire mesh from the screen door, running its blade at an angle along the wooden edges of the frame.

Half a minute later he switched off the light and hobbled outside.

36

The white Cadillac arrived with a roar and a haze of dust and exhaust that drifted across the low moon like an ominous cloud.

Carver watched through the cottage window as Raffy climbed out of the car, stretched his back and thick arms as if he'd been cramped too long, and grinned as his gaze fixed on the open front door. He was wearing shorts, his sleeveless black T-shirt, and white or gray jogging shoes without socks. Might have been a beachcomber looking for shells instead of a killer searching for victims.

The Caddie's engine was idling. Raffy reached in and switched it off, then slammed the car door. The sound was an explosion in the quiet night. Carver wished again he had the handgun Dr. Pauly had taken. Though the gun hadn't helped the doctor fend off Raffy. Maybe Raffy was invulnerable to bullets. Three nuts.

He yelled, "Carver, old buddy! Yeah, I know you're in there! Had a talk with Dr. Pauly about you just a little while ago. Time to have some of my kinda fun with you, fucking gimp!" He started toward the cottage, a moving myth of destruction that left in its wake very real death. Behind him the black ocean rolled like a dark mystery.

Using the umbrella for support, Carver limped out the back door into the hot velvet night. He left the door hanging open.

"Carver!" Raffy was inside the cottage now. "Hey, Carver! Gonna hide from me, you think? Won't do you no good, *compadre.*"

Carver could hear him moving around, slamming furniture against the walls, working up to where he wanted to be: higher than high and faster than the speed of reason. The sea pounded on the beach and the cicadas screamed. A towering palm tree silhouetted against the dim sky shook its fronds briskly in the breeze, like a giant, long-haired creature trying to clear its mind. Carver pushed his fear aside and held it there; he knew he had to control his own mind if he wanted to live.

And with an intensity that surprised him, he *did* want to live, wanted to go on and on being the crippled but breathing and feeling Carver. Right now, life seemed the sweetest condition of all.

"Hey, Carver? Where you go to, asshole?" Raffy's voice was louder, irritated. He wanted to get on with the game.

Carver dragged himself over the hard ground, beyond the mound of earth and the grave that had been dug for him. A crawling insect tickled over his bare arm. Gnats flitted around his nose and eyes. He stopped and lay curled on his side, staring into the darkness of nightmares.

Raffy stepped out the back door. He expanded his chest and hitched up his shorts. Swiveled his head on the muscular column of his neck.

Saw Carver and smiled.

"Ah, there you are, fuckface. Hey, you look scared. Well, you got a right. I been looking forward to this, you know?" He slashed at the air with the edge of his hand, leaped high and did a few spinning, lightning karate kicks. Giggled like a school-girl out of control. "Chop a gimp like you in half, I wanted to. But I won't do that. Not for a while, anyway."

He moved toward Carver with a slow swagger, clenching and

unclenching his huge fists. "Got nothing to say, scared man? I seen 'em like you before, find out they got no guts and just wanna get it done with. Like a shit-spooked rabbit caught by a dog and dangling there in its jaws. Know it's all over but the formalities, so they go limp. Natural thing to do, I guess. Well, it ain't gonna be that easy. Gonna be fucking *fun*, man! Though you ain't gonna think so."

Carver lay still and watched him approach. Raffy was obviously taking his time, stretching this out for maximum enjoyment as he relished Carver's terror. This was his amusement, the mainspring of his mind and the real reason he killed. The muscles in his face were taut and he seemed about to break out in his girlish giggle again. He wouldn't have laughed like that in front of someone he planned on leaving alive.

"Gonna pull some meat from the bone," Raffy crooned. "Gonna rip you where it hurts most, scared man. You know, we got all fucking night, you and me."

Raising the knife so its blade caught the moonlight, Carver said, "I'll see you get some sport out of it."

Raffy did giggle. "Man, you so right about that." His wide, white grin spread on his face and stuck there. "You gonna be surprised the tricks I can do with that knife. Nice of you to be holding it for me." He wasn't kidding; the knife represented little threat to him. But his dark eyes glimmered with the slightest caution and stayed trained on the blade. He couldn't totally ignore it. He had to be ready to dodge in case Carver threw the knife. "Cut off some small parts of you, won't even bleed much," Raffy said, crooning again, getting himself deeper in the mood. "Cut off some of you and make you goddamn eat it. Learn to fucking like it. Keep wishing you were passed out, but you won't be. Tell you, I learned some things from good old Dr. Pauly. Taught him some neat shit, too. Graduated the dumb bastard less than an hour ago. I mean, taught him his final fucking lesson. What I got planned for you—"

Raffy dropped from sight.

Made no sound.

Carver had been holding his breath. He exhaled now in a rasping whoosh of air. His hands were shaking.

He'd sharpened the pieces of his broken canes and embedded them pointed-side-up in the bottom of the grave. Then he'd laid the screen from the front door over the grave and hurriedly scattered loose earth lightly over it. A tiger pit. One that Carver had made sure was between him and Raffy.

High on drugs, concentrating on his prey and the knife, Raffy had forgotten what side of the mound of earth the grave was on and hadn't noticed any irregularity on the ground's surface. Hadn't noticed until it was too late and he'd crashed through the screen onto the sharpened walnut spikes.

Carver had expected a howl of pain and rage. An animal cry of surprise.

Anything but silence.

He crawled toward the edge of the grave, then used the shovel protruding from the mound of dirt for support. He stood up.

He edged closer and peered down into the pit.

Raffy shrieked, startling Carver, freezing him just long enough for Raffy to clutch his ankle.

The knife dropped into the grave. Raffy was pulling Carver down into the dark hole with him. The smell of raw earth was like a whiff of death.

Carver remotely realized he was screaming along with Raffy. Without thinking, he raised the shovel. Lost his support and almost fell. Propped himself with his stiff leg. Slammed the shovel down on Raffy's head. His arm. Again! *Again!*

Raffy maintained his crushing grip on Carver's ankle and laughed wildly. "*Bastardo!* You gonna fucking pay!" He inched Carver nearer the grave.

Carver swiveled the shovel and with all his strength chopped the sharp edge of the blade down on Raffy's wrist.

Raffy roared and released his grip.

Carver scooted backward, out of reach. Swallowed, and sucked in air deeply, in relief.

Raffy rose up from the black hole as if the devil were down there boosting him. He was free to the waist and using his powerful arms to hoist himself all the way out. He actually got a leg up, dug in a heel. Carver saw that a sharpened spike had penetrated his foot and was protruding from the top of his jogging shoe. Saw a glistening black trickle of blood on his side.

Then the soft earth gave way and Raffy grunted and slid back down. Into shadow. Out of sight.

Rose again, this time not quite as high.

Carver slammed the shovel down on his head. It glanced off and he almost dropped it.

"Think I ain't gonna get outta here, asshole?" Raffy screamed.

Carver thought Raffy might be right; despite his wounds he might be able to crawl out of the grave. Whatever his disadvantage, he seemed capable of anything.

Raffy hoisted himself up again, and this time when Carver brought the shovel down he tried to grab it.

He deflected it from his head but slipped down again into the pit.

"Sport, all right," he said, giggling. "You know I'm gonna have your ass, Carver!"

Carver began scooping dirt frantically into the grave, leaning on the shovel when he plunged its blade into the mound of earth, teetering in precarious balance as he flung each load into the hold. A regular, lurching rhythm.

"Hey, you motherfucker!" Raffy's protest suggested Carver was doing something outside the rules. Unfair.

Carver kept shoveling.

Raffy began hurling dirt out of the grave by the handfuls, but it was a hopeless struggle. He didn't have the shovel and he couldn't keep up. More dirt was going in than was coming out.

Carver's breath screeched in his throat and his chest heaved. He'd never worked so hard. Sweat dripped from him. His powerful upper body ached with each plunge and arc of the shovel.

His forearms began to cramp. The dirt dropping into the grave sounded like hail falling.

Raffy was quiet now, only grunting now and then as he tried to throw out enough dirt to slow Carver's progress, tried to churn his legs so he could stay on top of the loose earth Carver was shoveling in. But he was hurt too badly for that. Doing a clumsy kind of dance.

Maybe he thought Carver would fill in the grave until it was shallow enough for him to climb out. A desperate hope. The dirt was raining down around him too fast. And the harder he struggled the faster the flow of his blood and the weaker he became.

After a while the action of his legs ceased and they were buried up to the ankles, then the knees.

Carver shoveled faster.

Raffy saw he was losing the battle and snarled with frustration. Thrashed with immense effort and managed to fight his way higher. Carver admired the heart in the beast. He slammed the shovel down between the flailing arms, sickened by the vibration and melon-thump of it bouncing off Raffy's skull, off human bone and flesh. Raffy made a feeble attempt to snatch the shovel handle, but Carver yanked it back out of reach and resumed scooping earth. Shoveling! *Shoveling!* A brutal exercise in survival that lent raw energy.

Raffy was buried up to the waist.

Then the armpits.

At last only his head and one shoulder and arm were above the earth.

He waved the arm almost like a surrender flag, then dropped it. He was in agony and losing blood in the grave.

He wasn't going to climb out.

"Shit!" he groaned. "Look what you done!"

Exhausted, Carver braced his good leg and leaned on the shovel. He gasped, "Where's Birdie?"

Raffy stared at him with black, pain-glazed eyes and laughed.

"Birdie?" Carver said again.

246

Raffy spat at him.

Carver's upper-body strength was probably as great as Raffy's. He raised the shovel high and brought the honed blade down hard in a chopping motion on Raffy's hand, leaning all his weight into it. He flinched at the *chonk!* as a finger was severed.

"Where's Birdie?" he asked again, surprised by the calmness in his voice. The detached finger lay like a pale slug in the loose earth.

Raffy stared in shock at the bleeding stump on his hand. Didn't answer. A trickle of blood writhed like a snake down his arm.

Crouched on his good knee where he'd dropped after his effort, almost in a sitting position, Carver drew back the shovel as if to bring it down on the back of Raffy's neck.

And Raffy winced. Human at last.

He said, "She's with a friend of mine. Melanie Star."

"Address?" Carver said, not moving the shovel.

"Corner of Delta and Citrus. Old brick apartment building. Melanie's on the first floor."

Carver said, "You're a dead man," but he lowered the shovel.

"Whaddaya mean?"

"You're headed for Raiford Prison or the electric chair," Carver said. "If not the chair, I'll kill you soon as you hit the street after you do your stretch of time. You either fry and die, come out and die, or you're in for the rest of your years, and that's a kinda death. It's death whichever way. I won't forget about you."

"Guess you won't."

"You believe I mean it?"

"Yeah, I believe it. You got something to put on this finger, stop it from bleeding?"

Carver worked his way to his feet. Using the shovel as a cane, he limped away from Raffy.

"You gonna leave me here?" Raffy called. "We can work something out, you know? Motherfucker, I'm hurt!"

Carver opened the door to Raffy's white Cadillac and tossed the shovel inside. He remembered Raffy reaching in and turning off the idling engine, so he wasn't surprised that the key was in the ignition switch rather than in a pocket of Raffy's shorts and buried.

"Carver! Listen, man! Please! C'mon back!"

Gripping the smooth car roof for support, Carver lowered himself in behind the steering wheel and started the engine.

Raffy screamed.

Dirt and rocks pelted the insides of the fenders as Carver drove away.

Half a mile down the highway he heard sirens, and a bright yellow fire engine passed him going the other way, red and blue lights flashing and chromed pumping equipment bright with reflected color. More lights over the rise, and a sheriff's car swished past behind the fire truck.

The yodeling wails of their sirens faded behind Carver like the distant baying of hounds on the hunt.

On the straightaways, he used all the speed there was in Raffy's Caddie.

37

Sanderson's Drugstore was a stop on the way. Carver left the Cadillac double-parked on Ocean Drive with the lights on and the engine idling as he limped inside with the shovel. The girl behind the checkout counter stopped chewing her gum. Customers stared. A white-haired man holding a bottle of mouthwash backed away from Carver, almost knocking over a rotating rack of paperback novels. The rack squealed as if in surprise and did half a turn, to the mystery section. Carver thought, Stranger than fiction.

He made his way directly to the display of canes and crutches and quickly selected a wooden cane, leaning on it to test strength and flexibility, taking a few steps to make sure it was the correct length. Good enough, if not perfect.

He left the shovel leaning against the shelves and hobbled back to the front of the drugstore and the checkout counter. Tossed a twenty-dollar bill on the counter.

The girl at the cash register was unconsciously working her jaws again, red lips parted so her purplish wad of chewing gum was visible. But there was awe and fear in her eyes as they locked on the dirt-stained madman who'd wandered in with a shovel and was buying a cane.

"I was digging in my garden," Carver said. "Cane broke and I had to get a replacement right away."

The girl nodded and said, "Oh." She didn't halfway believe that one, but she wasn't going to argue about it. She counted out Carver's change and gave it to him, withdrawing her hand as quickly as possible, as if her fingers were burned.

He knew she was watching him as he limped outside and climbed back in the Caddie. As he settled into the seat he caught a glimpse of his face in the rearview mirror and knew why the checkout girl had stared and feared. The curly gray hair around his ears was mussed; his tanned face was darkened with dirt including a black glob on his bald head that reminded him of Gorbachev's birthmark; his eyes seemed a paler blue and were direct and wild. He'd be afraid of a man with eyes like that.

As he drove the rest of the way to the corner of Delta and Citrus, he smoothed back his hair and then wiped his shirt-sleeve over his face. Checked his image in the mirror again. An improvement had been worked. He looked less like a maniac and more like a chimney sweep.

There was only one apartment building where Delta Avenue crossed Citrus. Neither street was busy. The corner was in the depressed part of town where Raffy had pursued Carver's car and taken a shot at him. A steamy low fog had moved in, and the streetlights bending overhead glowed in brilliant swirling hazes that didn't reach the ground.

Carver parked half a block down on Citrus, got out of the Cadillac, and walked back toward the apartment. His arms still ached from shoveling, and the sweat-smeared dirt that covered them was beginning to itch.

The building was a six-family, gloomy structure with two stories. A light gleamed faintly above the entrance, near where the bricks were darkly stained from a neglected gutter leak. The windows had shades but not drapes, and a few of them had broken panes with cardboard taped over them. The rent here had to be low and the roaches probably ran the place. Melanie Star must have thought she was in paradise when she stayed with Raffy in Executive Tower. The hitch to that Eden was that she had to sleep with the serpent. Or maybe that was what appealed to her.

Carver pushed open the heavy, brown-enameled door and entered the vestibule. Somebody had swished a dirty mop over the cracked, hexagonal-tiled floor not long ago; a soapy ammonia odor lingered in the sweltering air.

He saw "M. Star" printed in the slot above the mailbox for unit 1-B. Folded religious fliers stuck out of all six locked mailboxes. Carver pulled one out and glanced at it. Prayer was the solution to all problems, it proclaimed. At the bottom was the name of a church and a form to send in if you wanted to make a donation. He tucked the flier back in the mailbox.

He decided to try the rear door of 1-B, and he quietly left the vestibule.

Carver had to take only a single step up a flight of rickety wooden stairs to be on the landing in front of Melanie Star's back door. There was a rusty barbecue cooker tucked in a corner against the wooden rail. A can of charcoal starter lay on its side nearby. The door was paneled and had four small windows in it. A heavy orange curtain hung loosely over the windows, but enough illumination filtered through to suggest there was a light on in the kitchen.

Carver was in shadow, not visible from the street or the block behind the building. He leaned nearer the door, listening. Heard nothing from inside.

He slowly rotated the knob and pressed in on the door, careful not to make noise. The bottom of the door gave a fraction of an inch but there was a lock of some sort, probably a sliding bolt, holding the upper half firm against the doorjamb.

It was time to forsake caution.

He backed up so his buttocks were against the wooden rail, raised his good leg, and kicked the door open. Somehow he'd knocked over the metal barbecue grill and it clattered down the step to ring on concrete.

The kitchen was empty. As he stormed through it, his cane crashing on the linoleum floor, Carver was aware of litter on the table, dirty dishes stacked high in the sink. On the wall over the table were three successively smaller ceramic mallard ducks, winging toward Lake Mediocre.

Then he was in a tiny hall. He stopped and glanced to his right. A bathroom. Cracked pedestal washbasin, yellowed toilet lid, wadded gray towel on the floor. Looked to his right. A bedroom. Violet walls. Four-poster bed with white canopy. Low dresser with mirror that reflected a hundred perfume bottles.

Melanie Star stood alongside the bed with her glamorous eyes wide and a hand raised to her mouth, one fingertip denting her lower lip.

Birdie Reeves lay curled in the fetal position on the bed's white cover, the gray skirt of her Sunhaven uniform twisted and hiked above her knees. Her eyes were open but she was staring straight ahead at the violet wall, as if listlessly mulling over whether she approved of the decor.

Carver moved into the room. The apartment was hot, but there was an air-conditioner in one of the bedroom windows, thrashing away at the heat and spitting out tiny ice crystals that glittered beautifully in the lamplight.

Melanie Star was wearing red shorts, a tucked-in white T-shirt lettered "Shit Happens," and red high heels. She extended both arms straight out in front of her with her fingers spread wide. She backed away from Carver, around to the other side of the bed. Tight muscles rippled in her long legs.

"She's okay!" she said, motioning with her head toward Birdie. "She's okay! Really! Please?" Her voice broke to a terrified whine, as if it were changing in adolescence.

Birdie hadn't moved.

"She's on meperidine, that's all," Melanie Star explained. "It's like Demerol. Won't hurt her. No kidding. Just to keep her quiet till Raffy's back."

Carver limped toward the bed. "Raffy's not coming back."

"Why not?"

"It's impossible. It'll stay that way."

Her voice hit that broken whine again. "He's not dead, is he? I know he's not dead!"

"You'll be able to visit him," Carver said.

He sat on the edge of the bed and bent over Birdie. When he touched the back of her hand, he was shocked by the coolness of her flesh.

"I only did what I had to," Melanie Star said. "To get what I needed. Honest, there was no other way for me."

Carver ignored her. He was tired of people telling him there was only one way for them in life.

Melanie Star said, "Goddamn it, what was I supposed to do? What do you want outta me?"

Carver said, "Birdie?" Trying to rouse her. In the corner of his vision he saw Melanie Star edging around the bed toward the door. He didn't try to stop her. "Birdie?" He heard the staccato burst of high heels on linoleum, the squeak and slam of the back door, fainter footfalls on the wooden porch and step. The rusty barbecue grill clanged on concrete again.

Birdie gazed up at Carver, smiled dreamily, and said, "Wheee!"

Carver said, "I know everything."

Birdie worked her elbows beneath her and scooted backward so her head was supported on a fluffed white pillow. She looked like royalty resting in the vast, canopied bed. Carver wondered how drugged up she really was. She said, "Know everything? Know I helped?"

"Know you killed," Carver told her.

She smiled faintly. "Helped is what I did. A mercy. What they wanted even if they didn't know it. You understand that, don't you, Mr. Carver?"

"No."

253

"Raffy'd give me the name of a resident and I'd shine up to him. Get something going, you know what I mean? Not necessarily sex, like, but intimate stuff. I'd sneak into his room when I was on the night shift, sometimes even when I wasn't on duty but'd come out to Sunhaven without being seen. Sometimes get in bed with him, like with my father. Do things. Let him do things. Kiss him on the ear and use my tongue, like was done to me. And then one day Raffy'd give me the word."

"What word?"

"To end it."

"How would you end it, Birdie?"

She sniffled. Her innocent child's eyes were moist but he didn't think she was crying. It seemed hard for her to find words, drifting between sleep and awareness, on a hazy plateau where she had little control.

"When I was real, real young," she said, "I read or heard about this long-ago princess, or maybe it was a peasant girl, that killed the evil king by letting a drop of melted lead fall in his ear when he was sleeping. I remembered that, Mr. Carver. In fact, it's still my favorite story. Raffy knew how I did it but he didn't care, long as it worked out all right." She smiled and looked around. "You ever see walls like these? So bright?"

"Is that how you killed the Sunhaven victims?" Carver asked. "Melted lead?" He was still trying to grasp this. He hadn't completely believed Dr. Pauly. Was he actually looking at a mass murderer?

Birdie said, "Sure. Me or Dr. Pauly'd see they got a strong sedative before they went to bed. Then I'd creep into their rooms. Oh, if they woke up they was glad to see me, even though they'd be in a foggy state of mind. Some of them said they loved me. Well, I loved them back. Really I did. I'd have this bunsen burner and this little glass beaker, and just a few ounces of lead. And I'd let the lead be melting while they was asleep or I was in bed with them. Most of them thought I was a nurse or something anyway, so even if they'd wake up they didn't ask questions. And if they did I'd just say it was a medical procedure for another resident I was getting ready to see. And when they was asleep I'd take this little glass funnel and lean over them and put the end of it in their ear, just like the princess in the story, and I'd pour the melted lead into the funnel. At times, if the funnel tickled at first, they'd think I was giving them a kiss, but then they'd just moan and kinda curl up. Sometimes their eyes'd fly open and they'd sit bolt upright and you could see they was confused and wondering what happened. Even try and struggle up outta bed. But that was only for a moment. It was quick. None of them ever made much noise, only thrashed around some." She licked her lips and sighed drowsily. "There was never any bleeding or anything."

Carver could imagine the melted lead, lumping up and sizzling through the brain like a slow-motion bullet, cauterizing tissue behind it so there was no bleeding. No obvious cause of death. The pain, if there was any after the initial burning, would have been paralyzing and occurred simultaneously with disorientation in the last few seconds of life, while the lead seared through delicate matter until it cooled enough to become a solid mass again and stop at the core of the brain. He said, "Sweet Jesus!"

Birdie said with sudden alarm, "They won't send me back, will they?"

38

McGregor laid a small lump of lead on his desk in front of Carver. It was the size of a .45-caliber bullet and shaped something like a comet with a short, curved tail. He said, "This one's from James Harrison."

Harrison's name had been only one of four that Birdie hadn't included in her list of residents who'd died at Sunhaven during the past year. The list had included Kearny Williams's name because she'd known Carver was investigating his death. The bodies had been exhumed and autopsied under court order. The order had extended to all male Sunhaven fatalities since Birdie's employment there. There was no other way. The news media had gotten hold of the story and were playing it big. All stops had been pulled and the investigation was roaring ahead. It had taken on a momentum that couldn't be reversed. Professional reputations and careers were on the line.

Carver sat in the cool breeze from McGregor's new window unit and stared at the streamlined ball of lead. He wondered if a real princess had ever actually killed her father the king that way.

"Fucking clever, huh?" McGregor said. "Might not have fooled a doctor curious about the actual cause of death, but it's a damned effective way to kill somebody without visible trace. Good enough so Pauly could sign the death certificate and not worry about being found out, so long as there wasn't a legitimate autopsy with thorough internal examination. Nothing would even show up in blood, tissue, or hair samples. Puts me in mind of that case in Fort Lauderdale where this one queer kills another by straightening out a wire hanger and running the sharp end up his ass all the way to the vital organs. There was some bleeding there, though. This hot-lead business seals the wound, the M.E. said. Cauterization. Not a drop of blood. Nothing suspicious unless you get inside the body and look hard."

"Nonviolent death in an old-folks' home," Carver said. "There wouldn't be an autopsy unless the family requested one."

"Exactly. And since the family was suddenly richer than before, they'd let the matter lie. Nobody'd even think the word *murder* except the heir in on the deal." McGregor dropped the lump of lead back into its clear plastic bag and deftly sealed the flap. "Hey, you see me on the TV news?"

"Which time?"

"Last night, six o'clock. I gave you a mention."

"Generous of you," Carver said. He'd stopped watching television and reading the papers after a week of seeing McGregor skillfully corner credit and limelight for the Sunhaven disclosures. Nobody was better at clouding and rewriting history than McGregor. Dr. Pauly had been found dead from loss of blood in a phone booth; Birdie Reeves had been discovered by paramedics who'd somehow been called to an apartment on Citrus Avenue; and Raffy Ortiz seemed to have wandered into a hole and got stuck. Lieutenant McGregor had been at the right spots at the right times, the essence of his job, and made the appropriate arrests. This because he'd kept his investigation secret, even from his superiors. The superiors knew better than to comment; they could feel McGregor pulling away and knew he'd soon be looking back at them. Their superior.

"These are the autopsy reports," McGregor said, tossing Carver a thick blue file folder. "Thought you might wanna see them.

Carver opened the folder and thumbed through the staple white forms.

McGregor said, "Interesting, ain't it, what a tiny piece of ho metal can do to the brain? Musta burned right through it lik it was a chunk of raw veal. Through where we feel love, hat fear, pain, pleasure. Through the place that controls whethe we can move our arms and legs and wriggle our ears. Throug where we remember. Makes you wonder what the old bastard felt. Wonder if some of them'd say it was worthwhile, seein they were near the end of the line anyway and mighta got t diddle with young Birdie."

"Makes me wonder what you feel," Carver said. "Or if yo feel anything."

"Hey, I'm human. Ambition. I feel ambition. And that's n way to talk to the guy that's gonna put Raffy Ortiz away forever keep him off you so you can go on breathing."

"The prosecuting attorney might have some part to play i that, too."

"Not without me, fuckhead. You might say I'm the principa player in this."

McGregor was riding high again, solid in his power and work ing on promotion. Full of his old gloating arrogance. Carve didn't like to see it. Had to get away from it.

He braced on his cane and stood up.

"You shouldn't leave yet," McGregor said. "I ain't showe you the newspapers. How they build me up high enough t run for fucking mayor if I feel like it. What they say about m in the *Miami Herald*."

"Too bad they didn't ask me for a quote about you," Carve said. He limped toward the door.

McGregor said, "You missed the news last night, watch tonight. I'm on again. *I'm goddamn back!*"

That afternoon Carver met Desoto for lunch in Orlando. Th lieutenant was pleased but somber. He'd asked Carver to tur

258

over a rock, and under it they'd found something nastier than either of them had expected. They were glad the rock was lifted and light was shining where there'd been darkness. Still, they'd seen what had been there, and that black knowledge saddened and somehow diminished them.

The restaurant was a tourist attraction that served fruit juice with everything, a noisy place. But Carver and Desoto had a booth in back, away from the sunburned travelers with their squabbling, impatient kids. Over coffee, Carver told Desoto the details of what had happened, as opposed to some of the information in the media.

Desoto moved his spoon in his coffee lazily, staring at the brown whirlpool in the cup.

"So she killed five men," he said softly.

"The psychologists say only one," Carver said. "Her father. Over and over again."

"Psychologists would say that. It's the way they think."

"Yeah, more or less."

"Raffy Ortiz. He'd find somebody like her. Use her. Makes you sick, eh, *amigo*?"

Carver said, "Seen the autopsy report on Sam Cusanelli?"

Desoto looked up, dark eyes vivid with interest. He didn't have to say McGregor hadn't phoned him. McGregor was a busy and important man these days and probably hadn't had time.

"Your Uncle Sam died of a cerebral hemorrhage," Carver said. "No sign of foul play. A natural death. His time."

"His time . . ." Desoto repeated.

He sipped his coffee thoughtfully. Then he put down the cup and smiled, adjusted his cuffs.

Carver could see he felt better.

39

Carver went to visit Birdie at the old city jail on Magellan Avenue before her trial.

He'd been waiting fifteen minutes in a small, pale green room containing only a scarred oak table and three plain, straight-backed wooden chairs. There were no outside windows; the light came from frosted plastic panels in the drop ceiling. It was warm in the room, and lingering desperation was palpable. It was where prisoners usually met with their attorneys, where hope was nurtured or crushed.

The door opened and a matron led Birdie into the room.

Birdie was wearing a Day-Glo orange jumpsuit that was too large for her. Her red hair was skinned back in a ponytail held by a gray ribbon in a tight bow. She wasn't wearing makeup and she might have passed for twelve years old. She smiled at Carver, glad to see him but not surprised. As if he were visiting her at summer camp, maybe brought her some cookies, and a flashlight so she could read under the covers at night. He planted his cane firmly and remained standing. Neither of them sat down at the table.

The matron, a buxom, middle-aged woman with a sad, kind face, ambled outside and stood at a thick glass window in the door, watching without seeming to stare. Quite a knack.

Carver looked at Birdie and wondered if she'd still have freckles when she was the age of the matron. Her guileless blue eyes had gotten years older in the past few weeks, but not at all wiser.

He plucked at her sleeve and said, "Some outfit for a princess."

She looked puzzled. Probably didn't recall what she'd said to him in Melanie Star's bedroom.

Then she said, "Oh, I know what you mean. I been reading the papers. All about me." She seemed perversely pleased by her publicity. Something in common with McGregor. It was more attention than she'd ever dreamed of receiving.

"They treating you all right in here?" Carver asked.

She shrugged her child's narrow shoulders in the orange jumpsuit that was supposed to provide a good target if she escaped. "Yeah, I gotta say so." She looked away, at a blank green wall, and then back. "There's something I never told nobody."

"Before you tell me or anyone else," Carver cautioned her, "you better talk to your lawyer. You're in deep trouble, Birdie."

"No, it won't matter if I tell you. And I want to, though I ain't sure why."

She waited, as if needing his assent.

He nodded.

"When they was dead I bent over and kissed them on the lips. Kinda to wish them peace wherever it was they were going. Know how come? 'Cause kisses go with death. Death is forever, and so's a kiss, Mr. Carver."

"I guess it is," Carver said, "in a lot of ways."

She stared at him. "You understand what I'm saying?"

"Part of it. That's the best I can do."

Birdie said, "Well, that's all I can ask and more'n I got a right to expect. Listen, will you tell Linda Redmond I'm sorry I let her down? And like thank her for thinking about me, and tell her I'm thinking about her?"

"I'll tell her," Carver said.

"Thanks. It was unfinished business. Sometimes I think that's the trouble with the world, too much unfinished business that can never really be worked out." Something infinitely sad crossed her features. "It ain't easy, is it, Mr. Carver?"

Carver said, "Hardly ever. For anyone."

There she stood, victim and killer, child and adult, testimony to the complexity of life and the simplicity of death. Smiling brightly up at him now. Her blue eyes burned and there was a sheen of perspiration on her pale, smooth forehead.

Good Christ, what would they do to her? What would become of her?

Carver propped himself against the edge of the table and held both her small, cold hands in his. He bent down and gently placed his lips just below her hairline. She'd recently showered with the prison's cheap perfumed soap and shampoo. Her hair smelled like lilacs.

He kissed her good-bye.